THE CONVERSATION

THE CONVERSATION

Mercedes Salisachs

Translation by Gretta K. Siebentritt

Jorge Pinto Books Inc.
New York

The Conversation

© Mercedes Salisachs

Published by Jorge Pinto Books Inc., website: www.pintobooks.com

Translation by Gretta K. Siebentritt

Cover design by Susan Hildebrand

Book design by Charles King, website: www.ckmm.com

ISBN: 1-934978-04-3
978-1-934978-04-7

To Isabel and Rafael Borrás, in gratitude
for many years of candid, intelligent
and unconditional friendship.

Man reveals himself through conversation,
not only in what he says,
but in what he does not say.

STEFAN ZWEIG

The first time I heard Antonia's name I was seated in her father's office in the building owned by the American multinational corporation Woultmand & Starky. I remember that just walking into that room, lavishly appointed and plastered with artwork, was like crossing the threshold of my most unattainable dream. It was an unimaginable achievement and one that never would have come to pass had it not been for the intervention of Douglas Raft, the company's CEO and advisor to Anton Mahler at the time.

Anton Mahler was president of the financial giant and ultimately one of those anthropomorphic myths whom very few people ever get to know on a personal level.

And there I was, standing before that prodigy of the financial world, brushing against the Louis XV table that dominated the room flanked by two enormous picture windows whose glass reflected a blinding sun that hurt the eyes. Whenever he returned to Spain after one of his constant trips to the United States and other parts of the planet, it was here that Mahler received those chosen few.

I suddenly glimpsed Antonia's photograph on the table. She was eight years old, blond, with light blue eyes and a pathetic expression that was a poor imitation of the smile the photographer obviously was demanding of her and that she, of course, was incapable of interpreting.

I remember that as I regarded the picture, Anton Mahler extended his hand to me, leaning slightly over the edge of the table without rising from his chair. "It is a pleasure to meet you. I've heard good things about you."

And since he could see that I was still staring at the photograph he explained, "That's my daughter Antonia. Pretty isn't she? Unfortunately her mother died when she was born. Her sister, who never married, has been like a second mother to her since the day she came into this world. That's why she lives in Spain. My wife was Spanish."

It came out all at once, as if he wanted to dispense as quickly as possible with the matter of the undeniable paternal negligence caused by his constant absences from Spain.

The glare from the windows prevented my seeing his face clearly as he was speaking, but from his manner I guessed that his expressions would be those of a cold man, a man indifferent to domestic concerns.

He shuffled the papers on top of the file and, clearing his throat, began to read in an unconvincing monotone. "Eladio Escalante: that's your name?" I nodded and he continued reading: "Awarded a scholarship to study Political Sciences and Sociology. A Masters in Business Administration from the ESADE School of Business (first in his class)."

He stopped there, glanced up and offered a slight congratulatory nod. Then he continued: "Branch Director of the Bank of Madrid. Director of IBM Cataluña."

Then silence. He leaned back in his chair and cleared his throat once again. Straightening, he crossed his arms and regarded me intently, which confirmed for me that my CV had caught his attention.

"Not bad. No sir, not bad at all. Douglas Raft was certainly correct. Clearly you're very capable. And in addition to your academic career, may I say that you come across well. People tend to place a great deal of value on appearance and yours is very positive. And I understand that you are fluent in several languages."

Mr. Mahler's face slowly came into focus as my eyes became accustomed to the glare and I was able to observe his features. They matched the reputation for aloofness that he was obliged to portray in magazines and newspapers with the passivity of a landscape, or a statue, or a monument.

Indeed, although Mahler was quite well known, to most people he was a figure lacking in human substance: similar to a person, but devoid of the attributes associated with the banalities of everyday life, family problems, or a sentimental side. He was a mythical figure in the world of global finances, a subject well beyond most people's reach. Perhaps that is why it struck me as so strange to be sitting there chatting with him as if he were just anyone.

His face, slightly pompous and square-jawed, was mainly defined by his piercing gaze and his self-satisfied way of pursing his lips.

I responded to his reference to my linguistic skills by saying that I was only fluent in English and French. Half jokingly, I added, "Of course I'm also conversant in Spanish, and I manage to defend myself in German with some difficulty."

I heard Mahler clear his throat again and he quickly repeated that my CV was impressive. "I would imagine that you are familiar with our company. Woultmand & Starky operates at several levels: television, radio, the print media, cinema, and of course, publishing."

Mahler abruptly left off being a man prepared to allow himself to be impressed by my business acumen and activities and began to talk about himself in a rather self-opinionated tone, as if the recently-mentioned industries were personal badges of honor. "I do have to admit, however, that the publishing side of the business is Woultmand & Starky's weakest link in Spain."

I explained that Douglas Raft had indeed brought me up to date. "There appears to be a lack of coordination between the Catalan headquarters and the Madrid office. He has also mentioned poor coordination between the key divisions that interface with the economy: marketing, accounting, and advertising, along with a lack of communication between administrative staff and the authors, editors, and distributors. And finally, there seems to be a critical dearth of strategic contacts in external media outlets."

Mahler nodded and quickly added, "That is correct. None of those things are operating as they should." And in a more relaxed tone, "It's not so much a matter of the substantive aspects. We have an excellent editorial director who is well-versed in identifying relevant works. Literature aside, what the Spanish publishing house requires is someone who knows how to direct the executive level staff. Up to now, the divisions I mentioned earlier have been operating with their own disparate criteria and coordination has been a disaster. What we are looking for is a man who can take over the direction of the various divisions and make sure they are operating as they should. At this point, no one is producing at capacity. People are working in a vacuum with no supervision and no sense of accountability. Basically each division does as it pleases at the expense of an effective overall performance."

He left off abruptly. He kept looking at me in that way he had, through half-closed lids, as if he wished to radiate a certain magnetism that would hypnotize me. Then he asked, "Do you understand what I'm trying to say?"

Of course I understood. But I did not dare show it. I might make a mistake. It was possible. And that would have brought all of my hopes tumbling down around me. "I'm not sure I understand what you're trying to say," I lied. Although reason told me there was room for optimism, it was hard for me to imagine the scene could be the first step—one I'd dreamed about so often—to becoming an employee of that company.

It was a dream I had been nurturing for years, as I endured day after interminable day of grueling routines, unexpected setbacks and ruthless professional backstabbing.

Mahler continued: "Our Spanish publishing house is extremely important but, as I said, its weak point lies in its internal organization. Put succinctly, what we need is a man with the right background who knows how to bring together all of these damned divisions and consolidate them into an economic fortress. You just might be that man. Of course, you would be generously remunerated, with all the perks. According to Douglas Raft, you are well equipped to do the job. The board of directors of Woultmand & Starky will be pleased if you accept the position—as will I."

For a moment, my mind went blank. It really was as if I were dreaming. I was finding it difficult to absorb what Mahler was proposing: "So you're asking me to become a sort of director of executives or executive director?"

Mahler nodded with a hint of a smile. "Exactly. You understand. A man like you with so many years of education under your belt must have finely honed organizational skills," he finished, half jokingly.

And for my peace of mind, he added, "I do not want you to think that boosting revenues is the most important thing. Profit-mongering is not my style. What I really want is for Autumn Books to function properly. I don't want the company's reputation to deteriorate. I want authors to be proud to work with us. Lately there have been a number of complaints which, unfortunately, have not been without basis."

"I'll have to think about it," I said. "I won't deny that your proposal is very tempting, but it is only fair that I notify my present employer and let them know what you are offering me."

Although I could hear my voice pronouncing the words, I had the impression that the person saying them was not me. My true self was a mute being, stunned into silence and smothered exclamations: a man struggling to come up with an astute rejoinder that had no meaning. But it was necessary to explore the nuances, weigh the hypotheticals, express reservations I did not feel. Basically, I had to prove myself.

Mahler persisted, "I think any doubts you may have will be gone once we go over the contract together."

I knew it. I always had. I never really doubted that my lifelong dream would one day come true. Especially since my mother was always saying, "I don't know where you're headed, my Son. The only thing I'm sure of is that you're going to kill yourself studying like you do."

She was right. But she also "killed herself" to put me through school. She gave up a lot so that I should achieve the goals I had set for myself.

I remember that after I first met Douglas Raft in the office of the ESADE business school, we quickly became friends thanks to my mother. "She is a person of few words and many actions," he told me soon after he met her. "Life hasn't been fair to her, yet she is clearly an exceptional woman."

Those words had a qualitative impact on my efforts. I remember my mother taking any job that came her way, no matter how humble or disagreeable it might be. The important thing was to save enough to cover my studies.

Of course she had little time left over for me. The days were short and the nights even shorter. Yet her support was always there. And of course, I never managed to find time to spend with her.

Douglas Raft would sometimes just stare at her as if he were contemplating a major artistic work. "Do you have any idea what kind of mother you have? I've never met anyone as tenacious as she."

Douglas Raft was not mistaken. His headhunting instincts—so valued by Anton Mahler—also enabled him to see the greatness in humble people: those who, in their mediocrity, were able to move mountains by the sheer force of their will.

While I was busy reminiscing about my adolescence, Mahler continued to regard me with the determination of one not accustomed to being refused. "In any event, it is a point in your favor that you are not swayed by first impressions," he commented. "That only reaffirms your prudence. The best way to avoid missteps is through caution."

His voice was no longer arrogant and his persistence ruled out any paternalistic generosity. "I've always trusted Douglas Raft's clinical eye," he finished.

I trusted him too. I can still see him as he was when I was young—my height, a man of understated gestures and impeccable posture—giving me advice and trying to instill in me the priorities and values that would cement my social life in the future. Though I did not realize it then, it was thanks to him that I learned to dress with a certain flair, to interact with people of a certain standing, to use the silverware properly, and to become accustomed to the forms of etiquette my mother either was not familiar with or had not had time to teach me.

U.S. born and bred, Douglas Raft had been living in Spain for a long while thanks to his high-level position with Woultmand & Starky. He was well aware of my humble origins and my mother's struggle to ensure that I would make something of myself.

He also knew that my father had been an usher at an upscale theater and that his salary, plus tips, had enabled us to live a decent life despite our poverty, free of the worries that beset us after his death.

"Douglas has filled me in on your background," Mahler continued. "In addition to your CV, I find other aspects very admirable. You know very well what it takes to climb that 'ladder.' And that's worth more than the hotshot who's had his way paved for him since birth. To take for granted what must be earned through hard work is one of the biggest mistakes life has to offer."

I made no reply. I let him go on. Apparently he was interested in my humble origins as much as my business acumen: my efforts to "climb the ladder," to rise up from the valley floor and scale the mountain.

I remember at one point he mentioned the need to come across as conscientious and self-confident. "To earn respect is a thousand times more honorable than to be born into it."

I thought suddenly of my father, when he was nearing death. "I have very little to leave you, Son." His speech was labored and he had a tendency to apologize for having helped bring me into this world. But he was mistaken. Though he never knew it, he had left me much more than the largest fortune. He had left me the imprint of his honor, his absolute lack of envy when his friends obtained better jobs, and his encouragement of my mother in her desire to make sure that some day I would actually "be someone."

"That's why I want to invest in you," Mahler went on. Although the wording could have been better, I could not help but be flattered that he considered me a good "investment." He instinctively tried to fix it. "What I mean to say, of course, is that investing in you is not just an investment in the financial stability of the company, but in the global outcomes as well, thanks to your futuristic vision."

And seeing that I remained silent he continued, "Only men who have 'been through the grinder' themselves are truly capable of having a futuristic vision."

I replied that indeed, there was little to envy about my childhood and adolescence.

I grew up on a narrow street in the downtown area. I frequently saw huge rats darting across the street with my friends, armed with brooms, in hot pursuit, proclaiming their glorious battle cry of "death to the enemy." I never joined in those chases, as the sight of a dead rat filled me with nausea.

"Do you believe that killing rats in the street can spark a futuristic vision?" I inquired jokingly. "That's what my friends did when we were little."

It is as if I am still seeing them. The street was our playground. It was an ideal venue for expending our boundless energy. No one watched over us or schooled us in ethics. People were simply scared of us, especially when our antics erupted into fistfights that scandalized the neighborhood.

We specialized in dreaming up practical jokes in very bad taste or else inventing contests to test our strength and end up beaten to a pulp.

Sometimes, when I engaged in some such excess in order to be like my friends, my mother would look at me as if I was from another planet. "But Eladio, how could you possibly be my son?" At the time, however, I was not in a position to gauge my mother's suffering. The important thing was to go along with the petty vandalisms perpetrated by my friends: snatch apples from the supermarket, shatter the street lamps with stones, ring doorbells and hide, train my slingshot on unwitting passersby, and visit the fury of the Vikings on any telephone booths that were still marginally functional.

"I have heard about those activities. Your mother gave Douglas Raft all the details," continued Mahler. "But I also know that you refused to play war with those disgusting creatures," he said, referring to the dead rats.

The truth of the matter was that my mother never scolded me. All she did was cry muted, impotent sobs whenever someone reported one of my escapades to her. It pained her terribly to think she could not give me a civilized upbringing. "If I stay home, I can't work and if I don't work, you can't study," she would tell me, with red-rimmed eyes, quivering mouth, her voice choked with despair.

In the end, it was those unshed tears and signs of impotence that compelled me to stop joining in my friends' mischief-making.

Now, as I reminisce about that time, I can see that everything around me was disjointed. Nothing was normal. Everything around me was dictated by destructive instincts that were not so much a result of pride or petty rivalries as the lashing out of children abandoned to their savage impulses.

One day I realized that the course I was on was tantamount to digging a grave, only to tumble into it and die. Especially when I observed my mother coming home at night, face drawn, hands swollen and red, hair disheveled, and a sigh caught in her throat as if she were trying to swallow a chronic dry sob. "I assume you behaved yourself today, right Eladio?" she would ask with the routine of a wish that never came true. That was why she never waited for a response. She would just look at me earnestly, her body slumped with exhaustion, her voice tired. "It's a matter of your not wasting your time. You have to stay away from those friends of yours who don't have your talent."

It was her confidence in me—the way she accrued on a daily basis the moral stores her husband had bequeathed her to marshal the strength to accept the most varied and unpleasant jobs (nearly always badly paid)—that made it incumbent upon me to emulate her tenacity.

"Actually it was my mother's example that instilled in me an 'insatiable greed' for knowledge," I told Mahler.

He burst out laughing and cut me short, "I like your reference to an 'insatiable greed for knowledge.' The acquisition of knowledge can certainly be driven by greed. That's why I need an executive with your background to organize the different divisions related to the economy. Someone like you, with brilliant ideas."

By then, talking to Mahler was no longer the extraordinary chance that my workmates had so envied me.

We both became increasingly articulate as we candidly shared details that earlier I would have never considered bringing up.

The part about brilliant ideas, however, did not ring entirely true to me. "Be that as it may," I suggested, "we have to bear in mind that a brilliant idea is no guarantee of lasting success."

Mahler refused to be outdone. "But lasting successes are always contingent upon brilliant ideas."

His response struck me as somewhat facile. "Many solutions can be identified without any need to be dazzled by their brilliance," I said. "Many problems can be solved using basic logic. For example, if there are no returns on investments, it's better to sell at a loss before a year has passed, because the tax write off is better. Yes, I know. You would say that sales at a loss are generally precarious because of the risk entailed, but that is not entirely true."

Mahler froze for an instant. I thought then that my proposals had displeased him. They probably did not dovetail with whatever expectations he might have had of me. Maybe he regarded my arguments as anticapitalist, or at least less than propitious for the capitalist market he vehemently espoused.

But I was mistaken. "You are right, Mr. Escalante. It is important to bear in mind the strategies of the new economy. Not long ago, the newspaper reported a quote from a renowned figure in the field, which I found unconvincing and even less instructive: 'dividends first, culture later.' I do not agree. Management must enjoy the latitude to adapt to different world cultures. Otherwise we would be running an autistic business."

Emboldened by his response, I continued to expound on my views. "We must also be cognizant that what works today might not work tomorrow and make sure not to lose sight of the risks inherent to certain types of accommodations."

I quickly added that the risk factor was necessary, but only if we could count on the able support of the executive staff. "If they are not trained in team work and cannot adapt to shared leadership, if what they're after is personal prestige and taking all the credit, then they'll simply have to go. It's no use being sentimental about it."

Our exchange was becoming increasingly fluid. Little by little the initial barriers began to crumble.

Over fifteen years have passed since that day and yet I recall every word that passed between Mahler and me. Indeed, it is as if no time at all has transpired, as if everything that came later was just a gruesome holocaust consigned to historic treatises that no one will ever read.

Even now, when everything is obscured by the nebula of what has been lost, our exchange that day remains imprinted on my memory. It is impossible to forget that preliminary encounter. I try to erase it, but it is always there, now no more than a heap of non sequiturs that gave no indication of inexorable consequences. It was impossible to imagine that our projects and ideas could flow headlong into such savage denouements and fatal traps. It is inevitable: memories do not lie. And now I try in vain to erase what can never be erased, though one would think a pre-historic encounter such as ours could be expunged in a fog of amnesia.

Elemental events of the sort that go virtually unnoticed at the time burst suddenly into my consciousness. True loves that quickly fizzled out. Illusions that had once seemed eternal now turned to dust. Echoes in the twilight seldom heard in the light of day. Translucent figures that never became flesh. And dreams.

So many dreams. And now I can only recover scattered words, split seconds with names that wound: dosage, stairs, water, lounge chair, umbrella, pools, balconies on the verge of collapse.... Mundane things that I, on that long ago afternoon, could never have imagined would plunge me into the darkness of the most unconfessable secrets.

I wonder now what would have happened if Mahler had not offered me the job, or if Douglas Raft had not taken it upon himself to recommend me so enthusiastically, hoping to reward in some way my intellectual achievements and my mother's tenacity in subsidizing my studies.

I do not know. The fact is that Mahler and I ended up connecting: he ostensibly bent on improving the operations of Autumn Books for structural as well as altruistic reasons, and I out of vanity, for having attained what I'd always aspired to. "Of course one must always prioritize the well-being of the professional staff by rewarding their technical expertise, which ultimately boosts profits."

Needless to say, I was not unaware that despite his veneer of disinterest and generosity, Mahler's aim was to boost the revenues of Autumn Books. The rest—his desire to improve coordination among the different editorial divisions—might well have been excuses to act the great benefactor, a man who is above greed, a true patron of the arts.

Mahler and I covered a lot of ground that day. Without either of us really being aware of it, we began to venture into terrain that had virtually nothing to do with the reason for my presence in his office.

I remember talking to him about my mother and the penury she had endured so that I could get ahead. How we moved when I had earned enough to escape the neighborhood where the rats reigned, notwithstanding the danger of being hunted down. Of our friendship with Douglas Raft. "He has always been much more than a friend to me," I told him. "I don't care what people have to say about his preferences. He'll always be a brother to me: an older brother who has always advised me with tremendous integrity."

Mahler nodded. He also had the highest opinion of Douglas. "Apparently no one can really accuse him of having tendencies any different than our own. He is very correct in his conduct and has an unfailingly dignified demeanor. He has never given cause for gossip. And in terms of intelligence, he is head and shoulders above those whose high opinion of their own virility is only surpassed by their ridiculous airs."

No. I never will forget my first contact with the man who would mark the rest of my life. Every moment had the feel of a contained fire, an eternal flame that would never actually consume us. Something fail-safe that guaranteed the solidity of a future brimming with promise.

Slowly Mahler's features softened. They no longer seemed tense or brusque. Any barriers that might have existed dissolved into mutual understanding.

And far from regarding the future as a flimsy and unstable prospect, it suddenly opened up before me as an opportunity to shoulder an important responsibility. "There's no doubt about it," he said as I was preparing to leave. "I am sure that you and I are going to develop an effective and fruitful collaboration, and not only a professional one, but a friendship as well."

We made our farewells.

I remember how happy I was after I left his office. In high spirits, I quickened my steps full of optimism and an urge to hug my mother. The streets were a blur. The only thing that mattered was to get home and tell her, "I've finally made it." And kiss her. Gather her tiny frame in my arms and thank her a thousand times over for all she had endured when I was little.

And to say over and over to myself, "I have succeeded."

Impossible to imagine then that the word "success" could consist of carrying a moldering corpse around on my back for the rest of my life, while every passing hour only reinforces the conviction of having fallen into the biggest trap of all.

The rain is gradually letting up but when Eladio Escalante opens the taxi door the humidity that envelops him is as dense as the recent downpour.

Preoccupied, he fails to notice the small puddle of gray water as he gets out of the car and the pirouette he must execute to avoid it nearly causes him to trip. "Shit." The taxi driver can identify with his passenger's ill humor: "Bad day to be traveling."

But Eladio barely hears him. His attention is on the string of carts in front of the airport waiting for the anxious, hurried hands of the travelers to pull them from the line.

Dodging the rain and virtually hopping, he grabs one and returns to the taxi where the driver helps him unload his luggage.

"Have a good trip."

"Thanks."

Despite the unpleasant day, the building is alive with people, steps, voices, and dragging sounds.

Be that as it may, the people milling around Eladio Escalante are just a blur. They are people just like him, thrashing about in their obsession to get out of the cold and rain.

Other than that, the faces are mostly colorless, expressionless masks that probably conceal circumstances that mirror his own: vague periods of fatigue, pointless ironies, lapses of judgment, and liberations from grave dependencies.

But looking around, it seems to him as if there is no single "somebody" among them. As if the turmoil of the unknown had turned the passengers into a mass of gray bodies with no distinguishable features or reactions.

The area is large but there are no echoes. The only thing that disturbs the air are the muted sounds—a mixture of steps, murmuring voices, and sudden bursts of monotonous announcements of flights, schedule changes, delays, transfers, or the name of some clueless passenger who is lost—that cut across the passageways leaving in their wake a tedious hum akin to the subhuman cries of a worn out civilization.

Eladio Escalante has never liked flying, much less when it entails crossing the Atlantic. He also dislikes the kinds of conversations that occur during flight, since they are usually superficial exchanges that fail to contribute anything new or compelling. Vacuous parleys devised solely to dispel the tedium of empty hours.

Whenever he is compelled to fly, therefore, he has always made every effort to avoid them. And if a seatmate happens to be too insistent, he never hesitates to cut the conversation short with an aloof expression and a fake yawn, as if he is so overcome by drowsiness that any attempt at conversation would be an imposition rather than a welcome relief.

He is approaching customs. Numbed by the monotony of it all, Eladio passes through the metal detector, gathers his carry on luggage and asks for Gate 25.

Although he has been told he can wait in the VIP lounge, Eladio decides against it. If he goes into the VIP lounge he will probably run into someone he knows, someone who will ask questions and offer their condolences. Although the people around him seem helpful and friendly, Eladio's main concern is that everyone leave him alone, not cause him to feel uncomfortable and, most of all, not force him to unleash the rabid dog of pain bottled up inside him.

Indeed, right now his only wish is not to be noticed and to get on that plane as soon as possible. Leave Spain. Put an end once and for all to everything that might revive those internal rages, the paranoid struggles to avert unhappy endings, and the looks of commiseration for the loss of his two "loved ones."

A man approaching fifty years old has a right to start a new life, to go down new paths where the past cannot trip him up.

That is why he wants to leave Spain behind forever and make New York City his next chapter.

It does not matter now that getting on the plane might be a trap. The traps that are now forcing him to leave Spain were bigger. At this point, the worst thing that can happen is that he will be dashed into the cold and desolate sea with no help or hope on the horizon. And death, to Eladio, is no longer an overriding concern.

What he is leaving behind has been far too bitter for him to be panic-stricken or tormented by the specter of death.

When his flight is announced he takes his place in line. In no time, he is showing his boarding pass and heading into the tunnel leading to the plane.

For an instant, there is only the sound of the passengers' nervous steps. They proceed in silence, falling naturally into the synchronized movements of prisoners chained together and marching towards a common destiny. No one among them will stay behind on land. Soon, land will no longer be something logical and necessary. The important thing is to break free of it, to rise over runways made of emptiness and to remain aloft for seven hours on a journey with no signposts, to a distant continent.

Next comes the flurry of questions, the anxious glancing about, the depositing of carry-on luggage and the nervous gestures to avoid sounding abrupt.

"Business," the flight attendant confirms, consulting her seating chart. And she points Eladio in the right direction. As he moves down the aisle he can see the passengers in coach settling into their seats, their expressions calm, their gestures relaxed.

He quickly finds his own seat. The flight attendants are extremely solicitous. They help. They stow his carry-on luggage. They take his coat for him.

Eladio drops into his seat and immediately notes that the adjacent one is empty. No company will be an unexpected pleasure, he thinks. Finally, silence, rest, a chance to sleep.

Most of all, the knowledge that no one is going to ask him questions or disturb him with impertinent queries or force him to put up with the insipid banter typical of chatty travelers. Eladio's personal doctrine has never been inclined towards the subconscious desire to fill in verbal gaps simply to ward off lethargy or monotony.

Eladio absently fastens his seatbelt and leans back into the headrest, closing his eyes. At last. It wouldn't be long until takeoff.

Although the door of the plane is still open, it would soon be shut, given the departure time.

But the minutes tick by and the door remains open. Eladio notices that the flight attendants are exchanging glances that are not entirely comforting. Something must be going on since the plane is showing no signs of preparing for takeoff. This damned airlines never seems to be on time, he thinks.

They finally explain that the delay is due to a major back-up on the highway. "Please excuse the delay, but the person we are waiting for cannot be long now."

Unpersuaded by these assurances from the flight attendants, the passengers' patience is beginning to wear thin.

"People should take the traffic into account," they grumble.

"No one should be allowed to hold up a flight like that."

Suddenly there is a small commotion at the door. Someone has arrived and, after a flurry of activity, the door is finally shut.

Eladio exhales in relief, the prospect of much-needed solitude taking the edge off his impatience. His hopes dim, however, as the newly arrived passenger moves towards the business class cabin. She stops next to Eladio's seat and, blushing and gesturing nervously, begins to apologize.

"I am so sorry to have caused trouble."

Standing there is a woman of undefined age with a nice figure, discreet mannerisms and a wistful smile.

"The traffic was terrible," she explains.

Meanwhile, the flight attendants are stowing her things and entreating her to take the seat next to Eladio and fasten her seatbelt.

The new arrival obeys, her face flushed with embarrassment and her breathing still uneven from all the rush.

"It was impossible to move," she continues, but the flight attendants are no longer listening.

Instinctively, Eladio turns in her direction thinking, There goes my peace and quiet. No restful flight for me.

At first glance she seems to be a woman of refinement, although not given to dramatic excesses. She has an elegant sense of style, yet there is nothing flashy about her outfit.

"Don't worry," he says reassuringly. "We've only been waiting a couple of minutes."

Suddenly the loudspeaker emits the predictable speech from the pilot.

"Iberia Airlines would like to thank . . ."

Then the routine information, schedule, time changes, details of the flight activities, and assurances that the passengers' every need will be taken care of. Next, the recommendations for using the safety devices. The background music is turned off. Then the sound of the engines. And gliding down the runway, while slightly nervous passengers grasp their armrests and press their heads against the seat backs.

Some pray. Most feign indifference. And of course, no one acts as if they are afraid.

Letting fear take over does not get you anywhere. The unflappable are busy reading. Others sift through papers, and most people close their eyes as if overtaken by drowsiness.

All at once, the plane lifts off from the ground, its nose pointed towards the open sky.

No one speaks. Everyone seems lost in their own thoughts. In the small business class cabin is a mother traveling with what appears to be a sick child, a large man splayed out over his seat, and two businessmen who begin to expound about their joint ventures as soon as the plane leaves the ground. The other passengers are nondescript. Corporeal masses, inscrutable from behind.

The roar of the engines finally dulls and the plane skims over the clouds while below the rain continues to soak cars, tracks, trains, roads, and everything else that relies on terrestrial gravity.

And suddenly the sun. A burst of sunlight that filters in through the windows and causes the passengers to squint.

Everything else out there is like a giant "nothing" that compels forward motion, precludes stopping, even for a second. There is no other choice if the goal is to survive.

Eladio absently leafs through the newspapers he has purchased in the airport. Although they all essentially report the same news, the way they present it allows for some diversity of perspectives.

It is interesting to analyze the incredibly varied content, all derived from the same information.

In any event, the alarmist news always prevails. Stories reporting already dead news or spreading dangerous conjectures designed to shake up the normal course of daily life. Daily nightmares hammer at the conscious mind until they become routine and unlikely to trigger a reaction no matter how horrible they are.

Nonetheless, Eladio still finds himself compelled to read the newspapers. Maybe because reading about distant tragedies seems to take the edge off one's own miseries.

One of the flight attendants approaches, her smile glued in place, ready to please: She asks. She offers. She notes the response, and rejoins her companions to prepare what they have requested.

Eladio has asked for tomato juice and his seatmate an orange juice.

Words often tell a lot about a person. From the way they are pronounced one can discern certain idiosyncrasies about the speaker. Surely the woman is from the United States. While her Spanish is fluent, there is a certain American cadence to it.

At first glance nothing about her really stands out, except maybe the self assurance typical of those who are free of prejudices and complexes.

Though she seems very feminine, it looks as if she has an independent streak too, he muses.

Soon the beverage cart is beside them and the flight attendant is depositing the orange juice on his companion's tray table.

Eladio abruptly turns towards his neighbor. They smile. They contemplate the pull-out trays as the flight attendant reaches across to hand Eladio his tomato juice.

But suddenly everything is disrupted. Somehow the flight attendant knocks into Eladio's hand and the contents of the glass spill onto his seatmate's skirt.

The effect is like an explosion. Both of them leap to their feet as the tomato juice silently oozes towards the floor like a waterfall of bleeding innards congealed with hate, vexations and reproaches.

But everyone remains calm. They look for solutions, they try to smile, swallowing the discomfort as they might swallow the now-spilled juice.

"Oh God, I am so sorry," apologizes Eladio, hastily brushing at the stained skirt with his napkin. "I truly apologize."

Meanwhile, the other flight attendants have hurried to their aid. Accustomed to dealing with the unexpected, they retrieve the fallen glass, mop at the puddle that is staining the carpet red, and try to pat the passenger's suit dry with towelettes designed just for that purpose.

"I don't know what to say. I am the clumsiest man on this planet," he continues.

Seeing him so distressed, his seatmate tries to ease his mind.

"Don't worry. It really isn't important."

But the stain on the skirt, only somewhat improved and lightened, continues to broadcast Eladio's incompetence.

"At least let me pay for the ruined suit."

The woman regards him smiling. She shakes her head, even giving the impression that she finds the incident amusing.

"Once I get it to the dry cleaners not a trace of tomato will remain," she says lightly. "Please don't worry about it anymore. These things happen. It wasn't your fault."

Her amiability takes him aback. He almost would have preferred her anger. "Now I'm practically obliged to talk to her," he thinks in terror.

But his companion does not seem disposed to start a conversation. Seated once again, she retrieves her book and resumes reading.

Eladio, however, is having a hard time concentrating on his newspaper. "Nothing more unpleasant than a surprise like that," he thinks. And no matter how hard he tries to concentrate on his reading, the letters waver and run together and the words refuse to organize themselves into concrete sentences.

Without interrupting his brooding, the flight attendant approaches Eladio and his companion to give them the menu.

"We will be serving your meal within the hour," she explains. "Select whatever you wish."

Both glance through the list. Eladio does not hesitate. His mother always said it was his ability to choose on the spot that had enabled him to climb up so many rungs.

His seatmate also appears to have made her choice, since after glancing at the sheet she leaves it on the tray table with a gesture of finality.

"She most certainly picked the chicken," he muses: "red meat is suspect these days."

But when the flight attendant returns to take their order, he hears his neighbor ask for the steak.

"Rare please."

Eladio turns towards her.

"Aren't you afraid to eat red meat?"

She shakes her head.

"If you are referring to mad cow disease, the meat we consume has never been as safe as it is right now."

Eladio decides on the chicken.

"Don't think I'm a hypochondriac. It's just that I've never been overly fond of red meat."

Antonia suddenly comes into his mind: she also liked rare meat.

"So you would like the chicken?" asks the flight attendant."

Eladio nods. He folds his newspaper and places it on the tray table.

He stares distractedly at his neighbor's hands. She has long fingers, but the nails are short and manicured. She too closes her book, using a Kleenex to mark the page.

It is not a novel. It is an essay on the aesthetics of visual harmony.

Eladio cannot refrain from brushing his hand across the book lying on the tray table.

"I know this book," he tells her. "It was published by Autumn Books."

"Have you read it?"

"No. But I work for that company. It is an important work, but it hasn't been very successful," he replies.

"I think it's a little jewel," she says. "But I can see why it isn't a best-seller: it is a comprehensive essay for specialists." And seeing that Eladio does not seem to grasp what she is saying, she quickly adds, "I'm an advertising director and publicity specialist."

"Interesting."

"Yes. I find my work fascinating." And after a brief silence, "I'm still working for myself right now but I'll soon be joining a production company based in L.A."

"Is that where you live?"

"Yes. I'm from the States."

"But your Spanish is perfect."

"My mother was Spanish."

She speaks self-assuredly, yet there is nothing strident in her tone. Her hands are resting on the book cover, her features relaxed, and her voice low, almost as if she were thinking aloud.

She turns to face him.

"And you? Somehow I don't think you're on a tourist trip."

"You are correct. I am an executive at Woultmand & Starky and the company has just made me CEO of Frederichstal Publishers in New York."

Silence again. The questions are piling up between them and curiosity struggles to find a path between caution and daring, although neither moves to interrupt the ineffectual act of not speaking.

A million questions are swirling around in Eladio's mind. Who is she? Is she married? She doesn't seem to be. No rings on her fingers. Does she have children? Does she like men or could she be a Lesbian? Maybe she's divorced.

But he does not ask. He waits. He allows his sudden absurd desire to "know" disintegrate into silence.

An unexpected bout of turbulence breaks the circle of silence.

"So you live in Los Angeles?" he inquires.

"Yes. I moved there after my parents died." And quickly, "You're saying that in Spain the type of books I'm reading don't do very well."

"Visual aesthetics are certainly not in vogue in Spain, especially when it comes to books. But even though essays such as the one you are reading don't tend to be commercially successful, they definitely enhance the publisher's reputation."

"You're right. Reputation is important."

And without pausing to think, Eladio offers her his hand.

"Since we're going to be together for seven hours, I suppose I should introduce myself. I'm Eladio Escalante."

"Daniela Rosenthal y Gómez," she replies, shaking his hand.

"Mrs.?"

"Miss."

They both settle back into their seats as if satisfied at having dispensed with an inevitable obligation.

They remain still for a few moments, as if lost in confusing thoughts they are powerless to avoid. They look around, trying to familiarize themselves with their surroundings.

Little by little the fear that has anesthetized the passengers seems to recede. Everyone is calming down and the plane is now an enormous machine advancing safely and soundly towards promising destinations.

Then there is the sun. A welcoming sun that feels supportive, as if the light were solid and could trace firm routes across the vast expanse.

Eladio now contemplates the dropped newspaper and the book atop the adjacent tray table. Both have remained silent. Sometimes, however, silence can beget strange forms of communication. At least that is what Eladio is experiencing at that moment. All at once he understands that his eagerness to isolate himself from his surroundings is fading and now that he has shaken hands with his neighbor, the possibility of remaining indifferent or half asleep has lost its appeal.

"Do you work in New York?" he ventures to ask.

Daniela Rosenthal turns towards him shaking her head.

"No, it's just a stopover for me. From there I continue on to L.A."

"A long trip," he observes.

She nods wordlessly, her dark eyes luminous in the rays pouring in through the window.

After a brief pause, Eladio continues, "Well I'll be staying in New York."

"For a long time?"

"For the rest of my life."

The response is categorical and leaves no room for uncertainty.

But Daniela surely does not grasp the import of what he has said.

"Do you have relatives there?"

Eladio shakes his head.

"Just friends. As far as relatives go, if there are any, I am not aware of them. I have no close family. And I have recently become a widower."

"I'm so sorry" she says. Had you been married long?"

"Just over six years."

He says it as if those lost ties still trigger a certain dependency on an idyllic past that can never be recovered.

Daniela is taken aback. She fears she may have been indiscreet. Sometimes the harder one tries to get it right, the more egregious the blunder.

Eladio perceives her discomfort and rushes to her aid.

"Fortunately I have no shortage of friends. And I work a lot. Work is a good conduit to solid friendships." He says it as if the obligation to complete a particular task might soften his solitude. "The higher ups at Woultmand & Starky are old acquaintances. I'm not afraid to start a new life far from my country."

Daniela nods as if to say she understands and empathizes with what he is saying.

Eladio, meanwhile seems to feel more relaxed now that he has shared that little confidence.

"I hope your new life helps you to recover some of what you have lost," she says.

But Eladio appears not to have heard. He is powerless to prevent the onslaught of memories. That chain of events that he will never be able to uproot from his mind no matter how hard he tries.

"My wife died barely a month ago," he explains. Sometimes I find it hard to accept that I'll never see her again."

Daniela feels uncomfortable. To do something, she shifts in her seat and tries to seem empathetic to Eladio's suffering.

"I understand that your loss must have been very painful," she says in a distressed voice.

Eladio does not reply, but his face tenses. It occurs to him that the response to what his traveling companion has just said would be more a reproach than a consolation.

Once again the scene of that death is replayed in his mind as if it had only just happened. There is Antonia, eyes open wide pleading for help, choking and unable to speak. And the blood is expelled from her lungs deforming the perfection of the lips he had kissed a thousand times.

"Six years is a long time," Daniela continues. "I can imagine how much you must miss her."

She says it in a distressed voice, as if she were casting about in vain for the right words.

Eladio realizes how much he has upset her and tries to remedy the situation.

"I feel badly that I've unburdened myself on you."

"To the contrary, I'm the one who intruded. Please forgive me."

"Please don't worry," he insists. "Saying what's on our minds sometimes helps us unload the things that weigh us down. Especially when the listener is a nice stranger."

Daniela acknowledges the word "nice" with an awkward smile.

"It's true," she responds. "To confide something personal in someone we will never see again can be a tremendous relief." And after a brief pause, "It's sort of like locking up our confidences with no danger of them ever becoming unlocked."

Eladio frowns, gazes fixedly at her and acknowledges that Daniela is as intelligent as she is attractive.

"That is a very astute observation. You're right: no friend is more loyal or safe than the one whose guarantee to forget is reinforced by distance and the impossibility of restoring the broken connection."

"I am still not so sure I'm so astute," she replied. "I am only intimately familiar with my limitations. But in effect, distance and the safety of a definitive parting is a good recommendation to ensure that one's confidences will remain secret."

"Don't kid yourself," he rejoins. "Smart people recognize their limitations. Only idiots seem to be unaware of them. That's why they're idiots."

Daniela bursts out laughing and the tension that had developed just moments before quickly dissolves.

"In any event," she says, "raw intelligence—in other words, sedentary intelligence that is not put to use, never has the dust shaken off it—is usually not foolproof in practice. I know so many sharp, quick-witted people who fall all over themselves when the time comes to really show what they're made of."

Eladio nods. But as he listens to her the bonds holding him prisoner to the past constrict: how to forget when the bonds tighten over his body, yoking his ideas . . . oblivion is always a chimera.

"You're right," he assents, his gaze wandering slightly. "Even those of us who consider ourselves wise are capable of the most spectacular missteps."

Daniela agrees, although she has no way of grasping the full meaning of what Eladio has said.

"It's inevitable. So often we mistake illusion for reality. It's the biggest threat we face: losing our compass." She gazes into the distance. "Humanity is imperfect. That's why we have the wrong idea about what is real."

Eladio does not reply. He simply regards her. Without being aware of it, he is analyzing her features. They are attractive although not in the conventional sense. And she is not wearing make up. Without presuming to be beautiful, her clean, fresh face is remarkable in the fineness of its skin, its straightforward countenance and the expressiveness of its gaze.

"In my field," Daniela continues, "we often have mistaken notions of reality, so we have to be very cognizant of that eventuality. More than once I've had to let go of what is generally considered reality so that what I'm aiming for in my work will end up being real."

Eladio gently clears his throat. He is disconcerted by the thoughtful mind that has been assigned to him as a seatmate. He had not expected that the circumlocutions of a routine trip could so quickly devise such a rich exchange.

"Have you been in advertising for a long time?"

Daniela nods and lets out a smiling breath.

"Too many. Enough to make a mess of all the desirable things in life, while earning more than I ever dreamed possible."

Eladio feigns a curiosity he does not feel.

"So I guess you worked so much in order to make money."

"No. There was another more compelling reason. To make money just for the sake of it doesn't get you anywhere. What I wanted was to be independent. Money gives you independence."

"Not always," he interjected. "It can also make you a slave. You just said so. As you put it, working so much has gotten in the way of the things you wanted."

"That's right."

"May I ask what that was?"

"To start a family, have children." And self-deprecatingly, "Basically, to experience the pleasures commonly known in Spain as the bourgeois life."

"And what kept you from your dream? I am not persuaded by the excuse about work."

"Believe it or not, money was an important factor at first. I had to support myself. Later I found I had become ensnared by my work without realizing it. I mean, I no longer worked to live, I lived to work. I fell in love with my profession."

"And are you still in love with it?"

"Enough to neutralize certain aspects of life that I probably won't ever have at this stage."

"Are you sorry?"

"Yes, I'm sorry."

"In any case, you're still young. If you've missed one train you can get the next one."

Daniela shifted in her seat again. She hesitates. She is afraid of being too frank. But in the end she opens up.

"The thing is, a few years ago I had the chance to get on that train. But once I was on it, I changed my mind. I stepped back down on to the platform and let it go." She confesses this with a rueful smile. "Actually that train wasn't on the right

track. The truth is, some trains just don't listen to reason," she is still smiling. "To be honest, the man I was going to marry was incompatible with my work."

"Did you love him?"

"Yes. I loved him. But we were like two different planets. Or the sun and the moon. Polar opposites situated in a vacuum that was only rarely filled by moments of understanding."

His expression humorous, Eladio tries to lighten the rather sticky subject matter.

"And might one inquire which one of you was the moon and which the sun?"

"I don't know. In any case, if I was the moon, the light of that sun may well have embraced me, but it didn't light me up."

"So you remained single, free and emancipated."

"Yes. And I am about to stop being all of that."

And noticing Eladio's expectant gaze, she continues. "I am getting married to a producer. We will be working together." She explains without waiting for a reply. "My maternal grandmother is still alive, but she is very ill. I wanted to see her—hug her again—before the wedding. That is why I went to Spain."

Eladio nods his understanding. "So you've finally found the man you needed."

Daniela assents without meeting his gaze and Eladio has the impression that this is simply her way of refocusing what she has just explained.

"Had it been a while since you had visited Spain?" he inquired.

"No. I escape every chance I get to get my fill of all the changes that are happening there." And since Eladio appears to be waiting for her to explain, Daniela goes on. "Not only Spain is changing. It's happening all over Europe. Even the U.S. is undergoing a lot of permutations." And after a brief silence, "It's strange the way civilized countries are always trying to emulate on another. For example, America is assimilating some of the good things about Spain, while Europe is busy absorbing the bad things about America."

Although she has said this with a certain degree of irony, Eladio seems to share her opinion.

"You're right," he agrees.

"Some roots, though, might appear to be dried up, but they are still alive. So you can't give up. That's what life is about:

hope. Unless you hope for something, whatever it may be, you can't really live."

"And yet sometimes 'hoping' can be as irrelevant as dreaming. There are things that never come to pass, no matter how much we may hope for them."

He has said it with his eyes fixed on the seat in front of him: his voice cracked and the pain inside him exposed as something beyond the limits of mere fatigue.

"But one mustn't be pessimistic. Dreaming is also part of life. Isn't that what Calderon said?" Eladio expounds, trying to restore a certain lightness. "I am referring to your wedding."

Daniela does not reply, she moves a hand towards her head and gently brushes back her long hair.

"If I were very young, I would believe in those types of dreams. But the age of fantasies is over as far as I am concerned. I am about to turn thirty-nine. I am no longer a child. Your illusions change as you approach forty. They become much too mundane to deserve to be called dreams."

"Thirty-nine. I would have sworn you were younger."

"Should I thank you for the compliment? She asks teasingly. "I'm not so sure. In any case, my perspective on life no longer includes figments of the imagination. I think I'm embarking fully on that chimera we call reality."

Eladio takes a deep breath and clears his throat again.

"And I have only just emerged from a nightmare."

He says this absently, without knowing exactly why. Sometimes human expressions act of their own volition, as if dictated by alien forces.

"That's natural," she rejoins. "It must be very sad to lose someone who has played such a central role in your life."

Eladio does not reply. He looks at her. He tries to smile, to allow a more neutral expression dissolve the depressing synergy that has arisen between them.

"I'm about to turn forty-seven," he confesses. "At this stage, I no longer expect great things from life either."

But Daniela does not accept this contention.

"A forty-seven year old man does not have the right to give up hope," she says firmly. "You're at the age when your second youth begins."

During my initial incursions into Autumn Books, the first thing I had to establish was a culture of the lockout. The executives were not producing as they should, nor were they putting in the hours. Important tasks were constantly being left half finished.

It was necessary to call a meeting of the executive staff from the various divisions and convey to them that simply meeting the established goals was not enough to ensure good outcomes. "You have to exceed the goals, expand them. Good planning cannot be confined to a schedule," I insisted. "Lack of motivation is the quickest way to fail."

I suggested that a salary should not reflect one's worth, but rather one's merits. "And merit is necessarily connected to what one is able to negotiate."

I insisted on the notion that a company should never be governed by friendships or family concerns: "the logical thing is to earn your salary based on market outcomes." And I added that in the future, regulations would be in place to increase the commissions in divisions that contributed the most to project globalization.

Based on those premises it was necessary to lay off some slackers who thought they owned the work and refused to cooperate with the other divisions to ensure that their efforts would also reap the desired fruits.

That rather drastic beginning provoked a certain degree of turmoil that Douglas Raft had already anticipated. "You just keep moving. Don't worry about the negative commentary."

I gradually put into practice my points of view even at the risk of inciting certain interpretations that at first seemed unpleasant. "We can't focus on winning the minor battles on the periphery of what others are doing. We've got to make sure that the autonomous divisions unite and support each other to promote good outcomes, not only for themselves but for each other. This is the secret to ensuring that we all win the war."

Sometimes, when I met with different executives, Douglas would listen to my presentations from the doorway. Although I could not see him, his unmistakable cough gave him away.

Later, when we were alone, he would encouraged me to forge ahead. "I really liked what you said about humanism." He was referring to my efforts to show the staff that humanism reduced to a single person rather than encompassing the entire team was an inhuman humanism.

Indeed, I had to draw on a variety of strategies with those who simply did as they pleased, without any thought for what the other executives were doing. I had to make it clear that they would have to change their autonomic tendencies in order to galvanize the synergies of team work.

I soon raised the urgent need to merge the Madrid office with the Barcelona headquarters. "If we don't merge to mutually reinforce their successes, just as the different divisions have merged to strengthen the financial panorama, then Autumn Books will always be a divided company. It will always come up short and will be ill-equipped to transform itself into a financial force to be reckoned with."

Mahler lost no time in applauding my proposition. He had just returned from one of his trips and as soon as Douglas had briefed him on my interventions he had made haste to receive me in his office.

I recall the office now, just as it was the first time I entered the building of Woultmand & Starky. By then, however, I was no longer impressed by my surroundings. There was the Louis XV table sandwiched between the two windows which, on that overcast afternoon, neither illuminated nor cast shadows on the features of the supreme chief.

That time, Mahler went so far as to rise from his chair to shake my hand. "Congratulations, Escalante. What you've achieved in the short time you've been with us far surpasses any expectations we might have had."

I can also see Douglas Raft's satisfied expression, reveling in the small triumph of having recommended me as director of administration.

That afternoon, I raised with Mahler the idea that the publishing house should establish branch offices in all of the financially viable franchises throughout Spain. "No matter how much we distribute and promote the books, I'm convinced that we can boost sales exponentially if we make it so that the publications also come from the offices situated in strategic locations across the peninsula."

Mahler appeared to waver at that, however. "You realize, of course, that the strategy you are proposing is somewhat obsolete. The approach now is to sell a certain number of copies instead of trying for an exhaustive distribution. That way, once we've reached the quota, we can get rid of what's already been published and put out new books. Especially if the authors are young. Today's economy stresses the image of the authors over the content of the publications."

While it was true that the formula he described was yielding major bonanzas in the publishing world, I dared to differ. "I am aware of that Mr. Mahler. The approach you're describing is certainly in vogue, but I can guarantee that it's shortsighted: bread for today, hunger for tomorrow. Readers are not stupid. To insist that all books are cultural icons, when most are nothing more than an anticultural mishmash is just a cheap trick. There will come a time when people will get fed up with reading so much trash. One has to know how to distinguish and promote authentic literature. That's why I think it would be useful to create a chain of branch offices. There are highly skilled people all over Spain with the know-how to assimilate new market technologies. All they need is a little boost and they'd be eager to develop their own criteria and become responsible promoters of quality books."

Mahler appeared to hesitate. He was still clinging to the terms adopted by all of the mainstream publishing houses. It was Douglas Raft who backed me up.

"I think Eladio is right. The nouveau 'use and discard' system discredits the company, cheats the reader and discourages the writer. It wouldn't take long to return to the old system of establishing an editorial foundation. You have to classify the materials based on their caliber. Spotlight the worthwhile books and support capable writers to make sure their works are recognized and they are not passed over along with the run of the mill authors."

We covered a lot of ground that afternoon. I remember when I finally went out into the street the air smelled the way rain does just before it pours down on the city. It was winter and a cold front was trailing in icy gusts, as if from some floating iceberg made of earth.

At the time I had no idea that my lectures on the need to create human teams and genuinely evaluate a book's content would come to be seen as some sort of editorial renaissance.

As it was, Douglas Raft soon let me know that my arguments had struck a chord with Mahler. I had a green light to run with my ideas. It was a time of travel across Spain, of contacts with trained professionals, of meeting people who saw me as some sort of patron of the arts willing to cut the umbilical cord that bound them to their small worlds of unfulfilled dreams and depressing convictions that they would never ever reach the port of their desires.

That strategy helped solidify the rise of Autumn Books during the ensuing years and its prestige grew along with its profits.

By then the president of Woultmand & Starky had become much more than a boss to me. When he returned from his trips, Douglas Raft encouraged me to accept Mahler's invitations, not as a business associate but as another friend among the many who surrounded him at social events.

It was at one of these gatherings that I met his sister-in-law. Luisa Escartín lived with Mahler's daughter Antonia, the girl who still inhabited the frame on the Louis XV table in his office. Luisa was still young then, despite her dour expression and awkward smile.

At the time, nothing that was going on around me gave the slightest inkling of what that world had in store for me.

I buried myself in my work. I was not thinking about the future. I knew a lot of people and in a way I felt privileged to be rubbing elbows with such an important crowd, so different from the people I knew when my father was alive.

The threats that life was hiding from us were completely absent from the incessant repartee among those influential names that my mother would frequently spy in romance magazines. "So you've met so-and-so?" She asked it as if my hobnobbing with certain individuals might mean their importance would rub off on me.

I still had not realized that all of those things were just specks, useless cinders that resisted dissolving into "nothings."

In my delusions of a man raised up by success, I regarded that world through the lens of one who has reached the peak of an unscalable mountain.

At the same time, in my new environment I occasionally lost my bearings when it came to women.

I am not sure why, but there was something about me that appealed to them. At least Douglas Raft was always assuring me of this fact. "The way you carry yourself, of course you're going to drive them crazy."

Douglas was clearly exaggerating. Sometimes I would look in the mirror, searching for the secret to the appeal they were always attributing to me. But the man reflected there was always just another face in the crowd who, by dint of imitating mannerisms, attitudes and niceties, had somehow managed to leave behind his humble origins.

Sometimes the women who were—according to Douglas—"after me," asked me about my parents. I never lied to them. I did, however, twist the truth slightly. "My father was in the theater business." "My mother was in charge of the domestic front." The truth was, "has-beens" did not count in my new life. Everything had changed. Even the conversations were different.

In that world, sexual debacles were all the rage, along with overenthusiasm, political inconformity and the often self-serving whirlwinds of adultery and deceit.

There was a lot of talk about politics, the universal conscience, new technologies and the need to shake off the moral constraints that so encumbered the daily interactions of normal people.

I admit I still felt uncomfortable whenever I violated one of the moral values my mother had drilled into me when we lived on rat street.

Usually, however, temptation trumped the more remote recommendations of my mother. And though she always told me, "Happiness is living by God's laws," when I sunk into the depths of such unsuspected pleasures, the happiness my mother portended slowly receded before my long-coveted freedom and independence.

The truth is that my sex life proceeded without impediments in a somewhat mawkish feminine landscape quite given over to frivolity.

It took me a while to figure out how deceptive that lifestyle was. What it actually took was for my delusions to fade into nothing more than stray impulses the day I met Antonia. She was the one who gave me to understand that the women I had been with up to then were shooting stars: worthless gusts of wind that were gone in seconds. Mere fluctuations marking glorious interludes in time, with no past and no future.

Antonia's presence was a thousand times more powerful than all of my sterile feminine contacts put together.

Other than that, besides work—which took up a lot of hours—I remember the intensity of a more or less hollow world and the sense of something pedantic closing in on my life.

Left far behind was the lingering fear of financial instability and the need to navigate the sordid reality of aloof distaste, the double-edged exchanges or the barely concealed gibes directed at one who did not really belong to a world ignorant of the tyranny of poverty.

Now, when I look back on that part of my life, I understand that nothing around me was unpleasant. It all boiled down to a life free of problems, disenchantment or disillusion.

I would like to know how many of all of the things I took in stride—things that could dazzle and excite—had a solid *raison d'être*.

But at the time I did not stop to dwell on "reasons." I was operating on instinct and my instincts told me never to underestimate the logic of utter well-being.

During the summer holiday, Douglas Raft invited me to visit his summer home in Marbella.

At the time, Marbella was all restless drone, shattered monotony, sensation on edge. The sun—which burned so intensely that its incandescence seemed to linger beyond nightfall—was its currency: the date who never failed to show up.

It mattered little that your hands were dripping with sweat after just instants in the suffocating heat or that emotions erupted for no real reason. The important thing in that milieu was the somewhat sticky immediacy of an endless parade of half-naked bodies, of minds half-distorted by sex, innocent cover-ups, the inscrutable petulance of extremely refined officials, and those experts of irony dedicated to provoking smiles with their seemingly ingenuous little slip-ups, if for no other reason than to ward off any hint of ennui that might threaten to take hold of some pessimist.

Although Douglas Raft's house was not in the same neighborhood as Mahler's opulent dwelling, the supreme chief usually spent most of his time with Douglas and me whenever he was in Marbella. The excuse was that his house—always teeming with his daughter Antonia's friends and his sister-in-law's dour cronies—was the refuge of the boring, the pedantic, and those whose sole purpose in life was to criticize the neighbors. "I just don't feel comfortable there," he explained. "I know they tire of me too, but I reserve the right to tire of those who in turn tire because of me," turning into a tongue-twister the irritation he felt when he settled himself into his own house.

Looking back on those conversations, I remember in my ignorance imagining that Anton Mahler's problem was his sister-in-law's staid lifestyle and the insipid pursuits of his daughter Antonia (still a teenager) and her friends. It was as if a fanatic of the sea were obliged to endure the arid climate of a remote water-deprived land.

The upshot was that whenever he was able, he appeared at

Douglas Raft's house to talk about the things he was passionate about—like finances, politics, the aurora borealises of skies papered with banknotes—and to visit with the people who frequently dropped by in the evening.

Occasionally Mahler would mention Berta, the nanny who had cared for his daughter since birth. "She's the only sane person in the entire house."

It seemed that this Berta would while away the hours talking with him about how to invest the savings she earned by putting up with bad moods, misbehavior, and the endless disturbances that turned the house of his sister-in-law into a psychiatrist's waiting room. "So many young people do nothing more than stir everything up and set Miss Luisa's nerves on edge," Berta would grumble.

That was more or less what Mahler had to say when he sought out the solace of our company.

But the complaints were always short-lived. Once he had completed his mission to spend a couple of days with Antonia, Mahler was done with his paternal obligations: what were feet for anyway? At the slightest hitch, the vacation was over and he would be off to God knows where leaving Aunt Luisa to deal with her niece's pals and Berta's holding the bag with her financial fantasies.

As I reconstruct that *modus operandi* now, it doesn't strike me as at all strange, but at the time I found it shocking. I could not understand how a father could be so afflicted with a constant desire to flee. The truth was that no matter how much appeal the world of finances might hold for him, no matter how hooked he might be, it did not make sense that he could do without his daughter as he did. "She's his own flesh and blood after all," I would say whenever Douglas stood up for Mahler.

The way he said it, though, left the impression that Anton Mahler was hiding something that he was not unaware of. I did not, however, feel it was prudent to interfere without invitation. "He must have some secret love affair going on," I would think, and I would change the subject.

I now understand his restlessness and his precipitous retreats and even his tendency to dwell on the stupid inconveniences in the household whenever his daughter Antonia decided to invite her friends over.

The whole picture is revealed now, a clear theatrical representation with no intrigues lurking in shadows. Even his sister-in-law's forced smile is no longer a mystery.

Everything that for years was just one continuous question mark is now a tangible image, detailed and weighted with logic.

And yet it took over ten years to completely iron out the wrinkle of the unknown.

The beginning of those impervious revelations coincided with Antonia's arrival in Marbella after a stint at a Swiss school to finish her education. Her father was planning to throw her a huge bash to celebrate her eighteenth birthday.

It's as if I am seeing him, his hat jammed on his head to keep the sun off his receding hairline, the golf clubs stowed in the cart, acting the part of pro golfer along with Douglas Raft, while I, in my capacity as a complete novice, tried without success to emulate them. "The party will be on the grounds of the Guadalmina Hotel. I want the best that Marbella has to offer to be there."

He said it with enthusiasm, as if this coming out party of sorts for his daughter Antonia was the social event of the season.

His usual flight instinct was nowhere in evidence. Everything revolved around his daughter. The mystery daughter I had yet to meet, who was, in my far off memory, just a picture frame on a Louis XV table, containing a photograph of a blond girl with light blue eyes and a forced smile.

That night, as we discussed Mahler's enthusiasm over Antonia's birthday party, I remember Douglas commenting to me something I had not known. "Mahler might appear aloof from his daughter, but he adores her. Antonia is a lot like her mother and no one meant more to Mahler than his wife. That's why he never remarried."

And frowning, he finally confessed, "The poor thing lost herself to drugs. No one knows how she got hooked, but when she died in childbirth, all of the doctors said that drugs had a lot to do with it."

I think that was when I first took an interest in Antonia as an individual.

It was an interest steeped in compassion. It was hard to imagine a newborn orphaned of the person who had given her life and growing up under the protection of an aunt who, much as she might love her, could never make up for a mother's love.

I asked Douglas what she was like. "Beautiful," he replied. "You won't find a more gorgeous creature in all of Marbella. I haven't spent a lot of time with her, but everyone who knows her describes her as intelligent, very witty and extremely sensitive."

Most of the tables were full by the time we arrived at the party. The night wore on slowly, amid hanging lights, glittering stars and soft music that seemed to filter through the trees and branches of the enormous garden that extended from the hotel entrance to the sea.

Of course Mahler had spared no expense to celebrate his daughter's eighteenth birthday. Everything exuded grandiloquence. Metaphors embodied in fireworks, mutating lights and harmonious sounds.

And suddenly she was there.

She was wearing a white dress, her tanned skin accentuating the paleness of her blue eyes and her blond hair framing perfect features that still retained a hint of the innocence in that childhood photograph.

She was immediately swarmed by a crowd of young people who gathered round in admiration to congratulate and flatter, to assure her there was "no one else like her" and that her beauty was out of this world.

And she was smiling. The classic smile of a woman at once shy and flirtatious, who accepts and demurs, flashes amused looks and reluctantly acquiesces.

I remember that Douglas Raft went up to kiss her and that was the first time I heard her voice. "How nice to see you," I heard her say.

It was the silky voice of a child already initiated into the fascinating adventure of being a woman. A voice as if extracted from an imposed calm incompatible with her air of a girl recently exposed to the adult world.

Douglas grabbed my arm and pulled me in her direction. "I suppose you've heard your father mention our illustrious colleague, Eladio Escalante."

Antonia looked at me still smiling, as she held out her hand. "How could I not know him? My father always talks about you. He says you've changed the face of Autumn Books."

Her manner of speaking exuded empathy. She couldn't help it: everything about Antonia flowed into the right comment, impeccable manners, natural harmonies, and radiations that filled the air with inexplicable wonders.

"I'm glad," I said. "It's always nice to know that a girl like you has a high opinion of someone like me."

I said it without realizing exactly what I was referring to when I referred to myself. The presence of that girl-woman was too overwhelming not to feel self-conscious.

At that moment, Antonia was, for me, a rare experience on the legendary evening that Mahler had organized. Nothing could compare to her figure, not too tall but incredibly well proportioned, or her loose hair barely sweeping her slender, well-formed shoulders, and above all, the impact of her gorgeous features.

If goddesses exist, not one of them could have held a candle to the diminutive goddess standing before me who, as she regarded me, seemed to spirit me away in dreamlike fantasies beyond my imagination.

Hard as I try, I have never been able to forget the impact her presence had on me.

I remember that for an interminable instant our mutual fascination rendered us incapable of pulling back enough to keep people from realizing that some indefinable scheme was being hatched between us.

Then there was the alcohol: a time bomb with a delay fuse ever ready to heighten attractions and inspire overwhelming urges.

Alcohol is often the great procuress of hidden feelings. Rarely does she refrain from applying her stimulants to dispel our sense of the impossible.

And the alcohol was there for us: willing to break ground, plot a treacherous course, help us along towards seemingly unattainable goals.

I do not know what happened, how it happened, or why it happened, but that night the only object in my world was Mahler's daughter. It was not a premonition. It was not even some vague fantasy. It was simply the conviction that despite the age difference, that child-woman was going to end up being the reason for my existence.

Daniela's reference to the second youth that might materialize out of Eladio's forty-seven years elicits a look of skepticism.

"I really don't understand how we can regard youth as any guarantee. Youth tends to be reckless, and as such, rarely gets it right. No. I don't believe in this second youth you refer to. I do, however, believe in a maturity that acts youthful."

Daniela frowns and looks around her, as if casting about for the right response. What Eladio is trying to say about youthful recklessness does not match the image she has developed of her lost happiness.

"But youth is what determines our course in life. That's why I sometimes think I made a mistake by rejecting a bourgeois lifestyle. Maybe I won out as a liberated woman, but I've never known real happiness, precisely because I chose independence."

Eladio does not reply. He simply looks at her expectantly, as if he is waiting for her to continue.

At her prolonged silence, however, he decides to try to draw her out of the strangely bemused state she seems to have settled into.

"And yet you've just informed me that you're soon going to become familiar with the bourgeois life you rejected when you got off that train."

Daniela turns towards him smiling broadly.

"Oh no. It isn't going to be a conventional union: you know, the so-called love of a lifetime. My fiancé and I have known each other for years. We're good friends. We love each other in our own way but neither of us expects any major sense of fulfillment in the traditional sense. Romantic love as I experienced it departed with the train I missed. Our future marriage is more like a merger of business and affection. Something like a pact, without all those oppressive illusions to get in our way."

"So you're still thinking about that missed train?" Eladio persists in a joking voice.

"I don't know. Why not be honest? Sometimes we confuse love for what we feel after we've let the object of our desire slip away. And yet the truth is, I haven't fallen in love since."

Eladio frowns and attempts a more transcendental approach.

"Be that as it may, I hope your marriage brings you happiness. Even though in this world, love always carries with it a large dose of indifference, indifference can also inspire a great deal of love."

"It all sounds so puerile. I have very few expectations in that regard. Why kid ourselves? No one ever finds true happiness. At my age it would be ridiculous to harbor impossible dreams. Leave that to the young." And before Eladio can reply, "How can one be happy when everything around us is just one enormous catastrophe? Impossible. The only thing I aspire to is a prolonged peace." And as if she regrets what she had *just said, she brushes her hand lightly over Eladio's arm and quickly removes it. "Forgive me. I tend to get carried away by my negativity. I was born that way and can't seem to get past it. But I don't think I'm infallible. Which is why I don't want to be a doom-sayer. Maybe you have known the happiness I barely glimpsed way back when. Who am I to deny it?"*

Eladio nods, his eyes closed. He must be thinking that his seatmate has been too much of a fighter to get caught up in dramatic illusions. One look at her and it is easy to see that her self-assured opinions are the product of a mind not given to oversentimentality.

"In any event, happiness—as we understand it in our more exhilarating moments—is always circumstantial" he replies. "So you're essentially correct. Any unanticipated situation can put an end to it."

Daniela settles back against the seat and stretches her legs. Once again, she seems to feel guilty for having touched a sensitive nerve in her companion. She must think that a man who knew happiness with a woman who has died could never accept that happiness does not exist.

A certain instinctive tension seems to take hold of them.

Most likely they are both thinking how bizarre it is that they have chosen to expose their innermost thoughts to a total stranger, as if they'd known each other all their lives.

Maybe it is because of the stain on the skirt. Or maybe the delayed takeoff. Or it could be that the intense sunlight filtering through the windows is bathing them both in an unexpected warmth. It is not out of the question either that Daniela's anxiety over having held up the other passengers has something to do with it. And her apologies, her cheeks flushed with embarrassment. And the spilled glass. And the flight attendants cleaning the floor. Or it could be that the confluence of all those things is conspiring to create the strange escape valve that seems to be operating between them now. The emancipation of hidden things, when it happens unexpectedly, can sometimes block what is considered logical and assign logic to things that make no sense at all.

Eladio now recalls something Daniela said when they first started talking. Something about how confiding in someone you'll never see again is the best guarantee.

Daniela's right, he thinks suddenly. The most faithful in-

dividual is the one who will never have the opportunity to be unfaithful.

But there are always some corners of our minds that—no matter how desperately they need to shed their detritus of pain—are certain to remain mental hostages forever. Nothing that corrupts life—try as it might to remain unnoticed—can ever escape that inevitable prison.

Eladio suddenly notices the ailing child in the seat in front of his. Right now he is resting on his mother's arm. And he remembers. Remembers that other little boy who used to turn to him for help, a bewildered look in his eyes. Eyes that did not understand. That sought and did not find. That required joys and only found sorrows.

A slight jolt of the plane causes his newspaper to slide off the tray table and onto the floor.

Picking it up, Eladio shows Daniela the front page.

"There's your future president," he says, showing her Bush's photograph. But Daniela shrugs as if to say that politics do not interest her in the slightest.

"In my opinion, both Gore and Bush are merely two ambitious politicians with similar platforms." And seeing that Eladio does not react, "Neither of them is capable of accepting that life is more than a fleeting, materialistic circumstance," Daniela asserts drastically. "The only thing American politicians think about is power: how to rule the world and accumulate wealth."

She says it with contempt, her gaze hardened, her mouth set in a bitter line.

Eladio regards her intently. Suddenly Daniela is a different woman: someone whose sensibilities appear to have collided with something too painful to remain impassive.

"See if I'm not right. To them the rest of us human beings are just plants. Yes, don't laugh. Plants rooted in the soil, trained to move in whichever direction the wind blows, or the breeze, or the rain they tolerate or cause to fall. In sum, we can only move when some political-economic element balances us. What I'm trying to say is that what our governors like to do is pull the strings of the human puppet, but none of them are trying to make it so that it isn't a puppet any longer."

"And yet, if those strings are not pulled, what would become of us? For better or for worse, somebody has to lead us."

Daniela looks annoyed but makes no reply. She merely contemplates the headrest of the seat in front of her and lowers her head with a contemptuous sound.

"You're not going to tell me you don't believe in democracy," *he inquires.*

"Of course I do. The ones who don't are the ones who use that brand of politics to turn democracy into a veiled dictatorship."

"So what would be your ideal?"

"Do away with greed. Use the money allocated for space exploration to help disadvantaged countries. Stop regarding an economic boom as a victory. But no: in America everything revolves around the damned economy. If the Republicans propose a tax cut, it's because the tax—which may never have been cut at all—doesn't have much of an impact on the powerful. And the Democrats propose a smaller tax cut, and recommend increased spending. It's a shame but they're all dancing to the tune of the dollar sign. Neither of the parties seems to recall that above and beyond the economic issues, there are certain basic values which are even more important, even if they don't have anything to do with fiscal management. Those values don't count. To the contrary, they're buried to make sure they don't disturb the flow of multinational interests."

"I guess you are referring to the advantages that benefit the richest?"

"No," replies Daniela unequivocally. "I am referring to the lack of interest in the metaphysics of the human being, the quality that each person deserves, the rights of men and women, the disregard for death. It's all well and good that Bush has come out against abortion, but what about his eagerness to preserve the death penalty?"

Eladio listens to her in silence. He dares not interrupt her, agree with her or, heaven forbid, contradict her.

Without realizing it, Daniela has touched an extremely painful nerve. Even unrevealed destinies sometimes erupt out of the blue. They show up unexpectedly and head straight for the soul, dodging reproaches, running roughshod over omnipresent pasts, spewing fountains of rot and emitting deadly radiations. So he says nothing.

He would have liked to agree with her. To show her that beyond conventional politics lie emotions and impatience and excruciating ruptures. Egregious things wrapped in ignorance, which is perhaps more egregious yet. Extreme motives for reprisals. And slavery. Yes, slavery most of all.

"In any event," Daniela continues, "Bush's motives are crystal clear and almost convincing, but just because you can explain your reasons for wanting something (such as the presidency of the United States) does not mean it is reasonable that you should have it."

Eladio remains silent. He now thinks that Daniela's views may have something to do with her religion.

"So are you Catholic?"

"Practicing even."

"And aren't you prohibited from practicing your religion?"

She bursts out laughing.

"Fortunately, America isn't like Spain. My country has never experienced religious intolerance. In fact, most Americans believe in God."

"And they don't have complexes?"

"To the contrary, the non-believers are the ones with complexes."

"It's exactly the opposite in Spain. Even though religion is no longer persecuted, people look down on believers. They're considered out of touch or a little naïve. It's a form of persecution in disguise, along the lines of a dictatorship cloaked in democracy. To an extent, Spain is still experiencing Marxist paroxysms and there's nothing it can do about it."

After a brief lapse, Daniela ventures,

"I take it you're Catholic too? I've heard that in Spain even the hardcores and atheists baptize their kids and see to it that they make their first communion."

"And hold funerals and sponsor processions and use religious traditions as an excuse for orgies," Eladio joked. "Yes, I'm Catholic, but not practicing. There really are no practicing Catholics." He's said it flatly, as if Daniela were not listening. He takes a deep breath and attempts a smile. "Sometimes life turns the things you once believed important into a heap of ambiguities. When I was young, I practiced. I believed. I had faith. My mother took it upon herself to drill into my head that human beings without religion ran the risk of turning into a herd of foul-mouthed beasts. And should that moment ever come, the earth would turn into a cemetery of the lawless, or in the best case scenario, a base comedy performed before an autistic audience."

"Your mom was right. Is she still alive?"

"No, She died. I think I mentioned that I don't have any family left."

"You did. I'd forgotten. What was your mother like?"

"Simple. A very simple woman. But smart, hardworking, tenacious." Eladio looks around as if he believes he might catch a glimpse of her. "She told me something once that I've never forgotten: 'Just remember, Son, when we set a goal for ourselves that is based on the short span of a lifetime, any effort to get ahead turns into a marathon with no victors. Only the vanquished. Only losers. The routines may be more or less satisfactory, but they lack hope. We live in time and time can never be anything more than an insignificant measure.' "

"She said that?"

"She said a lot of things. She also said time was the enemy of man."

"Why?"

"Because according to her, time turns hope into something trivial, meaning it distorts it. It deceives us. It leads us to believe that whatever elevates us is important. She used to say that we forget that time, no matter how long it seems, is always short, and that the important thing is to find success in the things that never end."

"And did you follow her advice?"

Eladio shakes his head.

"No. But sometimes I think my mother was right."

"And yet you don't vacillate? I don't get it."

"I don't either."

"So?"

"I go with the flow."

"Why?"

"Maybe because I'm used to it, or I'm lazy, or because everyone else does, or because I'm not scared of death. Who knows?"

I can see clearly now what was only a nebula at the time: a nebula composed of a thousand contradictory, but equally attractive variations.

42

In my apprenticeship as a sought-after man, I had passed the test of high society with honors. But still to come were the countless daily occurrences that seemed to insinuate themselves through the cracks of the unexpected.

They were things that came up out of the blue as if propelled by a little elf. Subtle things with no apparent cause. But now as I ponder everything that transpired, I can see they shared a common purpose: to introduce me wholly into Antonia's world.

Nonetheless, when I met her that night my first thought was that even though she was more beautiful than any woman I had ever met, I could never presume that anything real could come of it for me. Standing there right in front of me, she was as inaccessible as any shrine, because of the age difference as much as the social chasm between us.

Twenty-two years was too many autumns for the youth of that sculptural wonder to draw aside the sacred curtain of years that separated us.

It was impossible that the rules of logic could become so distorted and that folly should prevail over my entire history, pockmarked as it was by partially restored ruins.

That is who I was then: a much sought after relic. Someone who not only served to defend the massive economic fortress known as Autumn Books—and ultimately the transnational corporation Woultmand & Starky—but also occupied a tangential pedestal in the magnificent world of high society.

There was also the matter of my sense of responsibility. Much as my totalitarian impulses fought to govern my actions, my passion for freedom and loyalty to my boss stopped me from any missteps that might have caused Mahler's trust in me to erode. And then there was my conscience, which up to then had played a central role in how I set my priorities.

But that night, none of those thoughts crossed my mind. My surroundings were too dazzling and Antonia's presence too overwhelming to stop the alcohol I had consumed from obliterating my usual lucidity. The only thing that mattered was the need to spend as much time as possible with Antonia, to talk with her, to feel her close to me.

It is possible that our hopes were imposed by the atmosphere, but even so, we barely missed a dance together. We were oblivious to the comments we were provoking. Antonia clearly did not want to leave my side and I was beginning to think the evening might not just recede into the past—might instead become a continuous present. So I followed her lead, never imagining that my feelings could put an end to Antonia's innocence or to my own good intentions, which were still struggling to prevail over the soft music, caressing breezes, and the absurd sentimental traps poised to transform the birthday party of that wonderful creature into a newly erected Parthenon, or a Vatican fallen into magnificent ruin.

Everything about that night was a derangement of reason that made way for the most stimulating and blinding enthusiasm.

Antonia laughed, joked, offered ingenuous comments and sometimes allowed her cheek to brush against my chest when she rested against me exhausted after so many dances.

I also clearly recall being in my best form intellectually. Not that I was deliberately trying to impress her, but I drew on all of my creativity to shower her with compliments, toss off clever phrases and act the man of the world.

The bad part was waking up. The blurred awakening the following morning and my conversation with Douglas Raft. "It looks as if the Mahler girl has stolen your heart," he said looking me straight in the eye at breakfast. "No one at the party could possibly have missed it."

I told him that I did not care one whit what people said. "Who could imagine an eighteen year old girl falling for an almost forty year old man?" I said tersely. "If we spent some time together it was because she was interested in learning about the work I did with her father."

Douglas acted as if he believed me but I was not fooled. "I warn you she isn't just any girl. Watch your step, Eladio, because before you know it, you're going to feel bound to her and worse yet, with no hope whatsoever."

I replied that I was not concerned with futile hopes. "It was a lark. A summer reverie with a mermaid. And far from causing me any consternation, she has gone back out to sea never to return. It was nothing," I insisted.

Then Douglas asked me whether I intended to see her again.

I responded that Antonia was nothing more to me than a pleasant memory that did not set my neurons jumping. "The world is full of good looking women, so I'm not going to let myself get all worked up with those kinds of fantasies."

But Douglas Raft was not about to give up so easily. "Indeed there are lots of pretty women, but they lack Antonia's wit."

He explained to me then that although he did not know her very well, her father had always spoken of her. "Despite her gentle demeanor, she has character. She knows exactly what she wants. And if she wants something, she's not about to let anyone take it away from her."

He also told me about Aunt Luisa. "She was born with a capitalist ethic and she is afraid that someone is going to go after her niece for her money. Maybe that's why she keeps her on such a short leash."

I asked how he knew all of those things. "Look, Eladio, I've known that family since I was young. Her father adores her, no question about it. But his love is reduced to showering her with gifts and indulging all her fantasies. The aunt is not in agreement. She says that's spoiling her, not raising her. Maybe she's right, but sometimes poor Antonia seems so desperate for her father's affection. She gets it into her head that nobody loves her and then she cries her heart out."

I remember that Douglas was sipping his coffee as he spoke. "If Mahler loves her so much, why does he spend all his time traveling and leaving her on her own?" I asked.

He frowned and placed his cup in the saucer. "Look, Eladio, don't get so caught up in the whys of things. Mahler probably stays away because he can't stand his sister-in-law's rigidity. I would guess he stays out of her way because he doesn't have anybody better to take care of her. It is also possible that he agrees with her methods, but prefers to turn a blind eye."

I made it clear that I did not agree. I thought that living with your eyes closed was a very comfortable course to take. "We should all be aware of the reasoning of those responsible for our loved ones."

But Douglas was not to be put off. "Would it really help you to know the reasons for her rigidity if she was like a mother to a child of yours? No, Eladio. Don't go looking for trouble. The smart thing is to let it go, avoid problems, let domestic matters be handled by the person who is closest to Antonia and therefore deserves credibility and respect. The famous Aunt Luisa was, after all, her mother's sister."

It was a short conversation. The sea stretched before us became more compelling than the somewhat withering conversation that showed little sign of satisfying my curiosity.

The only thing I had been able to gather was that Antonia's father was fairly obliging, if sparing with his affections, her life one of chasing fancies, and her aunt some sort of bad fairy who imposed her authoritarian dictates to rein her in.

Yet hard as I might try, I could not put the party out of my mind: Antonia, in her white dress, returned again and again. When I least expected it, there she was, in some corner of the house, at the beach on the sand or in the intermingling forms at the water's edge, in sudden smiles, in everything that had anything at all to do with her figure, her beauty, and the sweetness of a women who has yet to live.

While I was aware that her memory was nothing but a crude snare, the impact she had had on me the preceding night had penetrated my mind like a bullet too deeply embedded to be extracted without tearing. As I struggled to put her out of my mind, my memory endeavored to relive the sensations I had experienced as I regarded her waist under my hand and the skin of her cheek against my chest, and recalled her way of acting the defenseless woman in need of support.

That was the worst part: knowing that between us a rare connection had been established that, for various reasons, we were forbidden to enjoy.

It seemed easy, but it was so very difficult. She ran in a completely different circle. The age difference set us apart. And then there were Douglas Raft's suspicions, and the risk that her father would reject me and the wrath of Aunt Luisa would be visited upon me.

How could I possibly find the path to get close to her?

And besides, wasn't I the one who was always bent on avoiding the trap of falling in love?

But whenever I thought like that, I was immediately yanked back to reality: I already have, I would tell myself. Why the hell else would I be longing to see her again if it were not that I had fallen inexplicably in love with her from the moment we met at the birthday party?

I could not explain it even to myself, but it had cost me hours of sleep and I had begun to talk to myself like a lunatic.

Marbella was too big a place to come upon someone accidentally, the restaurants too numerous to simply run into her. Especially since Antonia's lifestyle was naturally very different from Douglas' and mine. It was all one big rebus, impossible to decipher.

Even so, it was not long before I saw her again. It was in a bar in the vicinity of Mahler's neighborhood.

Douglas and I had met up with a group of friends there. People our age—men and women who I could never in my dreams have imagined associating with Antonia's friends.

All at once, I had the strange feeling that someone on the periphery of the group was watching me. I turned to see that it was Antonia. I remember that she had come in off the terrace and made her way into the room. As I watched her cross the room with the rare grace of a bird in flight, the pulsing sensation I had felt inside me the moment I first saw her, became a pounding.

That encounter led to others. Not a day passed that we didn't see each other, with no snags, impediments or obstacles to get in the way of prolonging the lost evening of her birthday party.

The murky pit of doubt was now filled with certainty. Mahler was the first to congratulate himself on the unexpected fusion of his daughter and the man who had succeeded in reorganizing Autumn Books through sound judgment and certain impositions that, while they may have seemed risky and counterintuitive, had handily produced the anticipated outcomes.

Of course no one spoke of engagement. My mother was the first to raise objections over the possibility of our bond becoming anything more than a friendship. "You don't realize it, Eladio, but you're slacking off. Don't let that child trap you. You'll fall hard if you do."

I tried to convince her that her fears were unwarranted. "I assure you that Antonia and I are just friends."

But she did not retreat. "Don't forget, Son: marrying a richer woman is as suicidal as trying to look in the window of a moving train."

And without skipping a beat, she went on to talk about appearances. "It isn't enough to have a beautiful wife. Beauty is the biggest ratcatcher of older men."

Aunt Luisa also assumed a dour expression whenever she saw us together. But she never tried to interfere. She simply approached our friendship as one approaches a precipice: clearly apprehensive but not about to venture an opinion.

Indeed, at times it seemed as if she considered "talking" a form of punishment, one that she always avoided. She was a woman of few words. She accepted my visits as one would accept an inevitable, slightly annoying circumstance.

My relationship with Antonia was still a regular friendship. Although the attraction was clearly mutual, I was bound by the sectarianism of the forbidden, by all the differences that precluded me from dating her.

On more than one occasion, she tried to turn a friendly exchange into a covert attempt to get me to fall into her arms. At the time, logic and reason were still sending me occasional alerts to prevent me from tripping and tumbling into a well that was getting deeper with every passing day.

I resisted. I can honestly swear I resisted.

But all of my resistance only left a bad taste in my mouth, along with a guilty conscience, since I could see that she was saddened by my efforts to keep her at arm's length.

More than once I saw her moved to tears when I deliberately flipped around some suggestive comment on her part. "As far as I can tell, I have come into this world only to have no one care about me," she said once.

In vain I tried to convince her that everybody loved her and that her father in particular, was extremely fond of her.

At that she began to whimper like a small child. "My father has never really loved me," she said. "He's always loaded down me with gifts to satisfy my every wish. It's his way of pretending he loves me, but he's always gotten along very well without me."

Such assertions left me disconcerted and a little overwhelmed. I could not bear to see her suffer.

So I ventured to mention her Aunt Luisa. "She may seem a little distant, but she has been like a mother to you."

But Antonia was not easily swayed. "A critical, despotic mother, without a drop of tenderness," she exclaimed, her voice altered.

I did not know what to say. Everything Antonia was telling me was consistent with what Douglas Raft had said earlier. Despite it all, I pulled myself together enough to avoid taking her into my arms to console her. All I did was stroke her hair and assure that sooner or later she would find a man who could love her as she deserved. "It doesn't make sense that a woman like you will always feel so alone and abandoned."

Her response confounded me. "Don't believe it, Eladio. My life will be short. Before long, I will be crushed to death."

I couldn't get my mind around such an assertion. I could not imagine how Antonia could possibly be so sure that her incredible body would be disfigured by such a death. "Those are just child-hood fantasies," I replied. "We've all had nightmares like that and they get stuck in our heads as if they were premonitions."

She seemed upset by that. "I'm serious, Eladio, I'm telling you. Don't ever doubt it."

That same evening, Douglas Raft hosted a party at his place. He had invited an eclectic bunch: the young, the seasoned, and a smattering of the ancient.

It was even eclectic in terms of social class. Douglas Raft knew a lot of people and he liked to mix up his parties, inviting guests who seemingly had little in common with each other. Everybody tended to have a good time at his parties structured as they were around such a diverse group of people.

It was a night of soft music, stars in the sky, and bright lights reflected in the pool. And alcoholic mixtures and maybe a joint, which of course I never smoked.

And Antonia.

There she is. I can see her clearly. She was wearing a red dress and her tanned skin glistened like the surface of the pool, like the sparkling trajectory of the moonbeams across the sea.

To deny what I felt when I saw her come in with her father and her Aunt Luisa would be like asserting that the Egyptian pyramids and the beauty of Petra in Jordan were nothing more than the imaginings of a deranged mind.

Antonia was just that: something ancient and extremely valuable that had the face of a young girl endowed with all the beauty in the world.

I found her as soon as I could. It was inevitable. I had no great designs. Just to talk to her. To listen. To look at her. To dance with her. Knowing that at any moment I might tell her I loved her and that my love for her might be as irrelevant as it was absurd, but at least it was sincere.

Occasionally I glanced over at her father. He seemed content. In fact, seeing his daughter and me deep in conversation, he winked at me as if to say that our mutual understanding pleased him.

People began to disperse at the first light of dawn. It was a dawn that retained the scents and luminosity of the night, its floral perfumes and the sparks of its meaningless fires. The fitting sequel to a night that transcended illusions, broke down barriers and above all, dared to believe in "tomorrows." Before one more day goes by, I promised myself . . . I could not possibly let another day could go by without telling her that I loved her and that my love for her was capable of overcoming any obstacle: the age difference, the financial complications, and the enormous gap between her world and mine.

The only thing that mattered now was to be sincere, to cast aside false pride, misplaced devotion and useless extravagances.

I remember that most of the guests had left and I was looking for her, hoping to have a few moments before she too departed. But Antonia was not to be found.

Someone told me she'd left with her father and her aunt. "They said their goodbyes quite some time ago," I was assured. I was somewhat perplexed by this, but did not dwell on it.

Meanwhile, Douglas (feeling slightly inebriated and optimistic) patted me on the back as if to congratulate me. "You're winning over your future father-in-law by leaps and bounds," he said, and went to his room.

The reference to Mahler only heightened my euphoria. At least he did not believe I was a poor match for his daughter.

I absently opened the door to my room and flicked the light switch.

At first I was unsure whether what I was seeing was real or a dream. Sometimes alcohol plays nasty tricks on us and invents dreams that seem real. But all at once the dream moved and reality took over. Antonia was there, in the middle of the room. Her dress was on the couch, her scant undergarments on the floor by the bed, and she was standing there, her arms outstretched towards me, her gaze pleading, her beautiful hair cascading over her shoulders and partially covering her breasts. "I need your affection, Eladio," was all she said.

My first thought was that this was what happiness was: having her there, indulging my fantasies, taking what she offered and convincing myself that making her mine was the most natural thing in the world.

But something inexplicable and overpowering told me to gather her clothing, curtly order her to get dressed, and demand that she leave my room at once.

The next day her father sent a message requesting that I visit his home.

I feared the worst. I imagined that in her displeasure at my attitude the previous night, Antonia might have offered Mahler a version of the evening that deviated from the actual facts.

But I saw immediately that my boss was unaware of what had transpired the night before. "I need to talk to you about the way you are keeping my daughter at arm's length," he began. "I guess you have figured out by now that she is in love with you. And according to the popular wisdom, you love her too."

I nodded, but allowed him to continue. "I've also been informed that you refuse to get involved with her for reasons that are merely topical and circumstantial: you're much older than she is, you are not in the same social class, and to top it off, she's my daughter."

I responded that he was correct. "I can't deny that I love your daughter. But I am not in a position to marry her. I am not her equal. That is why I keep my distance."

Mahler crossed his arms with an incredulous expression. "And do you just leave your feelings at the door? Do you think it is normal that she should suffer so much because of you?"

I told him I was suffering too, but that I would never in this world do anything to make her unhappy.

Mahler merely regarded me as if he would like to take a drill to my head. "Look, Son. I have no idea what the future holds for you, but if you don't go to her right this minute and tell her you love her, you can be sure that the future will have its revenge."

I have no idea what revenge he was talking about, but upon hearing those words, a lava flow of happiness welled up inside me. "So you would not object to our marriage?" I asked, still suffused with doubts.

"How could I object when my daughter's happiness is at stake?" he answered. And to seal the deal, he rose from his chair and came over to embrace me.

The rest was a whirlwind. It was a short engagement filled with transcendental plans, a sense of completeness and the certainty that life could indeed be a beautiful fairy tale.

The wedding preparations began as soon as we returned to the city. The reactions were mixed. Along with the effusive congratulations, were streaks of barely disguised envy, good and bad omens, and excesses of flattery.

Not to mention the friends of the bride: romantic creatures who regarded the nuptials as the golden dream of childhood fairytales come true.

Various pacts soon began to take shape. Anton Mahler, in his capacity as the grateful father, made me a major shareholder in Autumn Books. His view was that the company's revenues had risen exponentially because of me. He felt the least he could do was compensate me for that, not only with his daughter's hand, but also with a share in the economic bonanza the company was experiencing thanks to my managerial skills.

He also told me that he regarded me as a son. He said it in a trembling voice and there was no longer any trace of the Mahler I had met ten years before behind a Louis XV table situated between two picture windows ushering in the sun's harsh rays.

How clearly I recall it all. At the time, my life had been a steady stride forward, a sense of feeling complete, without the slightest shadow on the horizon to warn of an impending storm. "I'm telling you, Anton, that I will do everything in my power to make your daughter happy," I declared the next time we were alone in his office. "And I can assure you that my work will not suffer from lack of effort. You know me well enough to know how important this company is to me."

I cannot explain how, but I can still hear the orchestral hum of computers outside the room like a prelude to the wedding march that would soon be intoned amidst a host of guests, flowers, congratulations and euphoric predictions of good fortune and a lifetime of happiness.

And I can see Rosario, Mahler's secretary, smiling as she entered the office through a side door adjoining her small office to the main one. "My very best wishes, Mr. Escalante," she said.

"Thank you, Rosario."

At that moment nothing could have cast a pall on me. There was nothing ominous on the horizon. To the contrary, everything was bursting with light.

As the flight attendants prepare the meal, an enticing aroma pervades the cabin, chasing away the detritus of memory and lifting the passengers' spirits.

An appetizer is served: a glass of champagne, tapas, and steaming hand towels, properly rolled.

This breaks the silence that has grown up between Eladio and Daniela.

Instinctively, he raises his glass and offers an impromptu toast.

"To your future happiness," he exclaims, touching his glass to hers.

Daniela accepts the gesture and tries to maintain her cheerful demeanor.

"And to yours." She suddenly regrets her words. "Please don't take it the wrong way. I know that under the circumstances it's not exactly apropos to speak of happiness." And following a brief pause, "But even though happiness may seem like an impossibility right now, we shouldn't lose hope for the future. Life can change when we least expect it."

Eladio nods without enthusiasm, but smiles again.

"You're right. We never know what's in store for us." And as if talking to himself, "There are surprises," he murmurs into his glass. "One can't give up hope."

Then silence again, along with a fleeting sense of discomfort.

Daniela sips her drink and turns to him.

"Sometimes when everything is dark and we are sleeplessly waiting for morning, the awakening can open up new paths to us. We can't let ourselves become pessimistic." But realizing he has not taken this as she intended, she tries to rephrase her thought. "I guess a woman like your wife would be very difficult to replace."

Eladio nods, his jaw clenched.

"Indeed," he replies. "My wife was irreplaceable."

And he stares into the glass in his hand as if his interlocutor were in there awaiting his response.

"Was she very young?" asks Daniela.

"Very young and very beautiful. She also had the gift of entertaining everybody she met with her biting, and very clever wit." He says it in a dull voice, his gaze unfocused and the alcohol ingested already impregnating his memories.

Daniela regards him now with a somber expression. She is probably distressed by his pain and would like to find a way to draw him out of it.

"If I recall correctly, you said you were going to settle in New York to start a new life and you don't plan on returning to Spain. That could help a lot. I'm sure that living far away from the things that used to make us happy is the best therapy to forget what one has lost."

Eladio descends once again into silence. The words he is hearing seem to bother him. They are disjointed and intangible voices that don't "match up." They are meaningless sounds. Words that "imagine" because they don't "know." Vague reflections with no hope of intersecting with reason. They do not even come from a person who knows the truth of what she is talking about.

"Yet there are things that we cannot erase from our memory no matter how hard we try," he replies with a slight edge of impatience in his voice, as if Daniela's attempt to break the spell of his despondence has failed, has instead accentuated his powerlessness to ward off depression.

Once again Daniela tries to cover over her blunder.

"I don't mean to seem pushy, but the world is full of surprises that can bring about changes for the better," she persists. "Of course we always have to bear in mind the time factor. The worst things cannot be remedied over night."

Eladio nods.

"Are you referring to the possibility that I will remarry?" And before Daniela can respond, "Don't believe it. I will never get married again I can assure you of that."

Another prolonged silence broken only by the muffled hum of the engines, the clink of glasses, the bustle of trays and the flight attendants' gentle murmurs.

"No," insists Eladio. "I can't see myself starting all over again." And after another sip of champagne, "You have to be responsible. And accept reality. When life plunges us into certain quagmires, the chance of our ever remaining afloat again is slight. It is no use deceiving ourselves."

"It's also no use to let pessimism take over."

"It isn't a matter of pessimism. It is the certainty that no matter how hard we try to shrug off our painful burdens, some memories were designed to remain on our shoulders for the rest of our lives."

Daniela is not exactly sure what Eladio is trying to tell her. The only thing she grasps with dismay is that no matter how hard she tries, she has failed to raise her companion's spirits.

Suddenly Eladio reacts.

"I'm so sorry. I am ruining your trip. I shouldn't have let you sit beside me. Or put another way, it was selfish of me to burden you with my troubles. I hope you'll forgive me." And shifting his weight, he regards his seatmate. "Changing the subject, I would guess you've had your caricature done before," he says in a bantering tone.

Daniela is taken aback by the question, but Eladio hastens to reassure her.

"Don't be shocked at the impropriety," he explains. "It's just that while your face seems very uncomplicated and unadorned, anyone who gets to know you a little better would see immediately that you're not an ordinary woman. You probably belong to the very important persons' club."

Daniela cracks up. She cannot help but be amused at the wording.

"And what does that have to do with caricatures?"

"Well, they only do caricatures of important people, didn't you know that?"

"According to your theory then, the poor slobs who've never had the honor are unimportant people?"

"Indeed. And, for example, although I fly business class and have the appearance of a respectable person, I've never been deserving enough to have my caricature done," confesses Eladio in the same teasing voice.

"Does that bother you?"

"How could it not bother me?" he continues in jest. "Every single humiliation propels us into a constant state of crisis. On the other hand, if neither you nor I are relevant people, we have a better chance of becoming friends, didn't you know that? Which, in this case, I cannot help but consider a fortuitous turn of events." And with the last sip of champagne remaining in the glass, he proposes another toast: "To our friendship. May I call you Daniela? In Spain we would consider it silly for friends not to use their first names."

She nods, still smiling as she touches her glass to Eladio's.

"Yes you may, until I become a very important woman that is. After that it may be more difficult. I'm giving you fair warning just in case someone offers to do my caricature."

Eladio smiles broadly again.

"I was joking of course. There are important people who nobody knows, not even in a photograph. And one look at you is enough to see that you are not a run of the mill type. And just talking to you is enough to confirm that you're a head above the rest in terms of intelligence."

"Why thank you. You don't seem to have come from a tribe of idiots either," she exclaims laughing. "If I was advertising

something related to intelligence, I'd ask you to let me use your likeness."

"I never dreamed anyone would ever consider me an advertisement," he replied.

"Nor I that I would get to sit next to one on a plane," And quickly, "Don't be alarmed. I analyze everything through the lens of my professional de-formation. Sometimes I cannot forget I'm a publicist."

They have finished their champagne and the flight attendant refills their glasses. This time they do not toast. They glance at each other smiling and Eladio notices Daniela's large, dark and luminous eyes.

"I guess the Pharos of Alexandria must have shimmered like your eyes," he tells her, frowning. "I'm surprised I didn't notice earlier how they sparkle."

"Don't kid yourself," she replies. "It's the champagne. Alcohol tends to bring out that kind of sparkle."

All at once and without quite knowing why, Eladio is speechless. Maybe it is due to the champagne, or the sparkling eyes that are now gazing at him, or perhaps the subtle aroma that is filling the cabin and teasing the appetite.

"May I confess something to you?" he asks abruptly.

"As long as it isn't impertinent, you may confess whatever you like."

"I never allow myself to be impertinent," he says reassuringly. "Impertinent remarks are sterile. They have no future. They only serve to swell the egos of people with complexes. And I've always tried to steer clear of my complexes."

"Go right ahead then."

"When I saw you board the airplane all flustered and blushing, my first thought was, there goes my peace and quiet. To tell the truth, I was looking forward to a quiet flight, meaning that I'd have the chance to enjoy the blessed boredom that overly busy people like us rarely get to experience. I longed for that boredom. Needed it. In reality, boredom is what stimulates the mind: it gives us the space to think. And suddenly everything is all turned around. I don't want to be bored anymore. I want to talk. Maybe, as you suggested a few minutes ago, the champagne has magic powers to stimulate the senses. But the truth is I like talking to you. I am intrigued by your manner. I don't know why, so don't even ask me."

Daniela furrows her brow, still smiling. She probably does not know what to say. Sometimes our minds go blank for no logical reason and the words play hide and seek, while the rationales that had seemed so solid a minute ago crumble to pieces.

"Oh no. You're thinking that I'm trying to flirt with you," he continues. *"All I'm trying to do is satisfy my curiosity a little. Get to know something about your life. Get a sense of your personality. You're probably asking yourself why the devil I should care about the avatars of your existence. But for whatever reason, I do. I think it was the way you reacted when I told you about Antonia, my wife. I appreciated your discretion, your serenity, and especially the way you tried to cheer me up."*

Daniela laughs gently and shakes her head as if to say she appreciates her companion's good intentions.

"I too was looking forward to a quiet flight," she responds, still laughing. *"Sometimes the rambling conversations you get into on transatlantic flights can turn into a real nightmare."*

"I hope this isn't one of them," Eladio interjects. *"If I seem like a dullard, I beg you to save yourself. You have several options: pretend to sleep, read a book on the aesthetics of visual harmonies, put on your headset and watch the movie, or send me straight to hell. I promise I won't get mad."*

Daniela bursts out laughing again. Her companion has executed a completely unexpected about face.

No longer the dejected widower, Eladio is now a man of wit and humor. Someone who invites you to relax, to talk freely for no other reason than to enrich the hours, which are as stark and empty as the vast expanse they are crossing.

"If I remember correctly, you said that you're about to get married, but that your future husband is just a good friend, you're not in love with him, and you'll live in Los Angeles."

"That's right. The wedding is in two months. It will be a simple ceremony. It won't be traditional, but the rituals and sacraments are important. My fiancé is also Catholic so we know our union has to last a lifetime."

"Without love?"

"To the contrary. With a lot of love, but without a lot of sentimental illusions or selfish vulnerabilities. Love is one thing and being in love is quite another."

"What's the difference?"

"Being in love is like an incredibly egotistical toy that breaks in no time. Love, on the other hand, rejects egotism. It prefers to give than to require. It isn't demanding. It gives in, helps out, and most importantly, it forgives. That's why it's possible for it to last a lifetime."

"So this wedding has been designed to be foolproof."

"That's right. We've thought about it a lot. We will have very few guests and no banquet or any of the other conventional things that become so tarnished and lamented during the divorce, once the enthusiasm has waned."

"So you're saying it will be an unenthusiastic wedding," he confirms, smiling.

"Maybe. But while enthusiasm might serve to cast harsh light on dark spaces and invite insipid declarations that promise the world, it is nothing more than a firecracker that quickly fizzles out."

"And yet you're taking an enormous step."

"We're aware of that. That's why we don't believe it is necessary to gild the lily the way those who don't believe in the longevity of marriage do. It will be a very intimate ceremony."

"You won't even wear white?"

"For what? The dress symbolized virginity when women got married without 'knowledge' of their husbands," she joked. "But in this day and age, why should the dress be white? People getting married for the umpteenth time wear one. The truth is, I'd feel ridiculous wearing white at my age."

It was a winter wedding, but Antonia wore a silk dress. A white silk that clung to her body revealing the perfection of her figure and the enchantment of her graceful gait each time the fabric swished back and forth with the rhythm of her slow steps, perfectly timed to the music of the *Wedding March* that filled the nave.

The church was a swarm of people all dressed to the nines and predisposed to identify with the ingredients of the happiness that everyone was predicting.

Antonia did not wear a veil. The veil was her long wavy hair adorned with a crown of white roses.

And Mahler resembled a Casanova (if slightly balding) more

58

than a father of the bride willing, for the sake of her happiness, to renounce his right to keep her by his side always.

Even so, the emotion seeped out of his pores. He could not help himself. Certain that his daughter was the most beautiful woman whom God had ever created, he walked into the church and offered her his arm with the air of someone showing off a trophy won with tremendous effort and crafted from harmonious rhythms, corporeal perfection, unassailable sweetness and indisputable chastity.

When they approached the altar and Mahler placed his daughter's hand in mine, I was immediately transported to some sort of paradise lost.

I found it impossible to absorb that this perfect gift could belong to me. Not even the slightest shadow of adversity clouded our union.

It was true. Antonia was there, her sweetness imprinted on every expression, every glance and gesture, and in the smile that never failed to astonish. I considered myself the luckiest man alive.

I suddenly glanced towards my mother. They had seated her on the left side with the wedding party. She was wearing a dress that Aunt Luisa had taken it upon herself to pick out for her. Obviously a very stylish dress, for some strange reason it did not look at all elegant on my mother. All it did was accentuate her humble origins.

The truth is, I was embarrassed when I saw her, tiny and thin, looking somewhat distracted and completely out of place in her luxurious surroundings. I could not accept her lack of *savoir faire*. Her stilted and servile behavior was totally out of place with the rest of the guests.

I also felt ashamed, not just of her but of myself. Ashamed of having obliged her to play a role that didn't suit her. Ashamed of my own discomfort at seeing her so out of place, so timid and inhibited.

Now, as I go back over the events of that day and recall my excitement, my ridiculous pride, my attention focused exclusively on the grander aspects of the ceremony, I can see how painfully isolated my mother must have felt. And yet I lacked the self-confidence to go to her, show her the consideration and recognition she deserved as the positive force that had succeeded in turning her son into a much sought after, respected and happy man.

My memory fails when I try to place her at the reception. Of course she had been seated in her place of honor at the wedding party's table, but I have forgotten the true essence of what we talked about, what she might have thought, all of the things that must have made her feel humiliated for being "different" and ignorant of the subtle rituals inherent to those who have never had to bear the burdens and misery that she had.

Perhaps I allowed my amnesia to develop over time. When we find something disturbing we are often tempted to put it out of our minds and keep it from casting a pall over the happy myths we have constructed around ourselves. And I resisted having that day somehow marred by any minor imperfections.

That is what my mother was on my wedding day: "a minor imperfection." She was a tiny corner of my own being, trying to remain unobtrusive so as not to do something untoward and end up the object of scorn.

What really mattered to me at the time was the splendor of my wife: the natural charm that everyone admired, the ready smile over the most trivial things, the way she greeted our guests with the natural poise inherent to the privileged, always finding just the right word to flatter.

I can still see my father-in-law chatting with me as if I were his own son. "Now we won't ever lose touch, right Eladio? We're not just a clan anymore, we're a family."

And meeting his gaze with the confidence born of sincerity, "Of course we are, Anton. An indivisible family."

And I glimpse Douglas Raft observing the scene between father-in-law and son-in-law with a satisfied air, a hint of irony in his expression. "Who would have ever suspected that your arrival at Autumn Books would develop into a Cartland romance?"

Although a good friend, Douglas was capable of a biting sarcasm. "You're seething with jealousy," I retorted, clapping him on the back as if I found the jibe flattering.

Shortly afterward, I noticed with some relief that he had sat down beside my mother and the two were engaged in what appeared to be a lively conversation.

Later, as we were preparing to leave and I was looking for her to say goodbye, Douglas told me that she had already left. "This kind of atmosphere doesn't sit well with your mother. She said to give you a hug and tell you that you were not to worry about her."

The rest is a blur of pounding music, overly effusive hugs, the signing of menus, fast dancing, alcohol-induced laughter and some rather suggestive paraphrasing of the priest's brief sermon on the sanctity of marriage.

And Antonia. Always Antonia. I can see her now, clinging to my hand as if she would never let me go, hauling me around the room, zigzagging among the tables so that the guests could see just what kind of man she had married. "Take a good look at him because from now on, whoever dares to flirt with him will have to answer to me," she repeated to her girlfriends.

She was, of course, joking, but there was an edge to it reminiscent of a wild animal defending her territory.

Needless to say, I too had my silly little moments with my friends. "You won't find another woman like Antonia even with a magnifying glass."

Nothing could be ridiculous on that occasion, or stupid or excessive. Most weddings are stupidly happy and usually flush with unlikely assertions, thoughtless reflections, and questions that were really answers.

You became blinded by the vertigo of happiness. And that is why you failed to see the most minimal shadow of a doubt. There could be no dusks, only dawns. Especially as the alcohol gradually imposed its agitated rhythm of instincts submersed in preconceived pleasures.

It was as if the free flow of promises and potential fears were translated into forms of daring applauded by one and all.

I can't deny that certain comments grated. "You've finally amounted to something, Eladio, you old thug," and "you shameless rascals always have all the luck." But I was too exhilarated to let them bother me. "Pure jealousy. Even we shameless sorts can be honorable."

No one meant any harm. Such expressions were dictated by the loosened ligaments of the tongue and were meant to be friendly rather than to offend.

When the party had turned into nothing more than a constant whirl, Antonia and I decided to disappear. There were no farewells. We simply split up and, under cover of the multitudes, wended our way separately towards the exit where a car awaited us.

No one knew where we planned to spend the night. It was a well kept secret that actually held.

Outside, the winter chill continued to launch gusts of rain and freezing wind and pedestrians huddling under umbrellas hurried in and out of the darkness between streetlamps and dictatorial traffic lights that resembled tiny welcoming suns.

I remember now Antonia's body entwined with mine in the comfortable back seat of the car that was perfect for a prolonged and nearly horizontal embrace that lasted from one green light to the intense red of the next one.

When we arrived at the hotel, we practically ran up the stairs to the room that had been prepared for us.

At that precise moment, nothing mattered except to close the door and forget everything we had left behind.

Nothing existed beyond the two of us. It only seemed to. What was real was the knowledge that we were alone in the comfort of a closed room adorned with flowers and a bottle of champagne on the table.

And the bed. And the need to fall onto it with the absolute certainty that no laws were being broken and no sins committed by doing what would have been considered a lecherous act before today.

Nothing else existed.

Everything else was the others: those who did not understand life as Antonia and I knew it, as we gave in to a fire that caressed rather than burned, that healed rather than wounded.

Nothing mattered except the common objective of two loves that had fused into one. To make pacts of desire. To close the windows and doors, once and for all, against possible storms, although they no longer even counted really since they followed their course outside the walls of the refuge that was joining us together forever.

And that is how our marriage began. Without any suspicious developments or acute complications.

But one thing did happen that I did not understand at the time. It was after the successful consummation of our union, when Antonia clung to my body and began to weep hysterically as if she had just been violated, drenching my chest in her tears.

> Now Eladio shares the opinion that the white bridal gown is nothing more than a corny tradition based on a worn-out idealism. Just another example of the romanticized trappings that people dream up with no real basis whatsoever.
> "I agree with you," he tells Daniela. "Wearing a white dress

in this day and age is usually a pretty shameful display of childishness."

And Eladio fixes his gaze on the seatback in front of him, suddenly lost in thought, as if what he has just said raises a somewhat thorny problem.

"A penny for your thoughts," she interjects. "You seem distracted. I'm wondering if I said something that might have upset you."

Eladio reacts at once and apologizes.

"It's one of my main shortcomings," he replied. "Sometimes I get distracted. I withdraw into myself and I can't to do anything about it. It's not your fault, don't worry."

Daniela raises her hands as if to say that no explanation is necessary.

"That happens to me too. But that was more than just a distraction. You suddenly left the plane and plunged into the great beyond. You're submersed in God knows what type of memories. Yes, don't look at me like that. The impression I have is that you were flying somewhere beyond the course of this flight.

Eladio smiles at the thought and tries to allay his seatmate's mild alarm.

"Apart from a very few shortcomings, I also have some good qualities," he jokes. I'm neat and punctual and I know exactly what I want. I've never been indecisive. In my free time, I listen to classical music, read anything that's well written. And I try not to be tedious, although I am very well organized. Oh, I forgot. I hate surprises. I like to be forewarned, to know what is coming. It's not that I crave monotony, but I prefer that to dealing with the unexpected. And when it comes to what people think of as boredom, as I said earlier, it stimulates me. I like it. It helps me think. What do you think? Do I pass?"

Daniela nods. "Even so, your famous flight has left me confused. It was as if you vanished into thin air."

"You're right. For a few instants I left the plane to land on planet reminiscence. It's like daydreaming. Which is still rude. Please forgive me."

Daniela shifts slightly in her seat. For some reason she probably cannot define, she seems to feel uncomfortable.

"It isn't good to get lost in those sorts of reveries," she says somewhat severely. "They're too distressing and they make us feel guilty for no reason."

"You're not off base," he responds. "But memories can be ruthless. They come on like a flash, they invade you and leave you paralyzed. It's as if resentments that were never avenged in the moment were taking their revenge now."

Daniela smiles once more.

"It's not only that. There are other factors besides what you call revenge. Like it or not, we are surrounded by lifestyles as despotic as any dictatorship. A different alarm is raised every single day. I'm not just talking about mad cows, or hoof and mouth disease or terrorism or nuclear threats. Life on our planet is just one never-ending threat. When it comes down to it, the fact of being alive is a miracle in the sense that everything seems oriented towards destruction. Even the things we consider the most indestructible. For example, if something as silly as a cold, or indigestion, or bad breath can put an end to the most solid love affair, how can we fail to be destroyed by the things around us? Buildings falling, fires, floods, earthquakes, nuclear accidents. Who knows what else? Any misstep can lead to grave danger." And to stop the conversation from continuing down this increasingly gloomy path, Daniela abruptly changes the subject with a forced smile. "Sometimes I wonder whether what we call progress isn't just a deformation of the word 'regress.' Everything is fraught with risk. Even sitting on a plane talking as we are can be a risk. You know what they call these seats nowadays? Nothing less than 'deathtraps.' "

Eladio chuckles.

"I guess you're referring to what they call 'economy class syndrome.' "

"Of course. There have been several cases of deaths caused by spending too much time seated during excessively long flights. Apparently you have to move around and stretch your legs to avoid clots. If we don't get up, who knows what will happen to us."

But Daniela's comments seem to have deepened Eladio's gloom. The word "clot" causes his response to catch in his throat and he sinks once again into silence.

"Did I say something wrong?" she asks in alarm.

Eladio shakes his head.

"Don't feel bad. No one can be guilty of what they aren't aware of." And coughing lightly, "it was the word 'clot.' Sometimes a word is much more than a string of letters lined up in a row. They can be little knife stabs." And shrugging as if to play down the import of his words, "My wife died of a clot. That's all. Silly of me. It was enough to hear you pronounce the word for Antonia to die all over again." But he recovers himself quickly. "I am so sorry, Daniela. I probably shouldn't be telling you these things."

"To the contrary. It is moving to see that a man who loved his wife so much can be affected by the mere sound of a word related to her death. Very few men are capable of keeping alive a love that has been lost."

Eladio's remains impassive. He does not speak. But the atmosphere has become weighted down and Daniela tries to relieve it.

"What did your wife die of?"

"A pulmonary embolism. It was unexpected. It was sudden. She became very fatigued and had chest pain, dyspnea. She was coughing up blood." And as if the memory he was describing were exerting pressure inside his head, Eladio presses his fingers into his temples before allowing his hands to drop back into his lap. "We rushed her to the hospital. After a thousand tests they diagnosed the damned clot in her lung."

"Oh my God, it must have been terrible."

"It wasn't at first. They treated her with heparin. The X-ray showed that the clot was keeping the blood from reaching some areas of the lung. But she responded well and was soon back home again."

"So what happened?"

"No one knows. According to the doctors, the treatment was failsafe. It was a matter of administering exactly the right dose of Sintrom. So for a little over a year, she had to have a monthly checkup to monitor her blood levels. After a certain time period, she would be cured. The embolism would not return."

Daniela remained silent. Surely she thinks that letting Eladio talk is the best way to help him expel the pain.

"Every month they did the test to verify the correct dosage. The results were always good. There was no warning of what ended up happening. Although they had warned us that a second embolism would kill her, no one imagined it would actually happen. The prognosis was good and she was clearly improving."

For a few moments the two remained silent. Everything on the plane is now an unsolicited response. Something sifting through the atmosphere like an illogical destination.

Finally Daniela breaks the silence.

"So why did she die?"

"There was no explanation for it. Three days before the doctor had given her a complete check-up. Everything was perfect. The Sintrom dosage required no adjustment. But even following scrupulously the doctor's instructions, the embolism happened. There was no way to save her."

And right then it is impossible to bandy about ideas, venture a comment, remark once again how painful the loss must have been.

Antonia is between them now like an impossibility still determined to root out the secret of life.

Meanwhile, the flight attendants are beginning to serve the meal and the aroma fills the senses with appetizing foretastes.

Daniela quickly rises and leaves her seat.

"I have to stretch my legs!" she exclaims.

And after two or three jogging steps, she heads for the bathroom.

Eladio gazes at her distractedly as she goes. Her step is firm and graceful, her figure slender and erect, she barely brushes the seats as she progresses down the narrow aisle.

Eladio also rises. His companion's absence is a good excuse to justify his own.

As he passes by the sick child, the mother smiles in greeting, perhaps to make sure the child has not been to much of a bother to him.

But Eladio acts as if he doesn't even see him. He nods a greeting to the mother and waits by the door until the lavatory is free.

When he returns to his seat, Daniela is already there, her tray table down, hair freshly brushed, and the book on the aesthetics of visual harmonies stowed in the seat pocket.

Eladio's newspapers have been put away as well. The ritual of the meal takes over. It is time to select a beverage and most *of all, a formula to erase the sorrowful memories and enjoy lunch with happier thoughts in mind.*

The smiles return and Antonia is forgotten.

Enough of the exhausting retrospection, the bitter nostalgia, and the attempts to arouse compassion that never leads to anything good.

The flight attendant soon arranges the placemats, glasses and silverware. The meal will be served momentarily.

Wine? Beer? Champagne?

Daniela asks for a Coke and Eladio orders wine.

Tasty-looking appetizers have been placed on the tray tables and Eladio's chicken and Daniela's steak also look delicious. The lost energy seems to come flowing back all at once.

"I am ashamed of myself," he says suddenly. "Up to now we've done nothing but talk about my problems. I apologize. I'm not going to burden you with all of my issues. Tell me more about yourself. Please."

"My life hasn't been all that interesting," she explains. "You might say I've always planned around a less scintillating occupation. Not like yours. I've never found the philosopher's stone of happiness such as you describe."

"Are you telling me you expected some sort of success that never materialized?"

"Something like that. Although to be perfectly honest, my ambition to achieve success has been gradually waning. One fine day I realized that terrestrial achievements don't even last as long as a tree and that was enough to shatter my previous assumptions," she said, making a joke of her own testimonial. "In any event, I can't complain. I've earned enough not to have to worry."

"To summarize, you're ambitious, but you've never been motivated by greed."

"What for?" she replies. "Greed is a con artist. It knows no limits. The more you have the more you want. What's important is to renew yourself. Air out your life. Make sure you don't succumb to inertia."

"And how is that accomplished?"

"By fleeing the commonplace. By refusing to run with the pack." And seeing that Eladio does not quite follow, "It's simple: you try to go against the grain, the fads. In any case, style is merely a reflection of manners and people's manners today

are pretty disgusting. That's why I usually lean towards what isn't in style. In a way, that's what originality is: going against what everyone else is doing. Besides, where is the elegance in what everyone is calling transparency, as in 'letting it all hang out'? Or whenever a meal is served, why do they always have to say, 'washed down with such and such a wine'? What are we washing down? The repugnant mixture secreted in our stomachs? Or why, when they talk about an attractive outfit, do they say it's extremely 'sexy'? Can sex be elegant? It may be exciting or it may be coarse and cheap, but elegant? No. That's a huge fallacy. The truth is I hate stock phrases like that. They always seem to me to be abrasive, vulgar, definitely not what I want in my publicity work."

The two remain silent for a few moments, busily cutting and chewing their food.

"So what made you decide to go into publicity?" he asks.

"I've always been drawn to aesthetics. When I was a child, I liked to imagine all kinds of fantastically beautiful things. As soon as I was able, I studied design but it wasn't going to earn me a living. So, since I needed money, I worked as a waitress in an upscale diner. That's where I met the man who is now my fiancé. He was a publicity agent. He's very talented and had been doing publicity spots for years, with tremendous success. So I described some of my ideas to him and he liked them. Before long he was asking me to work for him."

"And you accepted?"

"No. I just put together a montage for his company. I didn't want to feel tied down, or a slave to someone else's principles that I might not share. I preferred to be my own boss. I wanted to prove to myself that my ideas weren't totally off the wall." And with a self-deprecating smile, "I've always been reluctant to be beholden to someone else."

"There's a lot of merit in that."

"I'm not sure if it's merit or arrogance. Perhaps a little of both. The point is, I've always had an objective helping hand when I needed it and I've always worked independently." Daniela shrugs and continues cutting her steak. "I slowly built up a reputation of sorts and finally ended up directing my own company."

Eladio nods as if to say he admires what she has accomplished.

"Your fiancé is a lucky man," he comments between bites.

"Thank you."

"I'm serious. Few women are able to achieve what you have: your own business, self-sufficiency, not allowing themselves to atrophy."

"It's more common in the States. Women are raised to believe we shouldn't be dependent on a man."

"Still, your trajectory is admirable."

"But I have to confess that, although I've accomplished what I set out to do, I don't feel completely content. How often have I asked myself, 'Which is better? Knowing we are in control of our own actions or depending on someone to support and protect us?' "

"If the person deserves your trust, then support can be gratifying," he comments. "The union that you and your future husband have planned will surely have broad repercussions in all areas."

Daniela does not contradict him. She does not look at him either. Her gaze is fixed on the bit of meat on her fork.

"I'm not a child. I know very well what I'm getting into. As I told you before, I love my future husband very much, but I'm not in love with him. I can't even swear that he's as enamored of me now as he used to be. But sometimes business arrangements last longer than amorous ones. So that's why I'm marrying him." She has said it coolly, her clear-cut premises leaving no room for doubts. But she quickly explains, "Which isn't to say that it's a marriage of convenience. I would never do that. Our marriage pact is not based exclusively on material wealth. We love and admire each other in our own way and those are essential underpinnings of a union intended to last a lifetime."

Eladio is busily trying to separate the wing from the breast and from the way he wields the knife, it is clear that he is not persuaded by Daniela's assertions. Giving up on his task momentarily, he turns to face her.

"I would still like to know whether, in addition to the premises that you have clearly laid out for me, there are other factors capable of keeping your marriage from crumbling to pieces." And with a sharp expression he asks her, "Are you fond enough of each other to sleep together?" And seeing that Daniela is disconcerted by the question, he tries to explain

69

"Often the little things no one thinks about can put an end to the famous 'for a lifetime.' "

"I'm not sure what you're trying to say."

"I'm referring to the thousand little things that can contribute mightily to destroying the most solid of relationships. For example, Do you like his voice? Does the way he coughs bother you? Do you like his ties? Are you attracted by the way he walks, or eats, or laughs? Does he know how to use his silverware properly? Does he yawn loudly? And the tics, are they constant or sporadic? And what about the sudden fits of anger, the slight difference of opinion, the unexplained bad moods, the indifference, chronic obsessions, the same expression over and over again." And recovering his easy, half joking demeanor, "Don't look at me like that. I'm serious. We often don't realize it, but it's usually the things we consider superficial that slowly chip away at the foundations of the best laid happiness."

Daniela cannot help but laugh. Her traveling companion definitely does not seem to be just another face in the crowd. Up to then it had never occurred to her that such little things could undermine the solidity of a decision adopted after years of careful reflection.

But Eladio does not retreat.

"Even though your agreement may be that romantic love will be conspicuous by its absence, the little furrows that surprise us, no matter how trivial they may seem, are difficult to fill. There they remain with loose dirt tossed over them, waiting to trip us up." And after a brief pause, "Don't have any illusions about it, Daniela. As solvent as your communication may be, the perfection we all yearn for is virtually impossible to achieve."

"Yet you have been a happy man," she contends, a little annoyed.

Eladio's expression changes. His frown deepens and the fear that his truth will float to the surface seems to numb his words.

"Yes," he replies in a sober voice. "I've been very happy."

And nipping the conversation in the bud, he returns to his meal leaving no room for his traveling companion to ask him any more questions.

As I watched her crying and clinging to me like that I had the impression she might be disappointed at my lovemaking.

Antonia continued to weep softly and plaintively. Her tears flowed liberally and her breath got caught in her sobs. I tried in vain to find out why she was crying, but her ragged breaths kept her from responding. She just gazed at me, her eyes glistening with tears that lighted her pupils until they looked as if they were made of crystal. But not a word escaped her lips.

I decided to just hold her close. I let her know that I understood. I told her I guessed it had hurt since it was her first time and promised that I would try to be less enthusiastic the next time.

She slowly calmed down. Then she hugged me fiercely and moving her lips to my ear, said, in a low, slightly embarrassed voice "I'm crying because I'm so happy."

We slept through the night like that, hearing in our dreams the magic word that had caused such a flow of tears.

Waking up was glorious. I only had to look at her and Antonia was transformed before my eyes from a piece of heaven into a woman. She looked beautiful in the morning. Neither the tangle of blond hair nor the features slightly dulled from sleep could dim the perfection of the angelic creature who seemed to have been plucked from a fairy tale.

I have never felt as overwhelmed by happiness as I did at that moment.

That is how we began our honeymoon, in total harmony, free of any suspicions and misgivings. We considered ourselves the happiest couple on earth and wished only to embark on our new life together unfettered by servants, anxiety or suspicions.

Everything about that trip was perfect. Mahler had seen to it that we were made to feel completely at home in every hotel where we stayed.

Everywhere we went, someone specially trained to attend to newlyweds took care of us expertly and with meticulous attention to detail.

The trip was scheduled to last a month. One month of togetherness, twenty-four hours a day.

Every place we visited became a source of memories we both knew we would store in our minds forever.

Together we contemplated tranquil seas, exotic, far off lands, an infinity of novelties that were so foreign to us they seemed unreal.

We visited innumerable cities. I remember it all so well: walking hand in hand along streets emblazoned with lights or else badly paved roads where we had to tread carefully. Hearing voices with disjointed echoes that made us laugh. And the silences that nothing could penetrate except the contours of our words.

Those were days of wonder, of glances flush with complicity and affectionate caresses.

Sometimes we would chat as if we had never met before. Antonia told me about her childhood, experiences she had not shared with me during our brief engagement. "I never told you before, Eladio, but my mother was addicted to morphine. They tried to keep it from me, but I knew because I overheard a conversation between my father and my aunt." It seemed to have left its mark on her. The idea of having a drug addict mother was an ignominy she found hard to assimilate. "They told me she died when I was born. But the truth is she was already very sick." And after a brief pause filled with something akin to a suppressed sob, she added, "It's hard to grow up without a mother."

Seeing her distress, I drew her close to me and held her tightly. "Forget the past," I told her. "From now on I'm going to do everything in my power to make you happy."

She also spoke to me of her father. "They say he loves me but it isn't true. He leaves me at my Aunt Luisa's mercy every chance he gets. The only thing he's good at is showering me with presents and satisfying my every whim. He's basically just trying to salve his conscience."

And grasping my face between her hands she looked at me imploringly. "Promise me you'll be a father to me too." And making a joke of her own entreaty, "Okay, a somewhat incestuous father, but an adorable one."

That made me think that our age difference might have been part of what had attracted Antonia to me in the first place. "Even as a father I will try not to disappoint you," I told her solemnly.

Once she told me about her school friends. "They were older than I was. But my grades were higher and so they were jealous of me. It was hard for them to accept that a younger student could outdo them academically."

She didn't say it self-importantly though. To the contrary, she always talked without a trace of vanity, as if they were merely objective assumptions inherent to a sincere explanation.

"I really loved them though," she continued. "We got along and there was never any friction." And the more I listened to her, the more my admiration grew. It seemed impossible that an eighteen year old girl could be so discerning, could overlook the negative to avert needless tensions.

I was also impressed by her simplicity, by the equanimity with which she handled the normal day to day inconveniences that arise, and especially the maturity with which she evaluated the faults of others. "Those girls weren't bad really. Had I been in their place I probably would have been jealous of a schoolmate who showed me up."

I asked her if she was still in touch with them. "Of course. Friendship has always been sacred to me."

And she quickly brought me up to speed on her relationship with the woman who had been like a mother to her. "She is a good person, but she's not very clever. She lives in a bygone era. That's been my cross to bear. It's been hard to put up with her. She's constantly harping about discipline. One's 'duty' according to St. Aunt Luisa," she teased. "She kept close tabs on me, kept me fenced in."

And seeing that I did not interrupt her, "In spite of all that, I love her very much. I say in spite of it and why should I deny it? Whenever she gets on my nerves, I feel an unhealthy impulse to hate her. She has infuriated me so many times. No one has the right to cut off someone else's freedom for no other reason than to upset them. Don't you agree? In any event, all that is over now."

I asked her what she meant when she said her aunt had restricted her freedom. "Stupid things," she said. "Trifles really. But they hurt me. For example, when she wouldn't let me watch TV depending on what program was on, or wouldn't let me play with certain friends because the way their parents were raising them was very different from my upbringing."

But she said all of this without rancor, brushing it off as what she called, "old-fashioned eccentricities." "Of course my friends didn't come to my house, but I found ways to spend time with them anyway. It wasn't fair that I shouldn't see them at all just because of a closed-minded and stubborn woman."

She also told me about her dog, Heraclitas. "I named him that because he was a cut above the rest. He was a little jumpy, but I was able to calm him down. I knew how to handle him and he loved me. He hated my Aunt Luisa though. He even bit her once."

And when I asked how the victim had reacted to being attacked by a dog, she merely shrugged and said she didn't remember. "It wasn't important."

She rarely let go of her obsession about her mother's sister. It would resurface when I least expected it. "She was always going on about lost values. She's a religious fanatic and hasn't realized that the world evolves. She doesn't get that all of those inviolable principles of her youth are now just relics, with no more value than an antique."

Her obsessions were not confined to Aunt Luisa. Indeed, perhaps the most powerful of her fixations had to do with how she would die. "I assure you, Eladio, I'm going to be crushed to death."

During our engagement, she had alluded to that danger on a number of occasions. "Walk around that balcony," she would say as we walked by dilapidated buildings. "It's going to come tumbling down when you least expect it."

I remember that shortly before we got married, I mentioned her fixation to her aunt. "Childish fantasies. She's been going around with that idea in her head since she was a little girl. You shouldn't pay much attention to her. Antonia is like a recently hatched chick. She needs someone to take care of her, pay attention to her and help her 'grow up.' "

I remember Luisa on our wedding day. There she is again in her black lace dress, with her innate refinement and her air of a mature and experienced woman, gazing at me with an entreating and grateful expression. "Try to make her happy, Eladio. And most of all, just try to understand her. She isn't totally grown up yet." And at my look of astonishment she persisted. "She acts like a self assured woman, but she is still a little girl. She is fanciful and her fantasies often distort reality. The slightest detail that is misinterpreted can hurt her terribly. Sometimes she has her own way of judging what is going on around her. That's why it's so important that you channel her, force her to see reason."

I have to admit that, at the time, I simply discarded Aunt Luisa's admonitions. In my eyes, Antonia did not have the slightest flaw or defect and I therefore regarded her aunt's insistence as completely unnecessary. "My niece is a wonderful girl," she went on, "but depending on which way the wind blows, her judgment becomes her worst enemy. She'll get furious with no explanation as to what has made her so angry. She simply becomes evasive, or retreats into silence, and of course she will never admit that someone else might be right."

But her words struck me as out-dated, echoes from the past. Nothing she said fit the Antonia I knew. I told her I'd never seen her niece behave like that. But Aunt Luisa did not back down. "It usually happens when you cross her. Maybe it's my fault. Maybe I was too strict with her."

The truth is I did not give her warnings or explanations much credence. Especially since, despite our short engagement, we both felt as if we'd known each other intimately for a very long time.

Sometimes Antonia and I would talk about our future. "I want to have lots of children," she'd say. And she enjoyed imagining perfect worlds for those children, extracted from foreign settings and immune from evil. "They will be the happiest children on earth, won't they, Eladio? No matter what. We'll never let anything hurt them."

I was dazzled by the things she said. It was astonishing that one so young could recreate so many reasonable sounding things. "You'll be the perfect father. You'll know how to love them just like you love me." And she would hug me as if those children she so desired were already there between us.

She also liked to talk about artistic subjects. She asserted that aesthetics were the "comfort" of art. She'd add that only the visual comfort that art afforded us could generate wellbeing. "Don't ever doubt it, Eladio. Aesthetics are important."

It's as if I'm seeing her, her beauty vanquishing all the aesthetics in the world and her self-assured way of expressing herself—a cross between lyrical and surreal—dazzled my senses even more.

I often asked her where she had gotten all those ideas. But she did not respond. She'd just draw close and hug me fiercely. "Don't you know that it's all just phrases I invent to impress you?" And she would add that her only intention was that I never forget her.

She also liked to divine the future. She used to say that we are all born with a path and that it was impossible to deviate from it.

And I would argue that God was not a dictator and that we all had the freedom to choose. "We can't deny our own free will." But she persisted, "Free will allows us to help our destiny along, but not change it."

So I brought up time. I said that what we call freedom and destiny are obliging aphorisms to justify our actions and the paths we take in time. "But if you dig deeper, you will see that time, as we conceive of it, does not exist. It was invented by humans because we don't know how to measure Eternity."

At that moment, Antonia stopped regarding me tenderly and I quickly grasped that she was not persuaded by my argument. "If time is the invention of normal men, then eternity is the invention of fanatics," she retorted brusquely. "I don't believe in eternities, or better lives after death. The important thing is to take full advantage of the parcel of life that we have been allotted, even if we have no idea why. The rest are all falsehoods invented to curtail our freedom."

Though we did not really argue, that was our only brush with the world of differences. "And why do you think that those of us who believe in Eternity try to curtail freedoms?"

Her face clouded, her blue eyes seemed to darken, and clutching me, she whispered into my ear as she always did. "I don't want to think about anything that might separate me from you. Eternity is synonymous with death. And I want to live. I'm too young to entertain the possibility of another life. Maybe when I'm older I'll be more interested in thinking about it. But all I want to do right now is live with you here on earth and forget all those old folks' tales." And with anguish in her eyes, she implored me not to let her fall into the void of nothingness. "I don't want to die young," she told me. "Please, Eladio, don't talk to me about unknown eternities. Take this terror away from me. Let me enjoy time."

Once the flight attendants have removed the food trays, they pull the shades down over the windows to dim the natural light so the passengers who have selected a movie have a better view of their screens.

Most people, however, are more interested in the duty free cart offering alcoholic beverages, chocolate, gems in intricate gold and silver settings, silk scarves and a host of other products.

Daniela regards the cart with indifference, while Eladio, curious, pays attention to the objects the flight attendant is showing the passengers. Distracted, Daniela leans towards the window and lifts the shade slightly. Below, the dense cloud cover has left very few openings through which to glimpse the sea. The clouds are thick and reddened by the most intense sunlight, even as they blanket the earth with shadows and rain.

Following the routine, Eladio and Daniela activate their screens and review the selection of movies.

By chance, they select the same one: *An Everyday Man*. It is a comedy and should provide some comic relief to offset the unsettling aspects of flying.

But when the movie begins, both leave the headsets on the tray table and settle themselves comfortably as if they prefer to sleep.

But neither seems to be able to doze off. Daniela stirs in her seat and addresses Eladio once more.

"It would be nice to have a nap. We'll arrive in New York at just about the same time that was on my watch when we left Barcelona and the change throws the body's whole rhythm off."

"You just have to resign yourself. Today is a long day and the suspension in time is actually okay with me. Once we get to New York I'll be able to start work straightaway."

"Without resting first?"

"I'll rest after getting in touch with the people I'll be working with," he replies. "The job I'm taking on is fairly daunting, so I don't feel as if I can allow myself the luxury of a day off."

"And what exactly will you be doing?

"It's very similar to what I was doing in Spain. Woultmand & Starky wants to reorganize Frederichstal Books in the United States. The company seems to have fallen into the same traps that were hampering the performance of Autumn Books. We're also planning a merger with another large publishing house."

Daniela is about to delve further into Eladio's impending job but he is a step ahead of her.

"The task ahead is not a pleasant one. I'm going to have to lay off a number of employees to make room for more highly qualified people. Reorganization is not just a matter of changing approaches and systems. You have to build the company with trained professionals, offer different sorts of opportunities and lay solid foundations that enable the goals we are going to be proposing."

As he speaks, Daniela is nodding her head in agreement.

"Of course, these measures will have to be implemented

gradually. Abrupt changes can cause even the most solid structures to collapse," Eladio continues. "A measured approach is required to administer any business effectively. It is important that people buy into the changes without feeling railroaded. Once everything is functioning properly more aggressive tactics can be employed, but never before."

"So from what you're saying, I gather you are going to be the managing director of both publishing houses."

Eladio nods.

"My father-in-law wanted me to take on the task."

"I understand. In a way, you represent an important part of his daughter."

At that moment, the screen lights up and after the trailers, the movie begins.

"I believe you mentioned that you have friends in New York."

"A number of them."

"I'm happy for you. Your friends and the change of environment will help you recover your strength."

"I hope they also help me to find oblivion."

He says it with his gaze fixed on the empty tray table. His mind assailed by the image of those open eyes and blood-stained lips, an image he cannot erase.

"The worst part," he continues, "is the remorse."

Daniela looks at him with a curious half-smile.

"You're not going to tell me you're harboring deep and unconfessed secrets."

Eladio takes a deep breath. Avoiding her gaze, he responds as if he is addressing the tray table.

"Everyone is hiding something under the surface." And attempting a lighthearted tone, "Despite everything I've told you, I probably wasn't a very good husband. To say I've experienced happiness doesn't mean much of anything really."

"It's pointless to torture yourself with those sorts of fantasies. If you hadn't been a good husband you wouldn't be going round and round inside with the void your wife's absence has left."

"Sometimes those voids empty into pits too deep to climb out of and recover your former stature. Maybe I don't deserve to climb out of the pit."

"That is not the case with you. One only has to look at you to see how much you've suffered."

"How do you know?"

"I can infer it from the small print of your life. The font that hides all the things that are not explained by the regular font. Don't ask me how I figured it out. I don't know. I guess I must have discerned it in your expressions, the way you act, your discretion, the way you express your ideas, or perhaps in your problems or your sorrow."

"I never knew that human beings also had fine print that gave us away."

"No one can escape it. Sooner or later it all comes to light."

Both now glance distractedly at the movie. Neither of them has put on the headset and so the images on the screen are devoid of meaning.

They turn to look at each other and both start to speak at the same time. Their words, however, trail away at the unexpected clash of voices.

"What were you going to say?" he asks.

"Nothing special. I've lost my train of thought."

"But I do remember what I was going to ask you. I imagine at this point you won't mind my nosiness. As we agreed earlier, friendships that we know in advance are not fated to survive are the most solid of all. You can't betray my confidences nor I yours, even if we wanted to. So we can both unburden ourselves at will."

"I agree. A seven hour friendship couldn't possibly be damaging or traitorous," says Daniela with a teasing expression.

"It all depends," he jokes. "According to the Bible, the number seven can mean something akin to an eternity."

"You're right. I'd forgotten. But bringing it back down to earth, the 'seven' for this trip ends in New York. I'll board my flight for L.A. and you'll remain in the city of skyscrapers," she says firmly.

"Who knows," Eladio replies. "Life is full of unimaginable surprises. Maybe in the future, on some chance occasion, we might see each other again. There's nothing to stop me from going to Los Angeles. The city has airports and airplanes and in particular, a clear sky that invites connection."

Daniela shakes her head.

"It won't be the same," she asserts, her voice subdued.

"Why not?"

"Things change."

And without waiting for a reply, Daniela pretends to cough and leans back in her seat as if she does not feel like talking any longer.

"There's one other alternative," he teases. "Forget that our friendship began in the air. Make it terrestrial. Keep in touch. We'll probably end up throwing dishes at each other's heads, as people tend to do when they're fed up by a relationship that lasts just a little too long." And seeing that Daniela does not react to his joke, "Anyway, I still haven't told you what I was going to ask when we interrupted each other," he finishes.

"Go ahead. I'm listening."

"I wanted to ask you how much you think your marriage is going to fill the holes in your life? Aren't you happy in your job? Haven't you made it without needing a man by your side? Why are you getting married if you're not in love?"

Daniela closes her eyes and presses her lips together. It is clear she does not like the question that has been put to her. But she doesn't sidestep it.

"Simple. I want children. It might seem ridiculous to you that I've discovered that I want to be a mother at this stage of the game. But I do." She pauses, appears to hesitate. Then she continues. "Well maybe that's not it exactly. Maybe I'm terrified at the thought of getting old without someone there to take care of me. In the States, women 'alone' come to a sorry end."

"So you're getting married so that you can have children."

"That's what I said."

"You can have them without getting married."

"Of course. But as I said earlier, I'm a practicing Catholic. That's why I'm not thinking of being a single mother."

"So your marriage is going to be more like a business arrangement."

"From your perspective maybe that's what it is. But I don't see it like that. Besides, when you get to be a certain age, you have to make a decision. The clock is ticking and there's a time limit on the possibility of having children."

Eladio does not reply. He remembers. He hears the boy's voice. Sees the lounge chair by the side of the pool.

"In all likelihood our marriage—lacking in enthusiasm as it is—will deteriorate into a resounding indifference," she goes on. "Anything is possible. But if we have children, the indifference will have been worth the risk."

"The word 'indifference' isn't exactly what you inspire," exclaims Eladio.

"Maybe you're right. I don't know. All I know for sure is that everything necessarily comes to an end. We're mutants, don't forget. We spend our life in a state of expectation. We are constantly expecting something. The days go by and we keep on thinking that we still haven't begun to live. And in essence that's what living really is: expectation. Even old people are waiting for something to happen. When you no longer have any expectations, you die."

"Have you ever stopped to think that those children you want so badly might change your life? It's not enough to hold a baby in your arms, love it a lot, give yourself over to it every day, and think that it will always be the most beautiful thing in your whole life. Strange as it might seem to us now, children grow and develop their own ideas, intentions and defiance. Suddenly the genes they carry inside them burst forth and they can even end up as our worst enemies."

"You're painting a very gloomy picture, but it doesn't matter. I have faith in education. The downsides can be mitigated."

Eladio leans his head to one side and frowns, his lips pressed into a thin line. He does not seem inclined to respond.

"Maybe you're saying that because you don't have children," she comments in a slightly strained voice.

For a few moments Eladio seems to hesitate. The words are like a sword passing straight through his body. Finally he confesses.

"You're wrong about that. I had a son." Daniela stares at him in confusion, but dares not ask. Eladio continues, "He died just before his fourth birthday."

"Oh my God, please forgive my tactlessness."

But Eladio does not hear her. The boy is there again, smiling, his light blue eyes, so like Antonia's, regarding him as if for eternity.

"It was a senseless death. One of those things that no one could have anticipated, that happen for the sole purpose of destroying us." And after a choked silence. "I think I have never loved anyone else the way I loved him. I delighted in watching him. Just analyzing his every expression, seeing his smile,

81

knowing he was there beside me, was enough to make me the
happiest father in the world. It never even occurred to me that
with the passing of time he would grow into a man like me, full
of faults, problems, mistakes. Yes, don't look at me like that,"
Eladio insists with a trace of a smile that is more derisive than
anything else. "If destiny exists, I have the impression I have
done everything possible to throw a wrench in it."

Daniela has been reduced to a mass of disorientation
cloaked in astonishment.

"So you had a son."

"Seeing him dead was the worst thing that ever happened
to me."

Daniela remains silent, waiting for Eladio to continue, but
for a few moments the only sound is the hum of the engines.

Finally, Eladio decides to speak.

"And although what I'm about to say might seem monstrous
to you, I sometimes thank God for taking him."

I do not remember exactly when it began to dawn on me that
death was more than just an obsession with Antonia. It was a
nightmare. More than once I heard her talking in her sleep as if
death were a living, bodily thing that evidently was threatening
her with a weapon against which she had no defense.

Whenever that happened, I would wake her, wrap her in my
arms and try to soothe her. Between sobs she would tell me that
no matter how much I tried to protect her "that being" was eventually going to put an end to her. "It's constantly coming after me,
Eladio. It wants to kill me."

Her nightmares became more frequent after our return to
Barcelona.

Mahler had given instructions for an apartment to be outfitted
for us not far from his own. "That way we'll be able to get together
often."

But no sooner did Antonia walk in the door, than she began
to have qualms, as if the luxuriously appointed rooms were
haunted.

Everything struck her as hazardous: the beams that had replaced
the main walls: "they could split any day and cause the building to
collapse." She was also worried about the gas pilot light. If we don't
turn off the main valve, we might wake up in the next world." The

shiny floor was another threat. "A friend of mine slipped on her living room floor and twisted her neck. She died instantly."

The fact was, no matter where she looked she saw hazards, threats, traps, unexpected sources of mortal antagonism and horrors she could not articulate.

Then there were the signs. The bad omens she claimed were persecuting her: black cats, spilled salt, looks from clearly dangerous strangers. "They're giving me the evil eye," she would assure me.

Antonia was not, however, a hypochondriac. She was not particularly frightened by illness. Her terrors derived from external causes: sudden outbreaks of fire, devastating storms, hurricane winds and earthquakes. Rivers overflowing their banks. In her mind, any hypothetical insecurity became an imminent and inevitable reality.

Her fears made sense to me at first. An uncertain childhood with a neglectful father and an overly strict aunt had left her trapped in a persistent infantile state that was barely concealed by her intelligence and her ability to analyze the world with the irony of a mature woman.

I tried many times to reassure her, always without success. "The problem is, Eladio, you just can't see all the dangers surrounding us," she would reproach me.

I eventually figured out, however, the one thing that intensified all of her fears and that was her terror of being alone.

We were inseparable during our honeymoon trip and therefore all of those potential threats had not tortured her as they would later.

Antonia occasionally voiced her fears when her father was visiting us. They were always minor things, ideas that even bordered on the ridiculous. "Now, sweetheart, you can't possibly enjoy life if you dwell on such things like that."

But Antonia appeared not to hear him.

After Mahler left, she would snap into abandoned child mode. "How can I enjoy life with a father like that, always aloof, always withholding the affection I deserve?"

And when she put it like that, I was forced to admit she had a point. "But darling, you have my love now," I would say, kissing her. And she would cling to me, beg me never to abandon her.

Setting up our new household helped allay her fears for a time. Although inexpert in domestic skills, Antonia had an instinct for decorating. She enjoyed going shopping with her girlfriends to show off her role as the mistress and the lady of what she liked to call "our home."

It was a happy home, decorated in the style of certain homes in the United States that Mahler had always admired, particularly if French furniture and objects were interspersed in the décor. "France is the most beautiful country in the world," he would say. "Especially when it comes to their elegant sense of style."

The servants had also been carefully trained so that Antonia, in her inexperience, would not venture to issue jumbled orders or create an absolute madhouse.

Fortunately for us, Aunt Luisa was a frequent visitor. She was the one who discussed matters with the cook, trained the servants and judiciously doled out responsibilities.

But her presence did not please her niece. "She's so annoying. She gives me no peace, even now that I'm married. She has to meddle in everything and stick her nose into things that have nothing to do with her," she complained.

But it did not take me long to realize that if Luisa had not intervened in the daily flow of "our home," chaos would have prevailed.

Antonia did not know how to run a household, or cook, or deal with servants, or organize the cleaning. In her inexperience, she would unburden herself to the servants, treating them like members of the family one minute, and issuing imperious orders as if they were slaves the next. There was no middle ground in her domestic interactions.

Berta, the nanny who had taken care of Antonia since birth and had automatically joined our staff, often intervened in potentially stressful situations.

Berta was a sensible woman. Whenever she sensed tensions, she did not hesitate to smooth the troubled waters and keep the servants from getting the hell out of Dodge.

At the time, however, Antonia's disorganization did not worry me. All I really wanted was her happiness. To keep her from being carried away by her fears. I wanted her to know that I was always by her side to help her in every way.

Her father sometimes chided me for my devotion to her. "You're spoiling her, Eladio. She needs to grow wings, learn to do for herself."

He said it with conviction, though he knew very well that Antonia was ill-prepared to manage a household.

Antonia slept a tremendous amount and never ate breakfast. She rose only when she guessed I would be on my way home from the office for lunch. And when I opened the door, she would throw herself into my arms as if I were just back from an extended trip. "I've missed you so much," she'd say.

Now and again she would tell me about her friends. "They're jealous. They can't help themselves."

But that did not seem to upset her very much. Being married to me, being the daughter of the all-powerful Mahler, and living large more than compensated for the friendships lost "out of jealousy" as she put it. "None of them have what I have and they simply can't get over it," was her justification.

Besides, the cooled relationships with her girlfriends were by no means permanent ruptures. It seemed we were always socializing with different members of our set. The occasions were always elegant, designed to dazzle and surprise our guests, a feat that Antonia (aided by Aunt Luisa and Berta) accomplished expertly.

My mother occasionally helped out with the preparations for those gatherings, but she was never among the guests. She said she wasn't cut out for so much show and just liked to help the servants out and lighten their loads a little.

Antonia thanked her without enthusiasm. At times she even seemed to regard my mother's labors as a form of payment for the privilege of seeing her son married to her.

Yet none of these trivial things could possibly put a dent in my feelings for my wife. It was impossible not to love her.

Of course there were times when I was totally nonplussed by her behavior. And then I would have the inexplicable feeling that no matter how much time we spent together, I would never really know her. There was a certain indecipherable aspect to her behavior that did not fit with the rest of her personality. But far from being concerned, that mysterious question mark made me feel closer to her. It was something like stumbling unexpectedly on a hidden treasure. I convinced myself that love was just that: the ability to discern the hidden facets in those we love and at the same time, to be constantly surprised and amazed by them.

I remember Antonia's self-satisfied air whenever we attended a party in high society. She was confident no one else could match her, not just in looks, but also in her ability to deploy an indiscreet blend of irony and ingenuousness when, anxious to be the center of attention, she would loudly proclaim whatever innuendo and gossip came into her head, always skillfully enhanced by her gift for exaggeration.

And I admit that when I saw her like that, animated and thronged by admirers, my head would begin to swell too. Nothing was more flattering to me than to see her showered with flattery.

Her exhilaration often persisted after arriving home from one of those parties where she had reigned as queen. I would see her swaying in front of her dressing room mirror as if dancing to a song only she could hear. "You think I'm pretty, don't you Eladio?" she would say to the mirror, where my reflection appeared behind hers. And turning, she would hold out her arms to me. She wanted me to enfold her in my arms, to repeat over and over again that I loved her, that I couldn't live without her.

And naturally, I never disappointed her.

Only once did I refuse to play her game of seduction.

That evening I had been preoccupied about a problem at the office and Antonia's silly dressing room games (after a party where the alcohol had been plied a little too liberally among the guests) struck me as a bit much, not to mention highly unlikely to provoke the desired response.

Besides, I was exhausted and anxious at the thought of how early I had to get up the next morning.

I remember Antonia standing before me frozen, tense, her expression sullen. "What's wrong, Eladio? Don't you love me anymore?"

I quickly realized that my attitude had upset her. I saw her shrink into herself, hurt and upset. "Or maybe you're no longer attracted to me."

I was stymied by her pathetic look, could not understand her hasty assertion, which was so at odds with my feelings for her. "Come on, Antonia. Please don't be so childish," I said.

I now realize that the worst thing I could have done was to call her "childish." I was only trying to make her see how exhausted I was and that I was worried about having to get up early to deal with problems at the office that simply could not wait.

"You're belittling me," was all she said, her eyes brimming with tears.

I went over to her but she rebuffed me, backing away quickly so I could not touch her. "You belittled me," she said again between sobs.

The rest of the night was spent in silence. As soon as she got in bed, she turned her back and refused to allow me even the slightest caress.

It was an uncomfortable night and it left me with a strange feeling of guilt that I was unable to shake for a long time afterward.

She was still sleeping when I arose and I did not want to wake her. I figured she had probably had too much to drink the preceding night. Alcohol can change your personality, make you more aggressive or more apt to lose sight of common sense than normal.

I called her in the late morning. Her voice was muffled, as if it were coming from deep inside a well. "You're not mad anymore, are you?" I asked in a light tone.

She replied that she was hurt, not mad. "You really wounded me."

Hearing her so dejected, I tried to be conciliatory: "If I've done something wrong, I beg your forgiveness."

But not even my apology relieved the strange sense of guilt I felt gnawing inside me.

Then I heard her voice again. "I never imagined that you would be capable of treating me with such contempt."

We hung up without reaching a resolution. "We'll talk when I get home," I said.

I remember leaving the office with a treadmill going round and round in my head. No matter how I looked at it, I could not figure out what to do to win her trust back.

Fortunately, everything had changed by the time I opened the front door. Antonia was there in the foyer, arms flung wide to welcome me. I hugged her. I asked her forgiveness once again and assured her that it had never been my intention to hurt her. "You know how much I love you," I repeated over and over again.

Although she seemed affectionate on the surface, I discerned in her attitude a lingering resentment she could not hide.

Her aunt was having lunch with us that day and needless to say, the conversation was rather stilted. Antonia was upset with her too. She still felt Luisa was meddling too much in our private home life. "You think I'm stupid and can't fulfill my duties as a homemaker," she reproached her.

But her aunt remained unperturbed. She simply continued to chat with me about things that had nothing to do with her niece's intimations.

Antonia suddenly rose from her chair in a fit of rage. She pounded the table with her fist and ran to our bedroom, slamming the door behind her.

Ignoring my bemused look, Aunt Luisa continued eating as if nothing had happened, but when I moved to go after Antonia, she motioned for me to sit. "Don't do it, Eladio," she said. "When she goes off the handle like that, it's best to leave her alone. She'll soon realize that her behavior was inappropriate." And seeing that I was still unsure, "She probably has her period," she told me. "Some women become absolutely insufferable when they are menstruating."

I was dumbfounded by this speech. My contacts with the women I had known when I was single had never led me into such ambiguous terrain.

Ignoring Aunt Luisa's admonitions, I ran after Antonia hoping to mollify her.

I found her face down across the bed crying her eyes out. I hugged her close, murmuring that I understood how she felt. "I've never doubted your ability to run the household," I assured her. "Don't worry about those silly things your crazy aunt says."

That time Antonia allowed herself to be placated. "She's always made my life miserable, Eladio. I don't ever want to see her again."

I began to think she was right.

"If you will allow me, I'll have a serious talk with her tomorrow," I promised her. My solicitous response seemed to calm her down. "Everything is going to be different from now out," I assured her.

When we returned to the dining room, her aunt was gone. She had left a note on the mantle. "Let go of your resentment, Antonia. You are on your own. I am leaving your house forever. I have no intention of getting in the way of your happiness."

Antonia did not get out of bed the next day. She said the unpleasantness had given her indigestion. "My stomach is acting up. That's what happens when people mistreat me."

But Aunt Luisa had been right: Antonia had her period.

Daniela surely did not expect such a harsh remark from her traveling companion regarding his son's death. She simply could not fathom how any normal father would be capable of thanking God for taking away what he loved the most.

She spent several minutes debating whether she should ask him why he had made such a radical remark or just let both of their thoughts become diluted in the ambiguity of what was already in the past.

It is clear from Eladio's expression that certain questions or comments might be too painful and she refrains from probing further.

They both seem to feel an instinctive reluctance to return to the subject for fear of being tactless.

There are, however, few distractions on an airplane and it is not always easy to come up with the necessary ingredients to smooth over an awkward situation. Anxious to avoid treading on precarious ground, both travelers contemplate the small screen, but they still do not put on their headsets.

They are able to decipher the comic scene taking place from the gestures and expressions of the main characters. The protagonists are in bed: the man is snoring loudly while the woman alternately makes clucking noises, claps loudly and plugs her ears, desperate to drown out the dreaded sound and avoid the plague of a sleepless night.

Daniela lets out a grunt that is supposed to be a muted chuckle.

"Don't you find it interesting that comedies always use snoring to portray a problem between couples, while in serious or dramatic films people snore away and no one pays any attention to it? When you come right down to it, snoring is an unrelenting torture, regardless of whether the couple in question is deeply in love or not."

"I'd never thought about it, but that's an astute observation. Movies distort everything. But it's true that there is nothing more mundane than having your beloved beside you issuing outrageous snorts, while your sleep is gradually stolen from you by the malevolent Parcae of insomnia," he exclaims, trying to restore a lighter tone to the conversation.

Daniela grasps his intention and smiles irreverently.

"It isn't fair," she continues. "The mundane truths should also be interspersed into what we call dramatic films. Why kid ourselves? Whether it's a comic pair, or a serious, compatible couple, snoring exists, it's disturbing, and, I would venture to say, capable of exasperating even the most fervent lover."

Eladio turns to Daniela with a trace of skepticism in his expression.

"I wonder if you have pondered what you just said in light of your upcoming marriage."

"Naturally. Charles and I have decided to have separate bedrooms. We don't want our miserable little foibles to upset the balance we've felt between us since we first met."

"A wise course. It's important to be cautious and circumvent the stupid crises to which we humans are constantly exposed. Like it or not, most anything can bring catastrophe upon us." And his expression jovial once more, "We must safeguard the catharsis of marriage at all costs."

They turn back to the movie. The headsets remain on the table as they both regard the soundless actions of the protagonists.

Rather than the snoring, it is now her husband's unkempt appearance—overweight, uncombed, yet looking extremely rested—that infuriates the sleep-deprived wife, especially as she regards him scratching his stomach, crumpling up his shirt and ultimately leaving it a mass of wrinkles.

They barely look at each other. She is at the stove listlessly cooking scrambled eggs, as the toast pops out of the toaster. Fatso nonchalantly takes his place at the table, evidently intending to read the paper while his wife fixes his breakfast. Of course the two of them are ignoring each other to the extent possible. The movement of their lips suggests that they have exchanged little more than a routine 'good morning.' "

Daniela turns once more to Eladio.

"This is an example of what a marriage should not be. Loving someone will not keep us from ending up hating them if the daily routine becomes a grind like that."

"But most people don't get that. They regard this kind of scene as a natural state that has no bearing on the longevity of our feelings for one another."

"There is a solution," she says. "To treat the person you're with as if you'd only just met them." And seeing that her response seems to touch on Eladio's disquiet, she quickly tries to put it right again. "That isn't to say that all marriages are destroyed by routine. Some couples reach the end of the line as much in love as they were on their wedding day."

Eladio nods, but by his sober expression it is clear that confusing thoughts are bombarding his mind with unpleasant images.

Once again he is lost in one of the silences that intrigue Daniela by their sheer detachment, yet leave her feeling slightly overwhelmed. She therefore tries to recover the lighter mood that had been disturbed by her earlier remarks.

"Don't mind me. What I just said is certainly an exaggeration. If love is genuine, then it will last and the more mundane elements will dissolve like sugar in water."

Eladio amiably accepts her response. He seems to be in complete accord with her clarification. "The bad part is no matter how often others get on our nerves, it never occurs to us that we might be getting on theirs as well."

"Are you saying that we're all self-centered?" she asks.

"No. I'm talking about the oblivious kind of indifference. That's our real defect: laziness. We forget how much we can wound those we love."

"If our intentions are good, then we shouldn't worry," she replies.

"It's a matter of understanding to what extent our intentions may be good or bad. The more certain you are, the more mistaken you might be." Eladio clears his throat, shifts in his seat and fights to maintain his composure. "When that happens, regrets follow." And as if those very regrets have triggered unpleasant memories, he inhales deeply and flaps his hand back and forth as if swatting at a fly. "Fortunately, perhaps now that I'm living outside of Spain I'll be able to forget mine."

"You think living in the States will help you shake off the remorse you describe?"

"Changing continents is changing your life."

"But you never stop being European. You can spy it a mile away," she teases.

"Don't believe it. Right now I'm just a survivor of the planet Earth."

Daniela does not reply. She is probably thinking that the hackneyed comedy on the screen is the reason behind the gravity of the conversation. The truth is, all comedy scripts are based on human misery. It's a matter of getting the viewer to laugh at himself, at his own mistakes, his little quirks. There are terrible falls, untimely drownings, unfortunate coughs, or torn dresses exposing key anatomical areas.

"Aren't we all," she rejoins, thinking of the survivor part.

The partially lifted shade now stabs Eladio's face with a shaft of light.

"It's interesting to observe these solar projectiles while there is a major thunderstorm in progress down there."

"And an enraged sea."

"And maybe I'm at the helm of an imperiled vessel, even though our plane is gliding across the smooth expanse of space without any thunderstorms in its path."

"No one is safe in any case. The unexpected can happen any second and put an end to all of our expectations."

Hearing her, Eladio has the impression that the person speaking is not Daniela but Antonia. A different Antonia but one still plagued by the same inevitable fears.

"It would be a shame should our seven hour friendship be lost in an icy stammer. Because the water of the Atlantic must be very cold," he says, trying to reduce the danger of a crash through humor.

"Yes", she agrees. "It would be a shame."

"May I ask you a personal question?"

She shrugs.

"Since we are presently at great risk of plunging into the sea, you may ask whatever you like."

Encouraged by her reply, Eladio loses no time in adjusting his position to face her.

"Have you ever been really and truly in love?"

A hint of a smile appears on Daniela's lips and quickly disappears into a short exhale.

"Yes. I think I mentioned it earlier. A long time ago. I fell in love with a man I barely knew. The truth is I had no reason to be in love with him. But I was, with the type of love that knocks you flat and you can't explain why."

"So how do you explain it?"

"I don't know. I never have quite. It just happens. It bowls you over. But it is still an illusion."

"Did it last long?"

"Enough to realize that it was an absurd kind of love. To love *someone you don't really know is a wonderful sensation almost always based on the improbable. As ephemeral as it is idiotic."*

"Yet you loved him."

"No. I was 'in love' with him. It's impossible to feel real love for people we don't really know. We can practice it in the sense of following the commandment to love thy neighbor as thyself. But that isn't the same as feeling it."

"Is that why you got off the train?" he asks, half in jest.

"It's possible. But I'll never know. The train kept on going— taking him with it—and I stayed behind on the platform to throw myself into my career."

"Did you ever see him again?"

"Never. The truth is I can hardly remember what he looked like. I do recall some details: the way he smiled, his way of looking at me, the way he walked. Things like that. And I also remember the illusions he could inspire in me."

"I suppose you've regretted your decision at times."

"Yes. But I've always consoled myself with the thought that if I'd married him based on 'love at first sight,' I'd have even more regrets now."

"You are a very pragmatic woman indeed."

Daniela purses her lips, unsure. "You don't know how many times I've asked myself whether pragmatism is an asset or a liability."

"Maybe it can be both."

"Which is the same as failure. Such dichotomies don't hold up long. Pragmatism turns into monotony sooner or later. Water always puts out fire."

"And yet fire can heat up water."

"No. When water boils, it burns. It hurts. It's not worth the risk of being scalded to death," she finishes.

A month later, Antonia discovered she was pregnant.

As soon as she found out, she almost seemed to regret her altercation with her Aunt Luisa the day she had left the table in tears. "Please Eladio, I need you to go with me to apologize. I was just under so much stress then. I admit it. And I want to tell her about the baby."

We paid her a visit that very afternoon. We found her in front of the television, sitting calmly, her expression neutral, betraying no sign that she remembered the inhospitable lunch that had turned our household upside down.

I can see the two women embracing as if nothing at all had transpired, hear the common sense and equanimity in their words: "I've missed you, Aunt Luisa." And she, "Don't worry, whenever you need me I'll be there."

I recall too that in a fit of generosity, Antonia had assured her aunt that "our home" had not been the same without her assistance on the domestic front. "Berta does what she can, but the servants don't respect her as they do you, and I'm too tired to keep up with all the domestic ins and outs."

It was her way of apologizing to her aunt for the previous episode and of conveying that she would like her to continue helping out with the household.

Luisa, however, brushed off her niece's apologies. Although she had turn off the TV, she remained staring at the screen as if she were still immersed in her program. While Antonia's compunction was evident, her aunt gave no indication of having any qualms or even any recollection at all of the violence to which her niece had subjected her.

Looking back on the scene now, I realized that her impassivity must have been the product of a long string of similar episodes which, by dint of repetition, were no longer capable of moving her.

The afternoon transpired calmly. Antonia had an enjoyable time making plans for the baby. "Will you help me set up the nursery?" she asked.

And her aunt assented with the same neutral expression she often wore when dealing with her niece.

Someone who was unaware of the true history of their relationship might have considered Aunt Luisa's attitude slightly overbearing and even unsympathetic to Antonia's excitement. I, however, was not at all taken aback by her demeanor, since I had already begun to see what Mahler's sister-in-law had been putting up with all this time in her efforts to channel her niece's infantile impulses.

Luisa loved her niece in her own way, of course, and had patiently borne the responsibility she had inherited upon the death of her sister. I am convinced she was somehow immunized against Antonia's irascibility. And much as she tried to hide it, it was also clear that she was weary of the constant battles.

"You'll have to share the good news with your father," she said. She tried to say it brightly, but it was clear she found the prospect overwhelming. She must certainly have thought that the newborn was going to become one more gratuitous weight on her already overburdened shoulders.

Mahler's elation upon learning that he was going to be a grandfather bordered on the ridiculous: "It will be a boy. He will be just like me and he will inherit his mother's beauty," he kept repeating.

I remember how he embraced me after his return to Barcelona from one of his interminable trips. "It's just what you needed to complete your happiness," he said.

The enthusiasm spread among all the employees, especially since Mahler organized a luncheon—for the entire staff of Woultmand & Starky—to celebrate the good news, presided over by himself, Douglas Raft, and the company's branch directors.

With regard to his daughter, the first thing he did was send her a bouquet of flowers, at the center of which nestled a package enclosing a small case which in turn contained a brooch inlaid with diamonds and rubies. "To begin to understand the joys of motherhood, even before the baby is born," the card said.

From that day forward, I became more than just a son and a valued colleague to Mahler. My currency had gone up considerably.

In addition to giving me a substantial raise when he learned I was going to be the father of his grandchild, he started to consider me as a sort of second Douglas Raft: someone who would never let him down and who was extremely well situated to enhance the reputation of Autumn Books, which had already improved considerably since I had taken over its financial organization.

Even the occasional difficulties that would arise (usually due to rapidly evolving technology that rendered each innovation quickly obsolete) stopped worrying Mahler. "I trust your judgment, Son. You'll figure out the next step." And he would lend me his objective support to surmount any unanticipated hurdle.

Nonetheless, I never accepted any type of help that I felt might make my job harder. "It isn't necessary, Anton. I've got it covered."

The truth is it was very hard for me as his son-in-law when he showered me with advantages that somehow diminished my own accomplishments and incited jealousy and resentment among my coworkers. "I don't like to take advantage of our relationship. I want you to treat me the same way you treat the other executives."

I have to admit that my position in this regard had no other effect than to elevate me even higher in my father-in-law's estimation. "Even with a magnifying glass, I could never have found a son-in-law like Eladio," he liked to comment to anyone in earshot.

But this also worked to my detriment in a way. The endless glowing remarks soon created an atmosphere of generalized touchiness. "As if you were the last man on earth with living sperm." They did not say it in a grudging way or as if they were intending to wound, but it was clear that Mahler's opinion of my virtues triggered a certain wariness that I would have preferred to avoid. Of course, his effusiveness even struck me as over the top, and I only tolerated them because I knew they came out of his love for his daughter.

On the home front, as soon as we learned that Antonia was going to be a mother, we decided that Berta would be in charge of the baby. Aunt Luisa approved of that decision. "There is no one like Berta to take care of a baby," she asserted. "She's an expert and will take better care of it than anybody."

Everything was very upbeat during that time, without the slightest hint of the painful episodes still to come. Life was a series of glimpses of the happy events to come. Just imagining the arrival of that tiny creature was enough to transform our existence into some kind of miracle, which promised magic moments and delightful certainties that could never dash our illusions.

In order to spend more time with Antonia, I often stole away from work to surprise her. "I get so bored when you're not with me," she would say.

It was difficult for me to make her see that my job responsibilities were vital. "I work for your father you know. It wouldn't be fair to give him short shrift."

But she would not listen to reason. "I'll tell Daddy not to keep you on such a short leash. I get the feeling that you live to work instead of working to live, and it simply isn't fair."

Of course, Mahler was oblivious to his daughter's machinations and I made sure he did not find out about them. It probably would have been painful for him to accept that his daughter's possessive tactics might be the start of an unhealthy obsession.

Therefore, whenever Antonia raised objections or acted annoyed at being left alone, I would try to reason with her. I did my best to assure her gently over and over that marriage did not mean spending all day together, exchanging adoring looks, saying nice things and trading caresses. "The bonds of love are also found in absences," I would tell her.

But Antonia paid no attention. All she cared about was that everything had changed between us since we had returned from our honeymoon. "You don't pay attention to me like you used to."

To salve my conscience, I told myself that her dissatisfaction probably had something to do with losing her figure. Antonia could not stand the way her body was changing. "This baby is turning me into a beach ball," she fumed. "Who knows if I'll be able to get my figure back once it's born."

Seeing her so out of sorts, Aunt Luisa was sometimes unable to hold her tongue. "You should be thinking more about your child and less about your anatomy."

On several occasions, I found myself trying to temper the older woman's diatribes against her niece. "Please try not to hurt her feelings," I entreated her. "She doesn't realize how those outbursts come across. Despite everything, Antonia is still very much a child."

I was stunned, however, when Luisa turned on me point blank one day. "But haven't you noticed, Eladio? Her belly may be growing but the rest of her body is a skeleton."

It was true: despite the pregnancy, Antonia was rail thin.

Worse yet, the doctor approved of her thinness. "The birth goes much better if the woman remains slim," he kept saying.

But Aunt Luisa was not about to give in. "You still have to eat nourishing food, and Antonia is not."

I thought she was referring to the constant vomiting. "But all pregnant women do that."

And with a trace of derision in her voice, Luisa conveyed to me in no uncertain terms that Antonia's vomiting was induced. "You need to be less naïve, Eladio. She is provoking a lot of that vomiting because she is afraid of getting too fat." And when I replied that Antonia ate a lot, her aunt gave a sarcastic laugh and confided that she might be stuffing herself with food, but she was also getting rid of it right away. "You're not trying to tell me Antonia is bulimic. I won't accept that. She's always wanted to have children. I don't believe she is capable of doing such a terrible thing," I retorted almost angrily.

And seeing Luisa shake her head with that knowing air of hers, I persisted, "Antonia is right to complain that you malign her."

That time Luisa did not even let me get the words out. "I would never try to malign her, Eladio. I love her as if she were my own daughter. All I'm trying to do is not shut my eyes to what is happening. I'm doing everything in my power to make sure this baby is born without complications."

I was confused, but she went on, "So open your own eyes. Pay attention. The child she is carrying is yours too. Protect him. Please."

There was no room for argument. With that, she left the room and I remained standing there in a daze.

At first I refused to believe that Antonia would worry more about her figure than her baby. But then I was flooded with doubts. It did not make sense that Luisa would issue such a serious warning with no basis whatsoever.

Yet it was also hard for me to imagine that all she had said was true.

In my brooding, I came up with all sorts of conjectures and twisted ideas.

I even entertained the thought that Luisa might feel a perverse jealousy towards her niece for having attained what she herself had not during her long spinsterhood.

But then her assertions would suddenly ring true, especially when Antonia's mood would change abruptly and she would became sullen for no apparent reason. My effusive displays of affection did no good. "You don't fool me, Eladio: I know I disgust you," she would rebuke me, furious with herself.

Once, she took it even further. "I wonder who you're chasing after while I'm sacrificing myself to bring your son into the world."

At first I was unruffled by her tantrums. It was inconceivable to me that Antonia could ever imagine I would cheat on her while she was going through such an obviously uncomfortable pregnancy. So when her accusations—always accompanied by periods of apathy and lethargy brought on by her lack of nutrition—became more frequent, far from upsetting me, I sometimes could not suppress a smile. I'd pull her close to me and assure her that no one could ever replace her in my affections. "You know I'm crazy about you."

Such assertions, however, began to lose their meaning as time wore on.

The worst happened when she paid an unexpected visit to my office. I remember that my secretary and I were going over some papers and we were both completely baffled. They contained significant anomalies and neither of us was having much luck figuring out where the problem was.

I can see myself, sitting elbow to elbow with the young woman, our backs to the door, as we poured over numbers, phrases and totals. It was a tangled mess and we had no choice but to find and correct the error.

We did not even notice when the door opened and soft footsteps approached.

At the same moment, the cause of the problem suddenly became clear. Elated, I put my hand on my secretary's shoulder and shook it with joy. "We did it. Now we can breathe easier," I said.

The young woman turned towards me with a look of satisfaction now that the marathon was over. "It made sense," she said. "And we certainly couldn't have just left it like it was."

Carried away by our bureaucratic triumph, I put my arm around her again and hugged her with perhaps an overly effusive display of enthusiasm.

The secretary was a plain woman, but she was very good at her job. The truth is, she had been like my right hand, but I'd never felt attracted to her and there had never been anything besides a strictly professional relationship between us.

I will say that despite her nondescript appearance, she was clearly very bright. She never raised her voice and when called upon to give her opinion, she always did so without pontificating. She would offer her ideas unassumingly, as if she were not quite sure of them, even downplayed their value.

But that day, when the problems we had spent so much time trying to decipher suddenly became clear, we both felt compelled to celebrate what to us was an enormous triumph: without undo fuss, without the slightest erotic intention, just the headiness brought on by success.

At that moment, we heard Antonia's implacable voice behind us. It was like the crack of a pistol.

"And what would that be?" we heard her inquire, imperious and hysterical. "So what I'd been sensing was actually going on right here within these four damned walls."

At first neither my secretary nor I had any idea what Antonia was accusing us of. Her haughty and severe voice kept us from grasping what she was insinuating. It was impossible to associate our honest satisfaction with her erratic jabbering. "So this is what you call work: picking daisies with your secretary. Getting all cozy with her where no one would ever suspect your outrageous behavior. And meanwhile, I'm turning into a barrel, as if you had nothing to do with it."

She dropped unsteadily onto the sofa: her chest heaving, her voice hoarse, firing off disjointed insults, her gaze unfocused, hatred seeping out of her pores. She would not be placated.

Hearing her cries, the room filled with people. No one understood what was going on, least of all I.

Fortunately, my father-in-law was out of town and did not witness the scene, although I'm certain he found out about it later. The employees who were privy to the episode did not hesitate to spread it around, spicing it up with all sorts of unfortunate details.

I'm seeing it all again: my wife tumbled onto the sofa, her swollen belly, her face disfigured by the almost greenish hue of her skin, her lips parted. She was gasping for breath as we stood round in a tight circle.

She had stopped talking. Half unconscious, she was making loud, gasping sounds as if she were choking.

All at once I saw Douglas Raft thrust open the balcony doors and order everyone to leave. "Don't worry," he told me. "This isn't the first time she's had one of these attacks." And at my look of shock and alarm, "I know these symptoms very well. They usually occur when something upsets her. She's probably had an attack of jealousy."

Even so, I rose to her defense, "But she fainted, Douglas. Jealousy doesn't make people faint." And I insisted that someone send for a doctor.

Douglas tried once again to defuse the situation. "Look, Eladio, there is nothing wrong with Antonia. She has not fainted or anything else. What she's having is a pure unadulterated hissy fit, thank you very much." And before I could stop him, he went over to her, clapped her once on the back, and slapped her across both cheeks.

Antonia responded at once. When she saw me she threw her arms around my neck. "What happened to me, Eladio? What am I doing here? Oh my God, what did I do?"

She wanted to apologize, but according to her, she had forgotten why.

Then she saw my secretary. The poor young woman was still cowering in fear, unable to fathom my wife's hysterical outburst.

Someone acting on Douglas' instructions brought a glass of water. Antonia took several sips and returned her gaze to my secretary. "Forgive me. I have behaved like an idiot," she said. "I thought you were someone else. I confused you with someone else."

It was her way of suggesting that there was no way I would cheat on her with someone as unattractive as she.

If my secretary was offended, she did not show it. She also did not show up for work the following day and before long, she had found a job with another publishing company.

The passengers still seem to be entertained by the film. The screenwriters had clearly made an effort to create a protagonist who would bring to life the typical man of today: a man who follows the beaten path. A man whose self-esteem is derived from such trivial pursuits as joining demonstrations (for any cause whatsoever), adding a few more inches to the line even though no one knows what it is for, filing with grief-stricken face past the corpses of famous people, complacently regarding whatever trash happens to be on TV, and writing letters to the editor of any newspaper just to see his name in print.

In sum, a "nobody" who has always dreamed of being "somebody," but who has instead been relegated to a life on the sidelines.

"Looks like a good movie," remarks Daniela.

"I'm sorry you're missing it because of me."

"Well, I'm making you miss it too."

But the headsets remain on the tray tables and neither of the two makes any move to put them on.

"From the little I've seen, the main character seems to be a faithful reproduction of much of humanity," comments Daniela with just a trace of sarcasm.

"Yet it is the majority that wields the reins of power."

Daniela does not appear to agree.

"Don't believe it. Just as there can be silences that speak convincingly and eloquently, there can be majorities dictated by minority self-interests."

"So you think that everything in this life could be a farce."

"Just like what is farcical about the life of that character," she says, motioning towards the screen. *"Like it or not, it's always a half-hidden minority that is pulling the strings of the established majority. It's a matter of the few knowing how to mass market the things they are bound and determined to impose at any cost."*

And as if to adorn her opinions with some sort of lyrical illustration: "Look at the sea. It seems innocuous, like an oversized minority that does not seek to influence. But the sea sometimes weeps and it sometimes laughs, it sleeps and wakes up, it can be feminine or masculine. It can get irritated and attack when it is enraged and the land becomes resentful even though it is the land that considers itself entitled to decide and to dominate."

"From your description I suppose you're referring to the famous and controversial globalization process?"

"In a way I am," she replies. "If it were completely restructured perhaps it wouldn't bother me so much. But the way it is being proffered is terribly dangerous. Once again, equity runs the risk of becoming just another commodity of the rich and powerful and that is nothing more than a shameful and unfair form of corruption."

"So you believe that life is made up of hidden conspiracies that we mere mortals are unable to grasp."

"Probably. Nothing happens merely by chance."

Once again, a smile plays at Eladio's lips.

"What about our meeting?"

"I don't know the answer to that one," she exclaims, laughing. "I'm not a psychic."

"Take the tomato juice stain for instance. Who caused it? Was it a fortuitous coincidence or was there a pre-programmed motive? According to you, something would have been guiding the hand of the flight attendant so that when her hand brushed against mine, the juice would spill all over your outfit."

"I guess the reasons for all the minor happenings we never stop to think about will become clear in the afterlife," she muses. "Here on earth everything is a mystery."

"So you think that when life ends, the surprises begin?" he asks half jokingly.

"I'm sure of it." And before Eladio can respond, "It will be in that still unknown dimension where we will discover the true significance of all of our small follies, the missed opportunities, the upheavals we could have prevented and didn't, or the mistakes we thought were accomplishments. And, most of all, our capacity for evil."

Eladio does not respond. What Daniela has just said seems

to make him uncomfortable. He clears his throat again, acts as if he is trying to get comfortable, and gives the impression of someone who is becoming increasingly anxious.

"Seeing things with excessive clarity can be one of the worst punishments," murmurs Eladio.

But Daniela is moved by his tone. "It seems as if you have endured a whole world of very painful misfortunes. You must forgive me. Without realizing it, I seem to incur in territories where I have no right to judge." And with no desire to rub salt into extremely painful wounds, she wants to show she empathizes with his misery. "I guess the worst thing was losing your son." And as Eladio appears composed, "How did he die?" she asks quickly.

"He drowned. He fell into a swimming pool and once they got him out, it was too late. They couldn't bring him back."

The strange thing is that Eladio has said it calmly, as if the death of that child had no effect on him whatsoever.

"Oh God. How awful."

Eladio nods in silence. He does not look at her. And Daniela has the impression that words are superfluous at that moment: that "saying something" would violate the laws of desperation, of everything a human being, despite his limitations, can endure when the bottom falls out.

"What was his name?"

"He was named after his mother and his grandfather: Anton."

"I can only imagine what the loss must have meant to your wife too."

But Eladio avoids speaking of Antonia. At that moment, it is the child who fills his thoughts.

"He was blond. He had blue eyes and when he smiled it was as if God were smiling with him. He loved to come running to meet me as soon as I arrived. He would jump up and throw his arms around me and you could breathe in the scent of his sweat. I remember it so well. A child's sweaty neck smells just like perfume, did you know that?" Eladio pauses suddenly, as if waking from his reverie. "I'm sorry, Daniela. I'm rambling. The memory of my son always causes me to ramble."

Daniela tries not to show how his wrenching description has made her feel. Although his voice is even, it is obvious that underneath the words nests the kind of pain that devours.

"Forgive me, please," he entreats her. "Once again, I'm ruining the trip with my problems. Let's not talk about my son anymore. Let's talk about the children you will surely have."

"The thing is, I'm not sure I'll know how to be a good mother," she asserts, as if to downplay what Eladio is suggesting. "I've spent so many years thinking only about myself." And shaking her head as if skeptical, "thinking exclusively about yourself is not exactly how a would-be mother should behave."

"But recognizing it is half the battle," he asserts, recovering his smile. "They say that motherhood is learned on the job, once the baby is born."

"Do you ascribe to that theory? I'm not entirely persuaded. Some mothers have no idea how to be parents. I know a number of them."

Eladio turns and looks straight at her. And he remembers. He has also known a mother who was incapable of fulfilling her role. But he is convinced that his traveling companion—while still a novice perhaps—has what it takes to bring up a child.

"I would like to get to know you better," he says on an impulse. "It's a shame to have to go our separate ways forever at the end of our journey. There is something about you that still eludes me and it bothers me to think that once we land, the possibility of finding out what it is will be gone forever."

Daniela shrugs and shakes her head, as if what Eladio has just said were inconsequential.

"We all have a hidden side. You also seem to be a man full of dilemmas and dissonance." And casting about for a suitable analogy, she adds, "Like one of those men who always says goodbye without budging from where he is standing."

Eladio bursts out laughing at the thought, but she continues, still smiling.

"I don't know why, but your true personality slips out of my grasp and just keeps receding farther and farther into the distance."

"Don't take it as a psychological defeat. It is precisely what we call distance that can bring people together. I think I said something similar to you just a few minutes ago. Even though we'd never laid eyes on each other before boarding this plane, I don't know why I have the impression that a longstanding and very solid bond was already there between us."

Daniela nods, her eyes wide as if she has just made an important discovery.

"Haven't you ever wondered whether the things we consider personal or subjective might be common to everyone?" And she quickly clarifies, "No, I didn't say that right. What I'm trying to say is that sometimes I think that everyone in the world, all of us, are just one person." And seeing Eladio's baffled expression, she tries to be more explicit. "I know it sounds ridiculous, but I've often had the feeling that we are all a single being. One with millions of different bodies, faces, facets and categories, but all part of a single human entity."

"Are you saying that no matter how different we might seem, none of us can consider ourselves unique?" he asks with an amused expression. "Or put another way, do you wonder, 'why am I me and not you?' as if being different might preclude our being one? Or maybe—just to cover all the bases here—you think that I'm you and you're me, but we just don't realize it?"

Now it is Daniela who bursts out laughing without taking her eyes from his face.

"Well yes. I've often thought something like that. Maybe that's part of the reason why influences can be so powerful."

Eladio frowns, lowers his eyes and stares at the headset on the table.

"What you're trying to say is that despite the things that distinguish us—or the different types of behaviors we deal with—we are all 'one.' If that were so, it would justify what you believers often say, which is that the sins of others debilitate humanity as a whole."

"That's not exactly it. But you can be sure that everything we do or don't do activates negative or positive mechanisms in all human beings. That's why no one can claim to be perfect. Our supposed perfection can be undermined by a million springs controlled by others."

"To summarize, if that were the case, then individual guilt would not exist."

"To the contrary, individual guilt adds to all the other guilts. But it is still individual."

"I'm not persuaded," he replies. "It rings of utopias."

"That's because you only see the downside. Individual merits can also mitigate the pain of others."

"How so?"

"By applying them to other people's suffering."

Eladio shakes his head in disagreement.

"To begin with, I can't understand a religion premised mainly on suffering."

"That's not how I would interpret it either. The One who came down to earth to lift us up out of the abyss could have come to this world to be happy. But he chose not to. And therein resides his greatness and generosity: in making our crosses like his. It's a way of letting us know that our own suffering is not gratuitous. There's a reason for it."

Eladio is no longer looking at her. He bows his head. What Daniela is saying does not fit with the blows life has dealt him.

"There has to be more to life than suffering," he exclaims without raising his eyes.

"Indeed, life is much more than that. And also much more than aspiring towards temporal goals: money, power, success, applause, titles, awards, adulation. In sum, all of the small miseries that loom before us like huge prizes."

"But you haven't hesitated to play the game of those aspirations you call miseries."

"I don't deny it. I also don't deny that I was wrong."

"So what you're proposing is to live as if you're dead. Leaving all illusions aside."

"To the contrary. What I want is to use freedom without becoming enslaved. If I recall correctly, Sartre said something along those lines: 'Man is condemned to be free.' But I refuse to be condemned. What I want is to find the kind of freedom that one day will shed all its boundaries."

Eladio wants to reply but can't seem to find the right formula. He seems overwhelmed by Daniela's ideas.

"I think we're getting a little too transcendental," she remarks. And to lighten the mood, she proposes, "Why don't we order another glass of champagne?"

Someone once told me that when we focus our gaze on someone, even involuntarily, a part of us stays with that person always.

And maybe they were right. That is why now, as I recall the scene of Antonia supine on my office couch, her eyes vacant, her deathly pallor, and Douglas Raft slapping her cheeks to bring her back, I have the sensation that it was I who did the slapping. As if, instead of reviving her, I had slapped her viciously to punish her for the scene she had just enacted.

I remember that Antonia was all sweetness and light when we arrived home. She was deeply ashamed. "I don't understand what happened to me, Eladio. I've never doubted you."

Yet her apologies had begun to sound to me like the distant tolling of indifferent bells. It was not the first time Antonia's "impulses" had thrown me off balance. Ever since she became pregnant, it seemed as if anything at all could send her into a fit of violence. Her actions were senseless, brought on by rages with no specific cause. Strange behaviors, which I tried in vain to justify—to give her the benefit of the doubt.

It seemed impossible that the creature I had so admired for her sweet and gentle nature could, for no coherent reason, suddenly unleash a torrent of verbal abuse, calling up a deeply-rooted hatred that even she did not understand.

Her ridiculous fears of being crushed to death also intensified. "That balcony is going to collapse." Or "That streetlamp is leaning. Stay clear of it."

Trash cans were also terrorist weapons. "Be careful, Eladio. Sometimes they just take off rolling of their own accord in order to run right into some passerby."

When, in my alarm, I mentioned some of these episodes to Berta, the good woman rose immediately to "her baby's" defense. "Pregnant women often have those kinds of fears," she would reply.

Only Luisa had a different take. "Don't kid yourself, Eladio. We've always had to tiptoe around her. Absolutely anything can turn into a disaster in her mind."

On one occasion, something happened that took me completely aback. We were having lunch at home when I received a telephone call. Since we did not have a mobile phone at the time, I had to leave the table in order take the call. The person was calling from New York, so I had to deal with the matter immediately.

When I returned to the dining room, I found my wife in tears. I asked her what was wrong. But before replying, she rose from her chair with an offended expression and said that lunches were sacred and should never, ever be interrupted, "much less to connect with a city where most of the people are black."

The remark was so totally out of place, it left me speechless. I even entertained the thought that Antonia was joking. So I let it go and returned to my lunch as if nothing had happened.

That time, I remember Berta trying to smooth the whole episode over with sentimental explanations. "My Antonia is a very vulnerable girl, Sir. But she loves you. Don't ever forget how much she loves you."

Berta knew her well and I was certain she was not trying to cover anything up. "You should have seen her when they put her in my arms right after she was born. She was an angel, Sir. Always smiling."

By that time, however, the smiles were few and far between.

She only seemed happy when she was invited to parties. She always accepted these invitations because they gave her the opportunity to show off and preserve her reputation as the centerpiece of any gathering, in particular because of her scathing commentary on all of the salacious events our circle so delighted in dissecting.

Antonia had also gotten into the habit of organizing dinners and get-togethers to—as she put it—relieve her boredom while I was away at the office all day.

The people she invited were the type who are sprinkled in glitter which, when rubbed off, exposes their underlying vapidity. Important looking people whose passions were limited to expensive automobiles, home entertainment centers, spectacular boats, and lavishly decorated homes. They loved to play poker and bingo, and they had nothing in common with people who read books or spent their leisure time in intellectual pursuits or keeping up with current events.

In sum: their proclivities lie in the direction of sex, off-color jokes, and making sure that they only wore designer outfits and Italian shoes, since the Spanish styles simply were not refined enough.

When Mahler was in Barcelona he almost never attended his daughter's gatherings. His excuses were very much like those I might have made, had I not felt obligated to be there. "I've got a lot of work to do and need to get to bed early."

But Mahler seemed basically pleased that his daughter kept herself busy with cocktails or dinners to dispel what was becoming her chronic ill humor.

"She's lucky she married you," he told me once. "You know how to handle her, Eladio. You have a special talent for keeping her stable."

I did not appreciate it when he talked to me like that. Though Mahler did not realize it, those kinds of comments only confirmed that my wife's mental state was not at all what I had imagined: she apparently had some deep-seated emotional imbalance that my attentions had helped keep in check only temporarily.

But Mahler was by no means stupid and whenever he caught himself making such a slip, he would hurry to add that he was referring to Antonia's pregnancy. "Once your son is born she'll stop fretting over such trivial things."

I too, needed to believe that. Especially whenever she was herself again and talked about the baby as any normal mother would: "He'll have a career. He'll live with us until he gets married. He'll be the most adored child in the whole world."

When we were alone that was all she talked about. We spent our time imagining that the little one was already there running around the house, all smiles and happy noises, or else playing with the arsenal of toys that we had been gradually amassing for him.

And the day of the birth finally arrived.

It was an easy labor and delivery and contrary to my expectations, Antonia handled the pain with infinite patience. Her energy never flagged. To the contrary, it was as if each contraction gave her the strength that her fragile frame should have denied her.

Of course she did not for one minute let go of my hand. Her staunch refusal to allow me to leave her side was the only demand imposed by her suffering. "Don't leave me now, Eladio. Please don't go."

As if I could have imagined leaving her. I think I never loved her as much as I did at that moment. I would have given years of my life to share the contractions, to buffer her pain with my own.

"How can you even think I would leave you? We're talking about our son, about you, the two most important people in my life." And I kissed her forehead, damp with warm sweat that only made her perfumed skin seem softer.

It dawned on me for the first time that, despite her childlike demeanor, Antonia was an adult woman, capable of carrying out the fertile and vigorous social rite that was giving birth.

Suddenly, the things that had so baffled me during her pregnancy were behind us: none of her ridiculous fears, or silly jealousies, or propensity to cry over nothing, existed any longer. The important thing now was her "heroic entry into motherhood," without complaint, without the panic one would have expected the contractions would cause.

Even Luisa seemed to regret her previous theories about her niece's irregular behavior. "The truth is, Eladio, Antonia is handling this exceptionally well."

And our son was born.

I can see him now in his mother's arms: blue eyes trying to get used to the light in the room, still damp wisps of hair already suggesting curls just like Antonia's. Smiles that were actually sighs dawning on his rosy cheeks. Tiny cries and pouts that hinted at God knows what strange fears, which Antonia and I immediately tried to calm by holding him and swaddling him in our love.

There was no way anyone could have anticipated the anguish to come or taken urgent measures to prevent his existence from one day plunging us into despair.

Yes, at the time it was irrelevant to imagine that anything might bode ill for the future. The days following his birth were filled with long lazy hours, bright suns and constant, many-colored lights. There were no downcast faces, no hurtful words. Not even the newspapers (always poisoned by misery) could cast a pall on those moments of tranquility and joy.

Even my father-in-law, usually loathe to visit, showed up every day to analyze and admire his grandson's progress, listen to his little cries, and wonder at his calm nature. "He doesn't take after his mother. Antonia cried all the time," he assured us, contradicting what Berta was always saying. "Anything at all could put her out of sorts." And so that his daughter would not feel offended, he always hurried to add, "She was such a sensitive little thing."

My mother also appeared to be delighted with her grandson. As was her custom whenever she came to visit him, she never used the front door. She always used the servants' entrance instead. She did her best, but it was hard for her to adapt to her new carnation as the honored grandmother and she tended to shy away whenever Antonia's friends stopped by to visit. She mostly enjoyed Berta's company. The two of them would engage in lengthy chats, during which she would become almost loquacious. Berta must have shared a hundred anecdotes with her about Antonia when she was a baby. "Her poor mother died in childbirth," she would repeat, but she always took care not to add that it had been the drugs that had killed her.

It was futile to insist that she join our guests in the living room. "Don't make my head spin, Son," she would reply, closing her eyes and shaking her head. "Just let me be here with Berta. She and I get along very well."

Luisa just plodded along as always, placid and contained, as if she already knew that all such outpourings of enthusiasm—even in the best case scenarios—were merely precursors to despair.

Sometimes when I noticed her so detached from all the excitement going on around her, I would venture to ask her about it, "But Luisa, what the hell is wrong with you? He's your grandson after all. I don't understand why you seem so apathetic."

She would either make no reply or, with her habitual chilly demeanor, inform me that even the most joyous events are soon overtaken by the daily routine. "Don't inflate everything, Eladio. Anything that has such a strong impact on us—no matter how wrapped up in fervent emotions—changes or wears thin sooner or later."

That time I would gladly have written off the famous Aunt Luisa as superstitious and ill-intentioned. How could she talk to me like that when we were surrounded by such joy?

My father-in-law, impressed by how well things were going at the office and at home, did not fail to insinuate to me that "my talent merited a reward that would not be long in coming."

I had no idea what he had in mind for me, and for all Mahler's mysterious comments hinting at grand things to come, nothing seemed more important to me than seeing Antonia happy and my son smiling in his cradle.

Douglas Raft also dropped a few mysterious tidbits portending grand promotions. "When the time comes, you'll have no choice but to approach the situation with the confidence of an experienced diplomat and the false sincerity of a prostitute." And though he said it jokingly, he could not help but inject a certain degree of truth: "Conspiracies that trigger envy, even when undertaken at a snail's pace, can end up being fatal."

Mahler's propositions were not long in coming, but I was reluctant to accept them. Such prebends can sometimes cause dangerous aftershocks. "It's better to give it some time so I can earn what you are offering me."

My position impressed Mahler. He had not anticipated my attitude. "You're as cool as a cucumber, Eladio. Anyone else in your place would be doing somersaults."

He failed to see that sometimes challenges can also be burdens. "What this firm needs are thinking minds like yours and not a bunch of technical experts incapable of articulating a clear idea," he reiterated.

When I mentioned her father's proposal to Antonia, she seemed happy about it. Then she said something that cut me to the quick. "My father always does as I ask. The slightest hint from me is enough to produce a miracle."

I found Antonia's comment very upsetting. It gave a completely different twist to the reasons behind my promotion. "You're not saying that you were the one who persuaded your father in the matter of Woultmand & Starky."

But Antonia did not answer. She just smiled. I insisted in vain that she tell me the truth. "Please, Antonia. I need to know. It's important to me."

I held her gaze. I felt humiliated and at once a little alarmed by her vague expression. "Can't you see that I cannot accept those kinds of favors just because I have a son with you?"

But she remained silent. And suddenly she was once again the adolescent girl whose father indulged her every whim.

I remember going up to her, taking her by the shoulders and shaking her gently. "Please, Antonia," I insisted. "Did you ask your father for this damned promotion? I really need to know."

All at once she burst out laughing. "And you fell for it," she said. "What would I be doing begging my father to give you a raise by making you CEO of Woultmand & Starky?"

I told her then that the salary was not the issue. The important thing was being named head of a multinational corporation. My dignity was at stake if either of those things had come about because of her.

With an uneven smile, Antonia kissed me on the cheek. "What do you call your dignity?" And without waiting for a response, she left the room to chat with her girlfriends on the telephone.

I remember how her shadow followed her like a giant eel as she moved down the hallway. She was still chuckling as if she enjoyed leaving me there with my misgivings.

My mother came for a visit that afternoon. I was on the verge of telling her what had happened, but decided not to. I did not want her to feel put out with Antonia.

My mother was one of those people who radiated the sorrows amassed during so many years of living in poverty. She could never be happy. After my father's death, it was one humiliation after another. She had put up with insults and hostility and made superhuman efforts to ensure that her son would get ahead. That is why I resisted adding to her miseries.

Now that she is gone, however, I sometimes feel terrible about all the things she had to put up with when I was a teenager.

Sometimes I even feel as though I never really showed her how much I loved her. But while I was never overly demonstrative with my affections, I did try to keep things from her if I thought they would hurt her.

So when I saw her come into the house that afternoon, I decided there was no reason to upset her with my misgivings about what Antonia had said.

It was Antonia herself who brought up the subject. The first words out of her mouth were, "You should congratulate your son. I have spoken with my father and they're going to make him CEO of Woultmand & Starky."

She said it with a mocking grin on her face that my mother managed to assimilate without changing her expression. "I'm happy," she replied. "Eladio deserves to have your father agree to your proposition. He will be an effective leader."

But my mother's voice did not sound normal. It sounded hollow, as if it came from a diminished woman. She suddenly began to cough. She had a habit of coughing whenever something disturbed her, perhaps as a way of changing the subject.

At least, that is what I believed at the time. I soon learned that the coughing (which I had believed deliberate) was the discordant reserves of her diseased bronchial tubes. It was only aggravated whenever something upset her.

Maybe it is the champagne that is making Daniela's eyes sparkle now. The movie is over and as she pulls back the window shade the light turns her eyes into two dark diamonds.

"Has anyone ever accused you of having eyes like two drills?" inquires Eladio, without moving his gaze from hers.

Daniela does not understand what he means.

"No one has ever told me such a thing." And perhaps entertaining strange suspicions, she laughs as if shrugging off the comment.

"I could tell you that you have pretty eyes, or that they're incredibly large, or that they shine expressively. I could describe them as provocative, or fascinating, or a thousand

other things. But none of those would be a completely accurate description."

"What do you mean by that?"

"What I just said: your eyes drill into the eyes of whoever's looking at them."

"And what is that supposed to mean?"

"It's hard to explain. It's as if you wanted to pierce the mind of the person looking at you with a needle."

Daniela is amused and tries to swallow the chuckle rising in her throat. "I'm not sure whether what you're suggesting is a compliment or a criticism."

"It's neither one nor the other. Compliments don't fit into this sort of conversation, and I certainly don't feel inclined to criticize. What I'm trying to say is that it didn't take me long to realize that your gaze drills into a person. It penetrates your mind without asking permission."

"I never imagined I had such powers," she continues jokingly.

"It is quite possible that had you imagined it, you wouldn't have them."

Daniela shakes her head as if to say that she is not taking any of this seriously.

She probably thinks the champagne they ordered is distorting the conversation. Alcohol can stimulate the imagination and create a sense of congeniality that evaporates once its effects have worn off.

"Now tell me, what sort of thoughts have my eyes drilled into in your mind?" she inquires. "Because I certainly wasn't aware of any."

Eladio is still looking at her. It is a strangely detached look that does not appear to be a come on; to the contrary, it is a cooler look, one that denotes curiosity.

"I don't know. But you must. You don't seem to be the kind of woman who is easily deceived by appearances."

"I've never claimed to be particularly incisive," she says lightly. "How am I supposed to know what the drill is hitting in that mind of yours?"

Eladio touches his forehead and tries to smile.

"Hidden memories."

"Good or bad?"

"In any case, they're not nostalgic. Maybe a little tense. But always willing to be dissolved into oblivion."

"I'm sorry," she exclaims. "So they aren't good ones."

Eladio seems to recover his equilibrium and confesses openly that whole drill thing was an excuse.

"I wasn't sure how to tell you what I was thinking, so I figured the best thing to do was to invent the drill. But the truth is that I have this sudden need to know you better, learn more about you. Don't ask me why because I have no idea. I guess I thought the best way to explore your true character was to make you believe you'd penetrated mine."

"With a drill?"

"Not exactly. With the very unique way you have. With your powerful notions. With your strict code of ethics that is so rare among liberated women."

"I think you have the wrong impression of me. The truth is, I have very little to be proud of."

"Maybe it's that 'little' that is the best thing about you." *There is a brief pause and Eladio continues to look at her as if he is seeing her for the first time. "What I'd like to know about you are the silly things. The insignificant details. For example, Are you punctual? Do you like things to be neat? Do you like to break the mold? Are you possessive? Are you ever overwhelmed by your obsessions? Can you sew? Do you like to cook?"*

Eladio suddenly stops. And from his silence it is clear he is not expecting a response. As if the questions he has posed were based on bygone answers that were lost forever.

Daniela can do without her companion's somber expression.

"Come on now. You're just full of curiosity." And breathing in deeply, "That's how it is with you men. You like to investigate, find out, dance all around the person just to satisfy your interest. And you say we women are the curious ones."

"It's not curiosity. It's interest."

"What interest could a perfect stranger hold for you?"

"None. But you are no longer a stranger. Haven't we already established that our interaction, precisely because it is destined to be brief, is more conducive to the sharing of confidences than a conventional friendship would be?"

"If that were the case, where might our mutual understanding lead us?" she queries as if talking to herself. "In the end, when we say goodbye it will be just as if we'd never met. Surely

the distance that separates us will grow with every day that passes."

"Is that okay with you?"

"I'm not sure. But I accept it. Maybe it will bother me for a while, but it won't change my life."

"Is it possible that you're one of those antisocial types who only need themselves to be happy?"

"I didn't say anything about happiness. I'm talking about communication. And solidarity. I'm not talking about developing a friendship either. Let's not kid ourselves. Friendships always contain a dose of selfishness, particularly when jealousy, demands, and reproaches take over. But solidarity is immutable: free of selfishness, anger, vulnerabilities, or demands. It aims to be helpful and it does not transcend the bounds of tranquility."

"So you're telling me that nothing is stable in a friendship. In other words, personalities change and no matter how much we try to understand each other, the inevitable changes will ultimately break up the closest friendship."

Daniela continues to shake her head wordlessly. Then, as if she wished to backtrack: "Don't fool yourself, Eladio. We are all 'appearances,' or put another way, 'we are what others believe us to be.'"

"But 'others' can be throngs of people."

"So can our personalities." And as if shaking off a disturbing thought, she holds up her hand, leaving it suspended in the air as if it were bothering her. "Don't mind me. My father always said I was an incorrigible dreamer. Maybe he was right."

"But you have to have ingenuity in order to dream: imagination, talent. That's all positive."

"So I must be positive," says Daniela, playing on Eladio's theory. "I appreciate your efforts to boost my self esteem. However, I don't think I'm positive enough to consider myself an optimist. I've never been very trusting and am not in the habit of giving in to chance emotions."

"That is definitely a virtue. Nearly all the blows we receive in life can be attributed to hasty emotions, a stupid excess of trust or to imagining a vast plain where there is only swampland."

They fall silent. Memories are unforgiving. They come back. They install themselves in the mind and eat at the conscience. The mistakes are magnified. Every misstep is multiplied. And the ill-timed imposes. Which means that speaking up right now might be a mistake too. "The best thing to do," thinks Eladio, "is to shut up." So as the words pile up in his throat—and abstractions are allowed to overtake the reality of what he was trying to say—he must cling to that godforsaken silence. Shutting up, however, can also be a form of indictment. So Eladio breaks the silence in self defense.

"Going back to the utopia of personalities, do you think a good person can do bad things? Or put another way, is it possible for a murderer to have a benevolent soul, independently of all that we consider evil?" he asks suddenly.

Daniela shrugs. "It would probably take an entire lifetime to answer that question. Things are never that cut and dried. There are circumstances, pressures, education, culture. So many factors that can influence human behavior."

"You're right. There are so many influences. Light, heat, darkness, color, radiation, the people around us, ambiguity, euphoria. Even where you live."

"Even cities?"

"Yes. And languages, and streets and pedestrians."

"Cities do have an influence," she continues. "For example, I live in Los Angeles. I like it. But I realize that it's an inhospitable city. It is incapable of mitigating the solitude that older people often bemoan. It's hard to find a quiet street. It's all thoroughfares, sidewalks and cars. Lots of cars. Meanwhile, the few pedestrians who venture onto the sidewalks simply ignore each other, as if they were so many wax sculptures. When I'm out walking, I often have the sense that I'm surrounded by an optical illusion—a huge lie—as if the city were nothing more than an endless desert."

Eladio listens to her carefully, but something is bothering him. "That is all very well, but you still haven't answered my question. Is it possible for a good person to be bad, or a bad person to be good? I'm not persuaded by your theory about having to live an entire lifetime to discover that. An entire lifetime can be an awfully long time."

Again Daniela shrugs. And he regards her hands. "That is what the hands of a virgin must look like," he thinks without knowing why.

The hands clench suddenly, the veins hidden under smooth white skin showing blue until the fingers separate and the hands return to rest on her skirt.

"I asked you the question because it means something to me. A long time ago I had a friend with strong ethical beliefs. He was always looking out for the welfare of others. And yet he ended up in jail accused of a crime."

"Was he innocent?"

"Yes. But the courts said he was a criminal."

"What was he accused of?"

"Killing his wife."

"Did he kill her?"

"Yes, he killed her."

"Why?"

Eladio pauses for a moment before answering.

"Because he was too innocent. Now do you see what I'm trying to ask you?"

And seeing that Daniela is awash in confusion, he continues.

"We're born. We open our eyes and take in our surroundings. We think we understand. But we don't really understand much of anything. We struggle not to betray our ideals and we rail against those who do betray them. We even try to make excuses for those who trample our hopes. But the war that others wage against us forces us to defend ourselves, to become something akin to savage beasts. I'm referring to the savage human. The kind of savage who, being a rational human being, ought to be more conscientious. Nonetheless, he does not hesitate to turn into an animal that is more reprehensible and cruel than the most irrational of beasts." Eladio pauses, swallows, and then continues. "You're telling me about cities, houses, deserted streets with pedestrians that belong in a wax museum, cars driving along ghost highways, but what you haven't told me is whether our essential personality is what sets us on a course towards peace or destruction."

Daniela is slightly uncomfortable. She probably has no idea what to say. She finally decides.

"Maybe personality doesn't even exist." And raising her hand, she indicates to Eladio that she has changed her mind. "Maybe it's possible that our true personality only emerges when our life is over."

"And in the meantime? What?" he asks.

"Meanwhile, we have to be guided by appearances. Maybe they're not so deceiving after all."

118

It is hard to pinpoint exactly when I began to feel uncomfortable in my marriage. I'm also not completely sure what initially caused the deterioration that was to come.

It was not boredom. Or insipidity. Or routine. Yet everything around me began to seem uncertain, as if spoiled by unforeseen droughts, especially when, arriving home from the office, I would be consumed by the fear of finding Antonia in one of her rages.

Her rages were erratic and did not seem connected to any particular motive. Insipid, peevish tantrums that dissolved into nothingness, after which no rationale or solid explanation was ever forthcoming.

At first I made excuses for her, attributing it to her youth. "She's young and inexperienced," as Berta would say.

So whenever I could see that she was down, I still tried to soothe her, coddle her, or apply more physical types of influence, often with positive results.

But when she was overcome by hate—almost always due to my absences—there was no placating her.

Antonia could not tolerate my being apart from her a minute longer than expected. I had only to experience some minor delay and arrive home slightly late for her to vent her hostility in a deluge of questions that left me exhausted: "Where have you been? Who have you been with? What did they ask you? What did you talk about? Why didn't you tell me you were going to be late?"

She was relentless in her probing and her suspicions—which were totally irrational—seemed boundless.

When she was in one of those irrational states, I would try in vain to sound her out, try to get to the bottom of whatever was provoking it. But Antonia would not answer. She would just look at me with disdain, as if I were hiding something terrible that made it impossible for her to let down her guard.

Her aggressive, spiteful behavior led me to question my own. Suddenly, and for no real reason, I began to feel guilty. It was an unspoken self-recrimination that grew in the contradiction between my natural feelings of defiance and my innermost fears that I did not know how to treat her as she deserved.

But the time came when I stopped doubting myself, especially after I mentioned to Mahler how his daughter was behaving. "I want to please her in every way, but I never manage to," I told him. "I have the impression that I have disappointed her."

My father-in-law was unfailingly sympathetic. "Don't fret, Eladio. Antonia is very impressionable and anything can throw her into a fit. But she still loves you. Don't ever doubt it, Son."

Maybe that was when I began to suspect that Mahler's insistence that I become his son-in-law might have had something to do with his daughter's character. Could another man have put up with the things I had to endure?

And then those notions would suddenly strike me as absurd, particularly when for no apparent reason, Antonia would revert to her old sweet self again, just as she was in the early days.

Out of the blue, she would come up to me all kisses and hugs and affection, behaving for all the world like a meek and modest wife.

It did not take me long to figure out, however, that such behavior was nearly always associated with her father's proximity. It was as if she feared that Mahler would find out about her aggressive and incoherent behavior.

In contrast, Antonia made virtually no effort to rein in her moods around her Aunt Luisa. With the excuse that the woman had never understood her, she would adopt an imperious attitude and hurl mostly unfounded accusations at her: "You never bothered to do anything for me. You've always been like those wicked stepmothers in all the stories."

But Luisa never lost her temper. Her niece could have been talking to the wall.

Those scenes faded into the background when the child was present. It's as if I'm seeing him—he was still not walking—crawling across the living room rug to grab onto my father-in-law's leg, issuing gurgling noises in an imitation of the word "grandpa."

The child was Mahler's prized possession. His life's great ambition made flesh. Nothing pleased him more than to have the little one hanging on him, to observe each new little discovery: his frowns when something confused him or his chortles when someone was teasing him.

Everyone doted on the boy and he, therefore, did not hesitate to shower us all with the same love that was being shown him.

Even Antonia seemed happy when she saw her father so delighted with the little one.

She would forget her strange impulses in her desire to seem

motherly. Nothing was too good for her son. "He's so different from all the other children, isn't he, Eladio?"

Her innate jealousy, however, eventually rose to the surface. This was particularly the case when she saw how the child threw himself into my arms when I arrived home. "I just don't see how he can love you so much when you're never around," she would chide me.

She also was not thrilled by Anton's evident adoration of his grandfather. "If you keep spoiling my son like that, he's going to become insufferable," she would reproach her father.

And loath to displease her, Mahler would extricate himself from the child, agreeing with her all the while. "You're absolutely right, Antonia. It isn't good to spoil them."

His reaction did not tally with his own habit of catering to his daughter's every whim. I truly believe that deep down, Mahler was afraid of Antonia. It was an unhealthy fear, one that surely dated back to those early glimpses of the narcissistic tendencies that would intensify as she grew up.

The truth is that he acted as if he felt as guilty as I did. I only had to look at him to see how he fought to maintain his composure whenever she was around. "You may not believe this, but if I travel a lot, it isn't because I like it. Everything I have will be yours someday. That's why I work so hard," he was constantly telling her, as if to apologize for his constant absences.

I began to think his trips were just an excuse that enabled him to block out his concerns over his daughter's erratic behavior.

For her part, Antonia showed no signs of being troubled over her father's absences and yet whenever any problem arose, she did not hesitate to reproach him. "My life would be completely different if my mother were alive." And as Mahler drew back, she would immediately turn on her aunt. "At least you understand me, but all my dear aunt ever did was heap punishments on me while you weren't around."

At first I too had believed that her mother's sister had had a disturbing influence on Antonia's upbringing. It took me a long while to figure out that the real injured party was Luisa.

One only had to observe the way she reacted each time my wife attacked her. She never reproached her for her conduct (unfair by any measure) nor did she play the victim. She simply remained silent, pretended not to hear, and invented any excuse to exit the room, leaving Antonia with the words on the tip of her tongue.

This state of affairs gradually opened up the doors to metaphysical compartments that I never knew were there.

The doors were well concealed. No more than a reverberation of undetected hideaways, dense vapors enveloping the unconfessable in their darkness. Things that had never seemed to be there before, or had gone unnoticed, had been there all along and they soon rose to the surface.

The worst of it, however, was not the virulent waves of her moods, or her incessant fear of being crushed to death. The worst part was her obsession with being thin: the way she would look at herself in the mirror and bemoan how incredibly overweight she was, how she could not go on like that. If she could not slim down on her own, she would have to have a stomach operation to stop eating.

I tried in vain to convince her that she was frighteningly thin: "Can't you see that you're nothing but skin and bones?"

But she would not listen. "It was the damned pregnancy that ruined my figure. I'll never get it back to where it was before." And every chance she got, she would install herself in front of the mirror. "Eladio, just look at what's happened to my figure," she would wail.

I kept telling her she was exactly the same, more beautiful than any other woman in the world, but my opinions no longer counted. The only thing that made an impression was the flattery her friends heaped upon her.

The dinner parties resumed. Cocktails that facilitated the showing off of her new dresses, the murmured gossip, and the "innocent" comments and jokes meant to highlight other people's defects.

Antonia was still queen when it came to such pursuits. Once again the fawning, the smiles, the bitingly clever remarks. And there she was, surrounded by anyone who would listen, tossing off superficial remarks that were meant to seem deep.

After such an evening, her high spirits would last two or three days. Living was no longer a chore. She did not have to criticize everything around her. She did not appear to miss her outbursts against the servants or anyone else she might consider her "enemy." Even her obsession about losing weight seemed to dissipate. And when she went out walking, she rarely looked up to check whether the balconies threatened disaster.

The only thing that could put her out of sorts when she was in such a mood was my mother's presence.

Immersed as she was in her frivolous and grandiose world, her mother-in-law's simplicity and calm exasperated her. "It's the way she just accepts life as if she were already dead. It just gets on my nerves," she would tell me. "Your mother has such a simplistic way about her. I often compare her to Aunt Luisa. At two totally different levels of course, since when it comes to refinement, there's certainly no comparison."

Her words cut into me but I tried to maintain my composure so as not to upset her further.

"Fortunately, you're not like that," she would say. "It's hard to believe you're her son. Are you sure she's the one who gave birth to you? How did you manage to keep from inheriting her vulgar manners? I fail to see how you turned out to be a man of any stature at all growing up with her."

When she talked like that, I would simply ignore her, pretend I didn't hear, but her words cut into me like a sharp blade.

What did Antonia know about the significance of the life of the woman who, according to her, did not deserve to be my mother? For instance, where she found the reserves to keep her head above water by taking any job whatsoever and sacrificing her own need for stability so that my studies could continue uninterrupted. And the way she feigned happiness to hide an empty stomach that left her depleted. And the polite, faintly condescending expressions of gratitude.

No. Antonia would not have been capable of appreciating how difficult it is to climb the ladder when all life has to offer is a slippery slope. That is why she did not understand my mother. Or rather, did not accept her. She could not imagine that her composure might be sincere and that her perspectives might have been shrunk by enduring such patronizing behavior without being in a position to demand an apology.

Clinging stubbornly to the assumptions inherent to a spoiled child, she refused to accept that my mother could be the glorious antithesis of her own way of life. From where Antonia stood, my mother's world did not even exist. It was merely a speck of dust in the grandiose world in which she lived. How could she possibly accept a mother-in-law who had resuscitated and worn the outdated clothing that her employers had passed along to her? Who had carefully mended her undergarments over and over again? And the purses she rescued before their owners could toss them into the trash can, and her aching feet, calloused and deformed by years of pounding the pavement to save on bus fare?

Sometimes Antonia would say that my mother was more like a ghost. "She hardly talks. No one ever knows what she is thinking." And on those occasions I found myself hard-pressed to refrain from a harsh retort. How to explain to her that my mother's debut in the world of opulence, which had always been an impregnable fortress to her, was perhaps the most difficult trial she had ever faced? Maybe it would have been easy to explain to her that what she called "physical carelessness"—namely my mother's failure to watch her figure even though she was still relatively young—reflected her desire to take advantage of each day's leftovers to make up for what poverty had denied her for so many years.

Her mind deformed by a life of luxury, Antonia could not possibly comprehend my mother's habit of eating all the leftovers before they spoiled. She overate to avoid wasting what would once have constituted a veritable banquet.

Antonia also found it hard to accept that my mother still bought her clothes on sale and never gave in to the impulse to buy anything impractical, even though she could now afford to.

And my mother would never let her own friends into our house. If they wished to see the baby, she would send them to the park where Berta would be waiting with him.

Antonia regarded my mother's friends as old busybodies who spent their time gabbing in second class cafés where social standing meant nothing and the conversation was too dull for words.

Although these women had managed to get "ahead," the only thing that counted in Antonia's mind was the "backwardness" of their youth, which had instilled frugal habits in them that were essentially meaningless when it came down to it. Placid individuals who analyzed the hazy past with the serenity and simplicity of those who have made it over what had once seemed an insurmountable barrier.

It was probably Antonia's obvious disdain for my mother's friends that led her to keep her distance from us.

When Antonia was not at home, however, my mother never failed to visit her grandson. "I'm not sure you even realize what a son you have," she would say, radiant with joy. "He is an exceptional child." And she would hug and kiss him, play with him tirelessly.

I never saw her as happy as when Anton rushed to meet her at the front door.

She always cut her visits short, however. She would leave as soon as Antonia came home, without complaint, never making a scene. She paid no mind to her daughter-in-law's impudence. She even went so far as to make excuses for her. "All couples need privacy," she would say.

In any case, by then Antonia was no longer staying home as she had done at first. Her habits had changed dramatically. Suddenly she was paying more attention to her appearance than ever before. Besides her passion for shopping for dresses, coats, shoes and all sorts of accessories to show off her refined tastes, she also spent hours at the gym, getting facials, and visiting diet specialists. "I'm getting too fat, Eladio. From now on I'm going to skip dinner." And to avoid temptation she would remain in the living room while I hurried through my meal alone in the dining room.

I often wondered what she was surviving on. The figure that had so attracted me when we met was now little more than a walking skeleton.

The worst part of her obsession was that she not only monitored her own food intake, she tried to limit mine and our son's as well. "There's nothing more dangerous than an obese child. When he's older, he's going to turn into an elephant," she assured me. "No fat. No carbs. No desserts, no donuts, no béchamel sauce. She said it in a clipped voice, with the severity of those in charge of extremely weighty matters.

Fortunately, the cook paid no attention to her. Berta was the first to make the necessary adjustments. "Just make sure he eats when his mother isn't around." So she supplied him "under the table" with everything his mother withheld.

Of course the love I had once felt for Antonia had become an alien sentiment by that time. It was simply outside the scope of my emotional wherewithal.

I felt particularly empty when I discovered her intention not to have any more children. "They're simply too stressful and they deform your body," she would say openly.

I cannot even remember how many times during our courtship she talked about wanting a big family. "I want to have a lot of children," she had assured me over and over again.

The truth is that in her urge to become the thinnest woman in the world, Antonia could not remember much of anything.

I don't deny it. Sometimes appearances are not deceiving," replies Eladio, "but it's always possible to distort them."

"I suppose you're referring to the inclination to manipulate the situation or to pretend we're something we're not, for whatever reason?"

Eladio nods and takes it a step further.

"We can even convince ourselves that the pretenses we engage in to make a good impression are the truth, rather than a barefaced lie."

"That would be deceiving ourselves. No, I don't believe in the notion of going to such extremes. Why pretend something that isn't true? What's the point of making a good impression if it's a false one? In the end, good impressions are not always necessary to live a normal life."

Eladio seems abstracted, detached from what Daniela is intimating. Absorbed in his thoughts, he frowns and turns towards her.

"Sometimes they are. Sometimes it is necessary to appear to be something you're not."

But Daniela does not accept her friend's categorical reply.

"When?"

"When we are afraid, for example."

"Afraid. Of what?"

"In the first place, of the shame of admitting our own deception and of losing the regard of those who trusted in us."

Their glances cross and miss as a certain incomprehension leaves them distanced and disconnected. Something they cannot name is bothering them, leaving them restless, levying who knows what kinds of unfathomable accusations.

The best thing to do would be to make a joke out of the discussion, but neither of them seems inclined to take a stab at the healing alchemy that laughter can create.

Finally Daniela ventures to break the silence with an impulsive comment.

"In any event, I feel certain that your appearance is not hiding anything negative."

"Thanks. But I still think that what you see in me is deliberately false."

"Why? I can't imagine why you would have any reason to want to deceive me."

Eladio breathes in deeply and moves to adjust the knot of his tie.

"The human being is very greedy when it comes to his pretenses. We all want others to judge us positively."

"Even though there is no reason for such a judgment?"

"No one likes others to be hesitant or distrustful because of what we seem to be."

Daniela smiles again and brushes Eladio's arm.

"Relax. Whether it's fake or not, you have a very positive appearance. I'm not sure why, but the truth is I trust you. It's probably a mistake. Maybe you have occult, malevolent designs. But you offer them in such a nice way. Maybe I'll end up disillusioned, but it will have been an intelligent disillusionment."

"And that's enough for you not to feel as if you were duped?"

"I think so. It would be worse to be disillusioned by my own idiocy. By having closed my eyes to the obvious. But closing them because they've been wide open for hours beside a person who seems sincere will not make me feel duped. I would feel sad though."

Eladio again regards the hands resting on his companion's skirt. Right then, they seem distended, as if numbed and vaguely inert.

"Has anyone ever told you that you have the hands of a lay sister?" he jokes, pointing to the back of one of them. And quickly, "It is nice that someone like you would feel inclined to trust me. In any event, even if my character is not what you think it should be, you can be sure that you are someone I would never try to deceive."

"Thank you. But why not me?"

"Because you are incapable of deception and, if I were to do it, I would feel like a total jerk."

Daniela regards him as if she is trying to suppress an irrepressible joke.

"And what makes you so sure I could never deceive you?"

"My sixth sense never fails me," he teases her. "I can tell you're very bright, but I just can't see you using your intelligence to lie."

"And how could you have figured that out?"

"Well, it's in the aura that surrounds you. In your voice, in the way you express yourself. You are what I call 'soft-spoken.' There's nothing shrill or artificial about your voice. Do you see what I mean, Daniela? Words pronounced in a voice such as yours are never insincere. There's also the way you eat, sip your soup, leave the silverware exactly perpendicular to the plate, the knife on the right and the fork on the left. Of course, it could be a drawback if you cut the eggs with a knife or eat lentils with a spoon, or slice your croissants with the silverware, but I am convinced that none of those things are really you. You might say I'm a fanatic, but there's no question in my mind that those kinds of things have a bearing on a person's character. Being who you are, you would never kiss a person you'd only just met, or use some slang greeting to address an older person you had never laid eyes on before."

"I never would have imagined that such trivial things could be so important, but you're right, all of the things you describe would be completely out of character for me."

Daniela leans back in her seat. She is not indifferent to Eladio's speech. She probably thinks that, though he is definitely exaggerating, what Eladio has said, mundane as it might appear, clearly has something to do with the difficult coexistence of any couple.

"I'll have to ask my fiancé if he is of the same opinion. Up to now it had not occurred to me that such little things could be so fundamental."

"And then there's the way we react when life takes an unexpected twist," Eladio continues. "Things like avoiding major upheavals, 'understanding' without resentment, asking without sarcasm, not over-reacting. Or avoiding the arrogant slap in the face, direct accusations, barbs, and most of all, the impulse to attack, to do damage, to humiliate."

"Well on that score, I have to admit I've failed on more than one occasion. And no matter how I try to preserve that 'soft-spokenness' you have so kindly attributed to me, when I get angry I can be very abrasive."

"Yet I'm sure your anger is not gratuitous. The bad thing is to get mad for no reason. Or simply because, for reasons we cannot possibly grasp, the furies we carry inside us suddenly burst forth with the ferocity of the demented."

"I agree with you there. I've never been a fan of creating scenes for no reason and I try not to be guided by animosity. For what? The only thing that accomplishes is that you alter your body rhythms and risk acting the idiot. That kind of erratic behavior is usually pretty pathetic."

Eladio is no longer contemplating Daniela's hands. The past is taking over in his mind: Antonia's incoherent episodes, her fits of rage over any petty thing. And the way she gossiped with her friends about the people on the periphery of her little circle, taking every opportunity to show what an entertaining woman she was, even if that meant picking apart the most solid reputations.

"I could tell," insists Eladio. "It's not just your voice. You have a rational calm that's evident in the way you express your ideas and opinions, the different facets of your personality."

"We all give ourselves away. You'd never guess the things I've detected in you."

"Such as?"

"Something deeper than your sorrow."

Eladio bows his head and asks without looking at her: "So I come across as a sorrowful man?"

"It makes sense. You've lost the wife you loved and you've lost your only son. It wouldn't be normal to be jumping for joy after all you've been through." And since Eladio does not appear disposed to elaborate: "Were you and your wife very close?"

"We were bound."

Daniela is confused by the response. She does not really understand what he means.

"It's not just closeness that counts in a marriage," continues Eladio. "There are ties that bind you."

"What sorts of ties?"

"Children, everything around you, vested interests, hopes, force of habit."

"Which leads me to believe that you were never unfaithful to your wife."

"Never," he says tersely "I couldn't have."

"In any case, I've always believed that being unfaithful once in a while might be reprehensible, but it doesn't necessarily mean you've stopped loving the person you cheated on."

"There was never anyone else between us," he said, his voice still terse.

Daniela can see that the conversation is taking an unpleasant turn for Eladio. With an air of impatience, he abruptly takes matters into his own hands, as if those still fresh memories were poking into the most sensitive areas of his conscience.

"Why don't we talk about you?" He asks, trying for an amiable tone.

"I think I've told you just about everything."

"You've told me about some of your reactions or takes on things, but not the details."

"You've held back on that score as well."

"That's possible." And returning to the previous thought: "I imagine there must have been a time when you felt disappointed, put upon, or punished. All of us have been spectators or actors in a situation where others have behaved badly. One look at a newspaper is enough to tell you that life is no bed of roses. Mothers who kill their children, brothers who rape their sisters, husbands who enjoy torturing their wives, sexual assaults for the pleasure of humiliating someone else. There are so many aberrations."

"Maybe I've been lucky, but I've never had to confront those sorts of problems."

"Considering your looks, it's hard to believe that you've never been harassed by a love-crazed man."

"I've never put myself in the line of fire. I've always tried to be cautious."

"So you think that when bad things happen it's due to the actions of the victims?"

"No. I don't believe that. In most cases it's machismo—or the belief that a woman is inferior—that leads to such tragedies. Of course, it's true that sometimes women get careless. You have to be so cautious. You have to think ahead and avoid provocations. Sometimes, maybe unconsciously, we ask men to refuse what we seem to be offering in a fairly blatant manner and that isn't fair. It certainly does nothing to ensure our safety. It deactivates our defenses."

"But one shouldn't discount the element of 'bad luck' either."

"Or drugs."

"Or ignorance."

Daniela nods. "I've seen a lot of examples of just how dangerous ignorance can be. It can lead men and women both into disaster," she adds.

Eladio remains silent. Daniela's assertion becomes wedged in his memories.

"In effect, ignorance may be the main factor in the worst cases. A direct path to true cruelty," she continues. "It confuses and misleads. We start to mistake instinct for emotion and believe that whatever hits us over the head must be reality."

Listening to her, Eladio has the feeling that he is no longer navigating in unsafe waters. Suddenly it is as if Daniela's voice were liberating him from those psychometric bonds that force him to oscillate between fear, responsibility and, most of all, the chronic self-hatred that has plagued him since Antonia's death.

"Of course." exclaims Eladio. "And men can also become victims of harassment, aggression and humiliation."

"But no one really talks about that."

"Because it would mean opening ourselves up to ridicule. That's why men who experience psychological and even physical abuse tend to keep their mouths shut." And since Daniela remains silent, "How many killers might have been victims themselves?" he finishes.

Although he has spoken in a muted voice, Daniela has heard him clearly. And all at once, everything seems to have been turned upside down. Eladio is no longer a man afloat in specific sorrows. His way of expressing himself has changed, as if to shield him from a reality that has nothing to do with the one she imagined.

"Are you familiar with a specific case?"

"Many. Men do not hold a monopoly on sadism, I can assure you of that."

Eladio's response raises a host of questions that Daniela dares not ask.

"Tell me the truth. Have you suffered some form of abuse?"

Eladio does not reply immediately. Then he seems to decide.

"There's always a degree of aggression in the roles we play. No man is exempt from that."

But his ambiguous reply does not satisfy Daniela.

"But I would imagine that you took the high road."

"I can't know for sure. The things we regard as positive may not be. And being right can be made up of many wrongs. What seems valid to us now may not seem so tomorrow." And inhaling deeply, "It isn't good to be too trusting."

"That's why I've always tried to go through life with my feet solidly on the ground," she replies, without quite grasping Eladio's meaning.

"And the person who is in the right is almost never recognized," he continues. "That honor goes to the person who comes out on top. Don't kid yourself, Daniela. We aren't perfect. We always make mistakes."

"So getting it right strikes you as that hard?"

"It depends on what you call getting it right. Sometimes victories go hand in hand with the most stunning defeats."

"What if what you call defeats were really victories?" she asks.

"Victories don't hurt, they don't intimidate and they don't crush your illusions of the future. No. It is impossible to confuse the two."

"And you? I mean, did they crush your illusions?"

A sudden lurch of the plane cuts the question short, essentially erases it. They instinctively grab the other's hand and hold tight. But the contact is fleeting. The plane stabilizes and Daniela rephrases her question.

"Are you afraid to die?"

"No. Death doesn't scare me. What scares me is life."

"And yet life can be wonderful," she remarks.

"I wouldn't deny that." And, as if to reconcile the tone of the conversation, he tries to reflect a peace he does not feel: "Right now it is. The problem is that moments such as this are short-lived." And following a very brief pause, "Thank you, Daniela."

"What are you thanking me for?"

"For having invented a seven-hour friendship."

I gradually learned how to defend myself. My bulwarks were rather desiccated, scorched by the sun with no mitigating ozone layer, but they enabled me to endure her. Negligible little tricks served as a shield that kept me from becoming too discouraged. This was especially true when Antonia, in one of her moods, would mount a masochistic scene to attract attention and place me in awkward situations.

The truth was that our relationship was deteriorating with every passing day. She would come up with a grievance at the slightest provocation. The most trivial thing served as an excuse and was magnified into a major drama. Anything could be an offense, or a slight, or an imaginary trap set for the sole purpose of infuriating her.

Suddenly and for no apparent reason, she would act rejected, misunderstood or, in most cases, offended. The important thing was to make herself into the protagonist of some situation, so that her ego would be acknowledged, stroked and admired. To that end, she deployed an endless array of artifices, most of which involved me. "Since you don't need me, I have no choice but to turn to my friends."

Her tricks seemed fairly benign on the surface. Arrogant eye-rolling when something did not turn out as she had planned or ridiculous complaints over petty things that she would blow completely out of proportion in order to humiliate me.

Soon she began to refine her techniques, making sure her scenes had the benefit of an audience predisposed to consider that her outbursts were eminently reasonable. Especially when she allowed—in a plaintive and melancholic tone of voice—that I was dependent on her and, had it not been for her, I would be just another low-level employee in her father's company.

She would say it in such a forthright and unassuming way that none of her friends dared contradict her, so naturally I was turned into the tyrant who was taking advantage of her.

When she staged those sorts of scenes, I sometimes pretended to go along so that people might think she was joking. Yet that strategy could also backfire. When she was in one of her real rages, she not only rebuffed the attempted humor, she turned it against me: "Do you see that? Even he has to admit it. He'd be nothing if it weren't for me."

I reached my limit the day I realized her beauty no longer had any effect on me whatsoever. To the contrary. What I could no longer forgive was that because of her beauty, which had so dazzled me when we first met in Marbella, I was now a slave to her perverse obsessions.

Worst of all were her derogatory comments. The way she would refer to me in front of her friends as if, far from being her husband, I did not even have a name: I was merely "the executive."

"Have you seen the executive?" Or "The executive has chosen to take off on a business trip and leave me alone."

Anything but my name.

The crowd found this very amusing and soon "the executive" became a familiar moniker at Antonia's constant get-togethers.

Of course, no one suspected that such references might be an insult in disguise and that, if she said such things, it was because she somehow felt I eclipsed her personality.

Blinded by their image of Antonia as a scintillating personality, funny and always willing to go along with the joke, they failed to grasp the malice in her half-spiteful half-teasing attitude towards me.

In spite of everything, before reaching the extremes we had by then, I had tried over and over again to recover the tranquility of the early stages of our relationship, always seeking rational explanations for her constant excesses. And I did it out of the love—albeit somewhat battered by then—I still felt for her.

I sometimes even lowered myself to ask forgiveness for having failed her. And far from appreciating my attempts to appease her, she would leave me there in the ditch and tried to make me feel even guiltier. "You're the one who has changed me. I've always been a reasonable woman. No one has ever gotten on my nerves the way you do."

It took me awhile to grasp that her accusations were patently unfair. Although Luisa never spoke disparagingly of her niece, whenever Antonia created a scene she made it clear that such behavior had been in evidence since babyhood.

Berta also confirmed a history of such diatribes when she realized what I was going through. "The poor child was born with her genes all messed up by the drugs her mother used. But she's a good girl, Sir."

The truth was that anything at all could set her off. For example, I could never yawn in her presence: "Oh, am I boring you?" Or walk past her without smiling: "Clearly I'm just a walking corpse to you." Or fail to compliment her on her outfit: "So I no longer exist for you?" The most trivial thing became another example of neglect that acquired tragic proportions.

Then there was the "refused plate" syndrome. It usually happened when we went out to eat with friends. Obsessed with the notion of not losing her figure while still pretending to eat, as soon as the waiter placed her order in front of her, she would poke at it with her fork and with a look of disgust, snap "This is not to be tolerated, Eladio. Look at the slop they've brought me. Please complain to them right away. Didn't somebody say that this was a decent restaurant?"

The first time I witnessed such a scene I thought she must be right. She was so adamant. But such episodes became chronic and I understood it was a ploy to avoid eating. "This swill has made me lose my appetite. Tell them I don't want anything else."

I would sometimes switch plates with her in an effort to avoid a scene. On those occasions, she would pretend to eat what food remained, but in fact, she merely played with her fork without swallowing a single bite.

But if, weary of the whole travesty, I pretended not to notice her grumblings, she would quickly become indignant and resort to another tactic to shoot me down fast.

Suddenly her eyes would roll back, she would grab her chair and claim to feel faint, so that I had no choice but to jump up and rush to her side, wave a napkin to give her air and show her every consideration until she revived.

For a while, none of these idiosyncrasies seemed to have any effect on her friends' undying devotion. No matter what, her genius for gossip, for ruining other people's reputations, for gainsaying the most solid beliefs seemed to hypnotize everyone around her. It was as if anything Antonia said was an irrefutable truth.

She was so poised and self-confident that even I believed her at first. I would be scandalized by her lack of scruples, but also amused by the labels she assigned to the people around her. Of course, the individuals in question never realized what she had said about them. She took care to make sure that her subjects were not present at the time.

There was only one exception to that rule, which was the label she had assigned me: "There is the executive." Or "Have you discussed your financial situation with the executive?" Or "You should never trust those executives. They always have a card up their sleeve to deceive the people they advise. Be careful with them. They're all smooth talkers, very dangerous."

I am not sure what Antonia really thought of executives, but she certainly wielded the term with nothing but disdain.

I remember the first time she pinned that label on me and I thought she was kidding. "Hasn't anyone ever told you that you smell like an executive?" And playing along, I responded, "And you, in contrast, smell like flowers."

I did not realize at the time that she was expressing her embarrassment at having married a man who lived off his salary. "Flowers don't shave, or wear Hermes ties, or marry rich women like you did."

Her intention was to humiliate me, but the only thing she achieved was that I turned the tables on her. "Have you forgotten how you chased after me? I didn't want to marry you. I didn't see myself as someone at your level, but your father pushed me into it. He said if I refused to marry you, you'd die of a broken heart."

Antonia defended herself as best she could. "Nobody knows what they're doing when their eighteen. You were older. You had experience. You should never have paid attention to my father's foolishness."

It goes without saying that by then, our relationship was little more than breathes of stale aromas, with the marks of putrefaction that would soon put an end to our best intentions. Uncertainty and confusion had evolved irrevocably into deflated passions, broken promises, and principles frayed beyond repair by neglect and by the lack of mutual respect.

Although I still had not come to despise her as I would later, it exhausted me just to be in her presence. I never knew how she was going to behave. The whole panorama seemed permeated with misery and misunderstanding.

Therefore, leaving aside the few occasions on which she still pretended that she was proud to be with me—especially in front of her father—there was nothing left between the two of us that could repair the damage done.

I often tried to analyze why Mahler's presence acted as a sedative, turning her back into the sweet and gentle girl of our courtship, but I never was able to figure it out. Perhaps she was afraid her father would reveal old secrets about her rebelliousness and volatility, afraid he would take my side.

So she would try to seem happy and give a positive twist to her attempts to humiliate me. "The problem with Eladio is that he lacks a sense of humor. He just doesn't get it. What he refers to as my 'tantrums' are just little games I play to strengthen our communication."

I do not know whether her father really believed her or not, but he certainly acted as if he did. It was his way of extricating from disagreeable situations he preferred to ignore.

The only ones to share my misgivings were Berta and Aunt Luisa, especially when Antonia's tirades began to involve our son.

All of a sudden, her yelling and fury were also trained on him for no apparent reason. In her mind, Anton was turning into "something" culpable for reasons she could not quite explain. Everything about the child now had a negative connotation: how much he resembled me, his huge smiles, they way he bumbled about in a manner totally inappropriate for "a child of good upbringing," the mess left behind whenever he "dared" go into the living room without permission.

Every single detail that had to do with the boy was cast in an unfavorable light: nothing was as it should be. It was as if in some indirect way she could not forgive him for the "deformation of her body" that of course only existed inside her head.

Naturally, my son was wounded by his mother's behavior towards him. He did not understand her sharpness. I can see him now: cowering, desperately seeking a glimmer of warmth in Antonia's harsh words. "Who gave you permission to leave your room? Get out. Go play with your dinosaurs." And she would shove him towards the door.

She also did not seem to care whether or not Anton overheard our arguments. It got to the point that her son no longer existed for her. She never refrained from hurling any insult that came into her head at me, even in front of him. "Fortune-hunter, despicable shit, social parasite, son of a whore." Any epithet served to unleash her tongue and cut the child to the quick.

Anton truly suffered. He was too bright not to be wounded by the insults his mother heaped upon me.

My God, how much incomprehension was reflected in the adult expression trapped in the eyes of such a small boy. It's as if I can see him coming towards me, hugging me close in sympathy. He did not cry. Anton almost never cried. It was as if he had been born without tears. Surely they were hidden deep within him, in the internal wounds inflicted by his mother.

Other than that he was a quiet child. He never rebelled, or had tantrums or got into things the way other children his age would. Yet one had only to look at him to see the sadness building up inside because of all that was happening around him.

I would take him in my arms to comfort him. I would press him against me and tell him that I loved him and would never leave him, and that we would always be together, no matter what.

But if he heard his mother's footsteps, Anton would wriggle out of my arms, jump from my lap and rush to hide in a corner of his bedroom.

And yet, despite the incomprehensible rages he witnessed, Anton loved his mother. This was brought home to me on one occasion when Antonia had a minor accident in the kitchen. She had burned her hand and the child was watching her in terror with tear-filled eyes and sobbing uncharacteristically.

The boy was clearly upset but he did not dare approach her. He just watched her, his chest heaving, as if his tears might cure her.

All he got in return, however, was Antonia exclaiming rudely in her irritation: "Will someone get this child out of the kitchen. He's just in the way."

She said this while studying her hand, with the long slender fingers and manicured nails she so diligently cared for. "I wonder if this burn is going to heal properly."

So aesthetics prevailed once again. Nothing could be more important than imagining whether that burn might leave a blemish on her smooth skin.

Meanwhile, the frightened child ran to his room to hide like a wounded animal.

Fortunately, Berta often made up for his mother's continual absences and erratic behavior. "Don't worry, Anton. You're mother's just fine."

But the child needed more than meaningless consolation. So whenever he could, he orbited around Antonia as if waiting for her to share some tidbit of the love she had shown him up until he was two or three.

Her indifference was such that I began to think our son bothered her. It was as if his presence set her on edge, or she was only putting up with him because it was expected: if she'd had it to do over again—given how things had gone—she would probably have preferred not to have given birth to him.

Her obsession with her figure—which she claimed Anton had ruined—was a constant source of frustration for her.

She would spend hours in front of the mirror examining all of her alleged imperfections, fluffing her long thick hair and practicing faces that might make her seem more attractive.

I still cringe when I recall the scene she created when—believing that no one was looking—she kissed herself in the mirror.

Opening her eyes, she suddenly saw the child leaning against her bathroom door. She turned on him and screamed, "Who gave you permission to leave your room? How often have I told you that you have to do what I say? Move! Get out of here. Go find your father. There's nothing of yours in here."

I could not restrain myself after witnessing that outburst. I confronted her. I told her that she sometimes behaved like a monster. I said she did not deserve to be a mother and that all she cared about in this world was to have all of her stupid friends fawning all over her, that her gratuitous and selfish despotism did nothing more than turn her into the ugliest woman in the world. I warned her that if she continued to visit her despotic rages on our son, I was going to file a child abuse complaint against her.

I know I lost my temper. I boiled over. Deviated from the conciliatory course I had set for myself. But when I saw how miserable the child was, I simply could not maintain my composure.

I hated her at that moment. And it was Anton's expression that had caused me to hate her. I could not stand seeing my son so at a loss, so fearful, so submersed in a chaos of doubts for which he had no explanation.

I soon found out what a grievous mistake I had made. Antonia did not even wait for me to finish. Overcome by fury, she came towards me, her eyes shining with anger, her lips quivering darkly. Without stopping to think, she threw the bottle of perfume she held in her hand straight at me, shattering it against my forehead.

All at once there was nothing but a cloying smell, the terrible burning in my eyes, and the stinging pain of glass shards encrusted in my skin. I grabbed her by the arms as best as I could, threw her down on the sofa and tried to staunch the bleeding with my handkerchief.

And then I heard the child's footsteps running down the hall, heard him scream in terror, "Mommy hit Daddy. Mommy made Daddy bleed."

I was about to run after him. Pretend his mother and I had been playing. Tell him that what he had witnessed was just a game between us. But I no longer had the strength to keep on pretending. I just stood there regarding Antonia where she lay on the sofa, the broken bottle on the carpet, my bleeding forehead staining my handkerchief, my tie and my jacket. "I suppose you're happy now. You've made our son suffer yet again."

Antonia did not reply. She did not look at me either. I saw her rise and walk towards me. She wobbled slightly. She raised a hand to her forehead and I could see she really was on the verge of fainting. "Forgive me," she said. And she fell into my arms, not caring whether my blood might stain her. "I don't know what came over me. Forgive me please." And she began to cry inconsolably.

That was the first time it truly dawned on me that I had married a pathetic human being who constantly craved the affection she had not received as a child.

I felt sorry for her. I held her close and begged her to forgive me too.

We made love that night. Sometimes sex serves to buffer the harsh feelings, even transform them into emotions that seem genuine.

The truth is, slumber consumed hate that night and by the time I woke up the next morning, hate had been forgotten.

For a longer period than I expected, Antonia was once again the accommodating woman of our honeymoon. It was as if there had never been a harsh word between us.

The worst part was arriving at the office with the wound on my forehead.

Of course I lied shamelessly. I told everyone that I had slipped and cracked my head on the edge of the fireplace.

At the time, I would have sworn that I covered up the true source of the injury to protect Antonia's reputation.

But it wasn't true. I know now beyond a shadow of a doubt that I was protecting my own.

"Seven hours," repeats Daniela. "In any case, New York is still pretty far off." And as if the passing of time were irrelevant, "I wonder if it's raining there. It was pouring when we left Spain, remember?"

Eladio does indeed remember. Hurricane-force winds. Frigid gusts blowing skirts, wreaking havoc with hairdos and turning umbrellas inside out.

He also recalls the hope that drove him to leave Spain and the yearning to find rest that had been building up inside him for so many years.

And his pledge to never again be fooled by appearances. And to keep silent. And to lean back in the seat, close his eyes and allow the wreckage of his life to gradually lighten during the course of the long trip, to fade away into nothingness.

"It might be sunny in New York."

"Do you believe in the influence of time?"

"No. Time is just the excuse we use to justify our changing moods," she responds. "Those changes that sometimes get the better of us and make us to behave like savage little beasts."

"Are you referring to gratuitous violence?"

"And unexpected depravity. And acts of aggression that are inherent to cruelty."

At that moment the sick child grabs his mother, whispers something in her ear, and she gets up to take him to the bathroom.

"See that little boy? He seems harmless. But who can be sure that at some point he might not turn into a little despot?"

"His mother seems to be worried about him."

"All mothers worry about their children," Eladio exclaims. "I still remember how much mine worried. It did not matter that I was grown up and a man by then. I was still her baby: a defenseless creature in need of her protection. She never said it in so many words, but it was obvious." And with a gesture that conveyed a sense of impotence, "My mother was very perceptive. She could guess at things as if she could actually see them. She could root out the big lies at the heart of the life's biggest truths. Otherwise she was a very simple woman. Simple in that her intelligence was not presumptuous. She must have suffered terribly when my father died. No social security was available to her and she had to take on any job she could find. She didn't care if the high and mighty turned up their noses at her efforts and paid her ridiculously low wages. She never got carried away by a desire for status. She reserved all that for her son. She wanted me to become everything she had never tried to be."

"Obviously she was successful," Daniela observes. "But how did she manage it?"

"By accepting whatever came her way: long hours as a domestic, caring for the sick who had no one else to care for them, putting up with the eccentricities of hopeless old people, taking in sewing. And, since she was very devout, she probably said novenas to help her get to the end of the month without debts," jokes Eladio. "One thing is certain: she never allowed herself to become discouraged."

Eladio takes a deep breath and looks at Daniela searchingly, as if he expects a reply.

But Daniela does not open her mouth. She merely arches her eyebrows slightly to indicate that he should continue.

"She never cared for luxuries. I think I told you that. She clung to her thrifty ways even after I landed my first important position. She tended towards the very basic. She always traveled third class and would find a cheap hostel to spend the night. Her friends were the same anonymous, modest people who, like she, made good use of the cast-offs of the rich. That was my mother."

"But by then you were helping her out."

"Of course. And despite everything, she was reluctant to accept my help. She used to say that being poor was much more gratifying than getting bogged down in riches. As I mentioned before, my mother was very religious and in her view, wealth was an obstacle to Christian principles."

"Well then she wasn't very conscientious when it came to you," Daniela teased. "I'm talking about your stature in the financial world."

"Her theories were not always cut and dried. She would say that Christ chose poverty but did not turn his back on the rich. According to my mother, the sin is not in being comfortably off, but whether that comfort is allowed to destroy one's faith."

"I see it has destroyed yours."

Eladio shakes his head and tries to explain. "I didn't lose my faith because of my job."

Daniela waits for Eladio to explain, but suddenly his thoughts have become confused, unpleasant, as if his mind has been enveloped in a dense cloud that is not easily dispersed.

"She tried to raise me in keeping with her religious tenets."

"But she didn't succeed."

"She did at first. Why should I deny it? Believe it or not, I was headed for sainthood, but ended up instead as one of those lukewarm subjects whom God spits out of his mouth. Isn't that what the Bible says?: 'neither cold nor hot . . .'. The kind of vomit that stinks to high heaven and then dries up. There is no doubt about it: being lukewarm is dangerous for those who consider themselves believers."

"It must have been hard on your mother to see you reject the things she had tried to instill in you."

"She never knew. She died before my son fell into the pool."

"So it was the loss of your son that took away your faith in God?"

"No. There were other things too. A whole host of disparate factors. For example success, praise, the ridiculous conviction that getting ahead is the only important goal in life. Then there was my wife. She had been raised without any religion. She didn't know the least thing about it. She didn't have the slightest notion of what was important in life. She had no concept of ethics or values. And that's contagious. And then the death of my son. The strange impression that with the loss of my son, my religious ambivalence had somehow been confirmed. My rebellion against God was enormous. I could not comprehend why he had given me so much, only to take it all away again."

Daniela lifts her hand to interject. "That was your mistake: asking why."

"I don't understand."

"Instead of asking why, you should have asked yourself 'for what purpose.' " There are no answers to the whys in this world. But there is tremendous consolation in believing that there is a reason for our pain."

"That's masochism."

"No: it's clarity. Masochism means to seek pleasure in pain. But pleasure for a Christian lies in the certainty that the pain serves to cushion other hardships. We must never forget that we are all in debt."

Eladio emits a knowing and somewhat ironic grunt. "What debt? I don't understand your value judgments. Now it turns out we're in debt."

Daniela lowers her head unassumingly. She probably thinks she is intruding where she has not been invited. But she does not retreat.

"I'm sorry. I didn't mean to get on my soap box. But the debt is real. Life is a gift. We must earn it in some way."

"And suffering? Where does suffering fit in?" persists Eladio. "How often have I thought that living is just a process of accumulating agony?"

"But that agony is what maintains the equilibrium that faith requires of you."

"And what does this equilibrium consists of?"

"In recalling, every once in a while, the agony of Christ."

They fall silent once again. The flight attendant approaches to ask if they would like another beverage. And suddenly the plane is once again an enormous metallic structure floating across the void, dragging its protocols, distractions, and canned drinks.

The mother and child have returned to their seats. The businessmen are blinking sleepily. The heavy-set gentleman loosens his tie and most of the passengers have put away the screens, probably overcome with boredom by now.

Only Eladio and Daniela remain deep in conversation, although a slight tension has inserted itself between them.

"After all this, I still have not persuaded you to tell me about yourself. It isn't fair," observes Eladio. "I'd like to get to know you better. Even things out since I've told you so much."

"My life hasn't been all that significant. You know the main parts."

"It isn't just a matter of the facts. I'm referring to your ideas, your unique take on life. Your opinions are not run of the mill by any means. Most of the people I deal with don't analyze life as you do."

"You might be right on that score. But I wonder, what value can my opinions have for a person who is predisposed to reject them?"

"You never know. Despite everything I've told you about my beliefs, I'm not going to tell you it doesn't hurt to have lost them."

"In any case, I doubt my opinions are important enough to change your thinking."

"It isn't a matter of importance. It's a matter of radiating confidence. And you radiate it."

"What I experience isn't so much 'confidence.' "

"Then what is it?"

"Peace. Repose. Even something akin to happiness, especially when I examine my conscience."

"That's what I want. A clear conscience."

"And you don't have one?"

Eladio sidesteps the question. He is awash in confusion, doubts, self-recriminations.

"Moving right along," he says, turning his response into a joke, and quickly: "Do you think we'll ever see each other again?"

"Who knows? In time, we'll probably end up as just a fragmented memory to each other."

"No. Maybe I'll become that for you, but rest assured you'll never be that to me. You may not believe this, but I've never had such a pure and solid friendship as the one I feel with you."

"Brief as it is?"

"Genuine friendships are not based on hours, days or years. They're time neutral."

"And yet what we know as civilization is prone to forgetfulness. Like it or not, it basically consists of collecting moments and then misplacing the collections," she jokes.

"You don't fit into any collection," he replies. "You're one of a kind."

"How can you see that?" asks Daniela with something like a guffaw.

"You don't see it, you just know it. It is clear from talking to you that you're not like other women. And then there are the other things: your sense of duty, your courageous way of confronting challenges, your simplicity, your lack of vanity. And your conviction that even though the things around you seem secure, they could come tumbling down any minute."

Daniela stops him with her hand. "That's enough. So much praise might turn me into the opposite of what you're describing," she continues smiling. "Even so, I still think that when you venture into the nooks and crannies of a civilization that creates multinationals, false globalization and corrupt policies, the memory of this trip will be nothing more than a speck of dust that will be blown away by the first financial victory."

"From which I have to infer that you don't think very highly of our civilization."

"You're right to a certain extent. There's no question that we're better off, but the advances that were hidden when civilization was prehistoric are also turning into prehistoric advances."

"So you're afraid of progress."

"Progress no. What frightens me is that what is often referred to as progress are things that are carrying us backwards," says Daniela with a taciturn expression. "I've witnessed too many sordid actions to feel proud of our much-touted civilized progress."

"Have they affected you directly?"

"In a way they have, especially if we accept the notion that all human beings are really just a single person with millions of different personalities. We think civilization makes us free, but it isn't true. We are governed by a freedom that obliges us to assimilate huge doses of wasted efforts, oppression, miniature dictatorships. Things that subjugate us, force us to swap ideas for ideals, or ideals for ideas. But ultimately we are still slaves of ignorance. Do you know the phrase from Robert Browning? 'So free we seem so fettered fast we are . . .' No matter how much we surprise ourselves with our progress, none of our discoveries are a human invention. They have been within our reach all along. It's just a matter of removing the lid and taking out what is hidden there. Naturally the lid is sometimes camouflaged and the discovery may take time. That's when the tenacious, the 'ants' get involved. The ones who set their sights on the Nobel Prize and sometimes even find what they are looking for. They become famous and then they die. And then a street is named after them, or a statue is erected. And then along comes the new generation and everything ends up being a base parody of what was, in its moment, a feather in a cap. Young people don't 'know' nor do they care to 'know.' The only thing they want is to 'advance,' as in progress. In other words, they just want to remove another lid."

"In other words, reach success."

"But success can never be authentic as long as there are still places where misery prevails over discovery."

"What would your proposal be?" he inquires, intrigued.

"Something as difficult as it is simple. Stop thinking about ourselves long enough to think about everybody else."

Often the darkness that enshrouds what we dare not confess, even to ourselves, keeps us from regret.

That is why as long as I could still relate my past to the present Antonia was offering me, difficult as it was, it all seemed possible and manageable.

No, at that point I still did not regret having married Mahler's daughter.

Regret came later, when the unimaginable reached its tragic climax.

Sometimes when I was very down, I would seek out artificial respites—unnecessary trips or doctor friends who prescribed several days' rest—so that I could reflect in peace. In my solitude, I would try to make sense of the turmoil around me. I understood very little of what was happening, but I had a burning need to know where the fault lay for all the chaos. In the end, I never was able to discern the true cause that was turning my life into a pit full of all sorts of anxieties.

I'm not going to deny that more than once I found myself on the verge of exploding, breaking with everything around me (my job included), forfeiting my father-in-law's trust and even risking less time with my son in order to separate from Antonia permanently.

But when I recovered my balance, I realized that the anger I was keeping in check would only serve to tighten the stranglehold on me and our life together would have gone on as usual.

My hands were tied for a thousand reasons and therefore, I kept the gag on. It wasn't just the fear of losing my job, my son, and my professional aspirations. The worst thing of all was being seen as a weak man: a pathetic sort who had allowed himself to be manipulated by a pretty woman and an overbearing father-in-law for years, just to get ahead. This was especially true because all of a sudden Antonia would unaccountably decide to change tactics and instead of staging violent scenes, she would become as gentle as a lamb.

The motive behind these transformations remained a mystery. There was no explanation for them. But they were real. From one moment to the next, Antonia would become all sweetness and light, an adorable being descended from some far-off Olympus. And in that instant, everything we had gone through—everything that had turned us into enemies—would come tumbling down and the world would be all rosy again.

The rationality that was so sorely missing during her tumultuous outbursts would be restored with no explanation.

This would occur out of the blue. Her expression totally different, she would take my hand, kiss me, beg my forgiveness, swear up and down she could never live without me. And the reasons behind these sudden transformations remained an enigma: they arrived like a premature heat wave or a hailstorm in summer.

There was no rhyme or reason. But I accepted it with the hope that one time, the change would stick. It no longer fazed me when she entertained herself in front of the mirror, scrutinizing the slenderness of her figure or when she would stop eating. I had gradually become accustomed to her behavior and the only thing I desired was that her character—too often tumultuous and nasty—would remain calm, normal, and free of that hateful aggression that was taking such a terrible toll on our son.

Of course when she was in such a state of grace she never said the word "executive." Sometimes she even treated Anton the way an affectionate, devoted mother would, especially if she feared our son might be in some danger: "Anton, stay away from the drainage areas in the garden. The vapors might be toxic." Or "Anton, don't get too close to the hedges. They're full of poisonous insects."

Frequently, these admonitions occurred in the adjoining yards of Mahler's neighborhood in Marbella. We spent the summers there and Anton was free to run about as he pleased, always under Berta's watchful eye.

Her warnings were absurd, similar to her fears when walking below a balcony that might crush her to death.

But Anton was happy whenever she took any interest in him at all. He never rebelled. To the contrary, he hurried to obey her.

There he is, just as I saw him that morning, dashing about the garden lawn as his mother rested in the lounge chair beside the pool.

The one thing that bothered me was that she strictly forbade me to go out into the garden with my cell phone. "All that silly contraption does is interfere with the moment and set your nerves on edge. You're supposed to relax when you're here."

I would give in to avoid an argument. She was right to a certain extent. It is true that there is nothing more frustrating than the incessant ringing of a cell phone designed to interrupt conversations, dreams and peaceful interludes.

Still, how often have I thought that my giving in to her somehow contributed to the tragedy that lay in wait for us.

Uppermost on my mind at that time was the need to keep her happy and avoid any sudden outbursts.

Her mood swings persisted, although they were somewhat more sporadic. It was as if an internal switch sent her impulses off in a different direction and something in her was transformed.

Sometimes there would be no prior indication that she was annoyed. She would simply rise from the lounge chair and, with a look of disgust, wrap her sarong about her and head for the house without explanation. Those particular episodes were most likely caused by some memory or some lingering resentment in the back of her mind.

And then the defiance that was always fighting to take possession of me for having fallen into the trap she and her father had set would rise to the surface right there in the garden.

I think I will never be able to forget. There are the oleanders with their toxic blooms, and the trellis of bougainvilleas overlooking the sea, and the thick trees shading the sandy area where Anton was playing hide and seek.

I see the pool, smooth, clean and clear, sparkling in the sun's rays.

And I hear Anton's voice repeating what he said whenever his mother, for no intelligible reason, would abruptly depart to punish us for God only knows what strange transgressions. "Daddy, Mommy doesn't love us."

It would have been futile to protest that it was not true. Antonia loved only herself. Nothing mattered to her except her own interests.

Berta endeavored in vain to get that obsession out of his head. But no matter how much affection she showered upon him, the child was not looking for substitutes. He needed his mother. He loved his mother. And therefore he could not conceive how his mother could abruptly put an end to their game and sequester herself in the house.

In Anton's mind it was as if everything in the garden stood still. It seemed surreal to me too. The people around us faded away and all that remained was the tiny figure of the disappointed child, staring at Antonia's receding figure as she left without even saying goodbye, leaving him completely bewildered.

I will not deny it: My lack of interest in my wife grew with every passing day. When I lay down beside her it wasn't so much making love as fulfilling an obligation: it was an embarrassing charade that I tried to avoid, despite her insistence.

Of course as soon as she picked up on my indifference towards her, she did not hesitate to throw it in my face. "You have a lover and you don't dare admit it." And to avenge herself for that alleged—and nonexistent—lover, she tried to create a sordid atmosphere to make me jealous, to get me to doubt her fidelity as well.

She made up patently false stories involving men who never existed. In her naïveté she was convinced that I "swallowed" her lies, just like her friends swallowed her assertions about the people she tore to shreds with her enthusiastic gossip.

She did not realize that people my age can easily see right through the lies of a younger person like her.

When I saw her so bent on raising my suspicions, I'd follow along, asking her questions as if I were interested in her fantasies. But she never gave a straight answer and naturally, she always left an escape route in case she backed herself into a corner.

The game soon became tiring. And the more she threw out verbal hieroglyphics to pique my interest, the more I remained impassive. And then, offended, she would burst into tears of frustration. Sometimes subdued and sometimes angry, her crying spells were frequent enough to rule out any genuine distress, which also relieved me of the duty to console her.

I was soon worn out. "Look, Antonia, if you like those men so much, go ahead and sleep with them," I told her, fed up with so much subterfuge. Indeed, I was cheered by the thought of the patience those hypothetical lovers would need when, once the lovemaking was over and done with, they found themselves having to put up with her tantrums, her demands, and her obsessions. "They will repent of their sins," I went so far as to predict.

I remember on one occasion that Luisa shed her reserve and spoke to me as if she were sorry that she had not warned me of her niece's true character. "I thought if she married you, it would all change," she confessed. And then she sang the same old tune of the drug-addict mother. "It's very hard to grow up without a mother."

I was unyielding: "My son is in similar straits," I told her. "What's worse, he is growing up without a mother, and she is alive."

Fortunately, my own mother, although she may have suspected some of the cruelty that had pervaded our marriage, never knew the extent of the effect Antonia's perversity had on me.

When she died, therefore, it came as a relief to know that she would never find out about the trap they had laid to compel me to stoically endure a partner who was not in her right mind.

I also like to think she was never fully aware of Antonia's derogatory remarks about her when she was alive.

Antonia never tired of belittling my mother whenever the opportunity presented itself, even in my presence. "Did you know that the executive's mother used to work scrubbing the stairs of the Marquis de Ripal?" Or "You should tell your mother to buy her clothes from the upscale retailers. That way she can flip her nose at the people she used to sew for." Or "You have to keep your mother from spending so much time with Anton. She's so unsophisticated and I don't want her to rub off on him."

Of course all of these charming comments were made when her friends were within earshot. They were tossed out offhandedly as if she was only trying to find out just how far my famous "sense of humor" went. "Come on, Eladio. Why are you looking like that? Can't you see I'm joking?"

But she was not joking. Antonia was incapable of joking. She was only happy when she was turning the knife, causing ulcers, and dismantling reputations.

The truth was she had nothing but contempt for my mother. To her—always chasing after luxury and grandeur—having such a humble woman for a mother-in-law was an inexcusable stumbling block.

If she came upon her visiting with me in the living room, she would often say, "Why don't you go into the kitchen and show the cook how to make one of those casseroles of yours?" Or "You'll have to watch TV in the play room. My friends will be coming over in a little while, so I'll be needing this room."

Naturally, her biting remarks were always delivered in a mild tone of voice, as if they were not orders at all, merely suggestions.

My mother would always hurry to comply. I never heard her voice a single complaint against her daughter-in-law. She was so used to having life throw rotten eggs her way that Antonia's nonsense could not possibly faze her.

Until the day that Antonia's desire to wound my mother suddenly disappeared. It was the day she learned that her mother-in-law had just died.

Hers was a simple death, without tragic overtones or mournful displays. She died just as she had lived: unremarked, as if on tiptoes.

The burial was a very modest affair mainly because most of the people in our circle never even knew she existed.

What I remember most is going to her house after she died and seeing her little dog wandering from room to room with the sorrowful look common to dogs that have been loved and then left behind. Every so often he would go over to the bed where she lay and clamber up next to her cold body, whimpering as if it might bring her back to life.

But the worst part of the entire affair was the way Antonia behaved.

The disdain she had reserved for her mother-in-law in life was suddenly transformed into a huge show.

The travesty of her mourning began as the visitors began to arrive to extend their sympathies to us. She was immediately overtaken by grief, uncontrolled sobbing, and incomprehensible lamentations.

If it had not been so pathetic and inappropriate, I think her comic delivery would have made me laugh.

In a heartbeat, all of the insolence, the jeers, and the mockery that my mother had successfully managed to skirt in life, mutated into expressions of grief, reminiscences, anything that might exalt the memory of the dearly departed mother-in-law, as if Antonia had truly revered and adored her.

I can still see her, clinging to her father, her face damp with tears, her painfully thin body quivering and her voice choked with sobs, repeating over and over: "Such a wonderful woman, poor thing. I'll never ever forget her, Daddy."

That night when we were alone once more, I remember going over to her, grabbing her by the shoulders and shoving her back onto the sofa with a hard look. "I think, Antonia, that I will never hate you as much as I hate you now. You are the most hypocritical creature I have ever met."

I immediately left the house and did not return until the following day. I slept at the office. It was my way of allowing the steam to blow off.

Once again, the flight attendants are moving through the cabin with the duty free cart.

"We still have a couple more hours before landing, but we're about to enter the American zone, so we will no longer be able to sell the merchandise duty free."

Daniela thanks her and repeats that she does not need anything.

Eladio, however, appears interested. He turns in his seat to get a better look at the merchandise. And he asks Daniela to help him select a gift for the wife of the literary director of Frederichstal Publishers. "She's a good friend."

The flight attendant shows him perfumes, jewelry, scarves,

Hermes handkerchiefs, Scotch, purses. All of the things women love, but which in fact are almost never necessary.

"How old is your friend?"

"About your age."

"Then buy her that scarf. She'll definitely like it."

It is a light-colored natural silk weave with a simple pattern that has been finished by hand.

"Do you like it?"

Eladio nods. He asks the price and pays for it and the scarf is duly wrapped and handed over.

But as soon as the flight attendant leaves, Eladio places the package on Daniela's lap.

"It's yours. I bought it for you," he says cheerfully.

Daniela is momentarily taken aback.

"Why are you doing this? You tricked me," she replies, still surprised.

"I wanted you to pick out whatever you liked best."

"But, why the gift?"

"It isn't a gift. It's a testimony."

"A testimony? To what?"

"To an important friendship."

Daniela still does not know what to say.

"You didn't play fair, but thank you anyway. I will treasure it."

She opens her travel bag and places the package inside without unwrapping it.

"I should give you something too," she affirms.

"You already have."

"I don't know what you mean."

"Your company, the way you think. The lesson in good sense and serenity that you're teaching me," Eladio finishes.

Daniela lowers her eyes. Her cheeks redden. She is clearly still confused.

"I have to tell you that the scarf you selected was my favorite," Eladio adds.

"I'm glad we agreed. And I like the tie you're wearing. I'm going to confess something to you: when I meet a man for the first time, the first thing I notice is his tie, then his voice, and finally, the way he walks."

"I hope I haven't disappointed you."

"I like your tie. Your voice does not irritate the eardrums. And with respect to the way you walk, we shall see once the *plane lands." And looking straight at him, she says teasingly. "Now you have to tell me what you notice when you meet a woman."*

Eladio lowers his gaze and shakes his head slowly, as if casting about for a reply.

"I haven't paid that much attention to women for a number of years. Antonia outshone them all. She was beautiful, had a model's figure, and walked with tremendous grace."

"I imagine she was very intelligent."

"In her own way. It was the type of intelligence of those who always manage to get their way, without knowing a whole lot about life. She had a gift for dazzling everyone she met. She was not refined, but she seemed to be. In the end it's the same thing.

"I would have liked to have met her. I'm sure we would have gotten along well."

Eladio does not reply. He remembers. He imagines. He sees his wife face to face with Daniela and tells himself that a friendship between the two would have been impossible. But he declines to say it.

"I'm sure you would have," he responds dryly.

For a few minutes both Daniela and Eladio are aware that their conversation is fraught with all sorts of nuances as if something hidden and mysterious were manipulating the course of their words.

"And your mother? Do you take after her?" Eladio asks abruptly.

"No. I'm more like my father. I've always loved animals. It makes sense, I suppose, since my father was a veterinarian. He taught me the language of living beings that don't use words," she says with a lively expression. "He loved to penetrate their secrets, scrutinize their reactions, decode their mysteries. In the end, I think I was just another one of them to him. Especially when I was little."

"And your mother?"

"She had an aversion to zoological species, but she helped her husband. She did it out of love for him. The truth is my father couldn't have done without her. They had a very happy marriage. They understood each other without any need for words. They could communicate with a glance."

"When did they pass away?"

"My mother died soon after I emerged from a rather excruciating adolescence. And my father became deeply depressed. He couldn't live without her." And again her face is clouded. "It was as if a marvelous destiny had died in his arms, putting an end to his future, his illusions, his desire to live." And looking straight at Eladio, "Probably similar to what happened to you when your wife died."

But Eladio does not meet her gaze. Her words not only bother him, they hurt.

"Did he stop working?"

"He gradually lost touch with the animals. We lived in the country but he couldn't enjoy it anymore. We moved to LA. He was getting older and nothing interested him. His heart was the problem and I was his concern. The combination was fatal. One day I found him on the sofa in his usual place, dead. The TV was on and the lights turned off . . . forever."

"So what did you do?"

"I took the little bit of money he left me and got by until I found a job. Similar to what your mother did, the difference being that I was young and didn't have a child to support."

Eladio just looks at her without asking questions. His admiration for the woman beside him has grown even more. Instinctively he tries to imagine her alone, disoriented, trying to figure out what to do. Just scraping along and trying to get ahead, much as his mother had done.

And though he tries not to, he cannot help but compare her with Antonia: a woman-skeleton, full of frivolous notions, looking for excuses to attract attention and fearing that balconies had been invented for the sole purpose of crashing down upon her.

"You know what I have to say to you, Daniela? I'm glad my tomato juice spilled all over your lap. Thanks to that stain, I've had the good fortune to meet one of the most complete women to have ever crossed my path."

Daniela bursts out laughing and regards the stain on her skirt.

"You've just given me an idea for an advertisement," she replies. "Why don't we call some refreshments 'friendship drinks?' Or, 'Put a stain of such and such a refreshment in your life.' Or maybe, 'The stains from this drink cleanse the mind and solidify friendships.'"

Eladio rallies his creativity and ventures into Daniela's territory.

"Why don't you call them drinks that leave an immaculate stain?"

"It's not out of the question. Whatever gets attention without losing what I call 'harmony.' In other words, a gentle hint can have a stronger impact than an advertisement full of violence and stale eroticism." *And indicating Eladio's tie,* "Your tie also deserves a compelling slogan: 'Buy intelligent ties.' "

"And what makes you think my tie is intelligent?"

"The presence of the man who's wearing it."

The two of them fall silent, their gazes locked, the charged silence between them blending into the sound of the engines' hum until, suddenly, she reacts.

"Anyway, don't think I'm going to hire you for an ad. I was just throwing out an idea. The intelligence I'm referring to goes beyond the normal definition of the word. It doesn't even have to do with intellect. It is a quality that seduces, beyond beauty or aesthetics. It's an intelligence of movement, of expression, of voice, of gesture."

Daniela cuts herself short, shakes her head, and looks back at Eladio with a playful smile on her lips.

"All this probably strikes you as extravagant and a little ridiculous. And you might be right. But those are the ridiculous or extravagant details that have led to the success of my business."

Eladio is regarding her with curiosity. He is not sure exactly what she means but he is taken by the quiet self-assurance in her voice.

"You know something? As I listen to you I find myself wishing this trip would never end."

Daniela clears her throat, pretends to cough, and then responds.

"Why?"

"Because I hate the thought of separating from you. Would you be upset if I told you that you fascinate me?"

Daniela chuckles softly but her laughter sounds forced.

"It's not a joke," *he persists.* "We've been talking for hours and, even though we don't agree on anything, for some reason I feel as if we're speaking the same metaphysical language."

"No," *she replies.* "It's just the opposite. We speak two dif-

156

ferent languages. Sometimes situations like the one we're in now compel us to imagine similarities that are nothing more than illusions. You know, Eladio? Life is full of extremely shaky convictions. It's better to err on the side of doubt."

"What doubts are you referring to?"

"The ones that are derived from fascination. Fascination can blind you."

"Okay, forget that word and replace it with another one."

"Like what?"

"Attraction."

"Attractions are also deceiving." Her voice is barely audible. "Not everything that attracts us, is good for us."

Eladio nods. Daniela is right. Attractions are deceiving. It's enough to recall the intensity of his reaction to Antonia to see that nothing can be more misleading than the insistent clamor of an attraction.

"I can't deny it," he exclaims. "It's true."

And once more, the plane: a gravity-defying machine suspended high above the harsh roar of frigid waves drifting across the vast, sun-drenched expanse.

When I returned home after spending the night in the office, I imagined I would find Antonia in a temper. I was anticipating the worst. I even imagined that in her fury, she might have gone to her father acting the abandoned wife and accusing me of being a terrible husband.

How many times had she, in a rage, threatened to tell her father how badly I treated her? "Don't provoke me, Eladio. Don't forget I call the shots. My father never refuses me anything I ask of him and if I ask him to fire you, you can rest assured he will."

There is no point in denying that I was intimidated by her threats. No matter how many times Mahler said that Autumn Book had taken a 180 degree turn thanks to my efforts, his daughter's influence over him could well cost me my job and all that came with it.

I also had not forgotten what Luisa had said about her brother-in-law. "He wants to avoid trouble. When Antonia is angry, he simply washes his hands and lets the chips fall where they may. He's capable of doing just about anything to keep from having to put up with her tantrums."

So that morning when I woke in my office, realized where I was and recalled the preceding night, I was afraid. It was a dull, disagreeable pang, and certainly not without basis. I was acutely aware that Antonia, wild with jealousy, could easily have reported to her father that I had spent the night with another woman.

But my fears evaporated when I opened the door to my house.

The first thing I saw Antonia standing before me in the foyer, her emaciated frame drawn into itself, her eyes puffy and red and her arms hanging limply by her side, dispirited and downcast.

"Oh my God what you've put me through. Where have you been all night? You look terrible." And she threw herself into my arms sobbing.

I understood then that far from being offended by my nocturnal absence, she was attributing it to my despair over my mother's death.

I tried to calm her down. I told her I was sorry for having taken my stress out on her. "I shouldn't have treated you like that. That's why I left the house. I felt ashamed," I told her. "I spent the night in my office."

I am not sure whether she believed me or not, but it did not take her long to resume the role of victim. "You left me alone yet again. I never imagined you would be capable of hurting me so terribly."

That was her weapon of choice: her loneliness. A loneliness that allowed for no extenuating circumstances, brooked no argument, accepted no apology or show of affection. "When we got married everything was different. You never left my side."

There was no way to make her see that it was one thing to be inseparable during our honeymoon and a very different matter to resume our everyday lives glued at the hip. "Don't forget that I have a job and what's more, my job is with your father's company. It would not be fair for me to drop the reins just because I am married to his daughter."

She also did not accept that I might attend lunches or dinners "just with the men." On those occasions, she would grumble, "As if your wife were not even a person."

The passing years had not changed her habits in the least. She never failed to interrogate me about every single minute I was not with her. She needed to know, to hear, to be privy to the most personal details of my actions, especially if her friends were not around and she was bored. Her questions were incessant: Where have you been? Who have you spoken to? What did they say? Why don't you ever talk to me about those things?

Her need to "know all" was more than a sickness. It was a veritable torture. Half the time, I could not come up with enough answers to satisfy her. How could I possibly recall every last detail of what one has said, done, or not said? I was sometimes exhausted by my efforts to make up answers for her. But if I did not do it, the risk of infuriating her loomed threateningly.

If she saw me hesitate, she would imagine herself the subject of hypothetical disparaging conversations. "I'm sure you talked about me. I know your friends. Especially that fairy Douglas Raft. Always looking for something to criticize. None of your friends are like mine: open and sincere. People of your class are different. They can't escape their humble origins or get over their little complexes that come from being nobodies."

To put an end to such diatribes, I would distract her with some frivolous banter that appealed to her vanity. I would say something about her figure, her outfit, her incomparable beauty, her fake nails. "Everybody thinks they're real." It was my way of placating her. "You are still the most beautiful woman in all of Spain, you can rest assured about that."

By that time, of course I no longer had any illusions left. Everything about her wearied me. Her beauty had no effect on me whatsoever and sometimes just seeing or hearing her, just knowing she was close by, was sheer torment.

Fortunately, I had Anton. His smile and his joy whenever I was around him made up for all of the turmoil his mother caused.

But Antonia, wrapped up in her senseless rages and fanatical ravings, would forget the child was even there.

Anton had a basically happy nature and when his mother's yelling subsided somewhat, his face would light up and he would attempt all sorts of antics to blot out the storms and the scorn he had witnessed.

We were especially close when he was sick. Although it may seem strange, that was when we had the chance to reinforce the subtle bond that was turning us into accomplices against all forms of violence.

Antonia refused to acknowledge those illnesses. She did not want to accept them. She would say that Anton was pretending to feel bad in order to get our attention and as if to reinforce this view, she would simply leave the house, usually not returning until evening.

So I would take advantage of the opportunity to spend as much time as I could with my son.

We played. I told him stories that I made up as I went along. We created Jurassic Parks and pretended to be dinosaurs just like the ones in his toy box.

Berta too helped entertain the child when he was sick. "He just needs affection, Sir."

Although Anton's good spirits when he had a fever may have seemed somewhat half-hearted—like those poor souls who cling to their illusions even after their hopes have been trampled—his natural optimism and desire to be loved buoyed him and even helped him recuperate more quickly than anticipated.

How well I recall those vigils: his burning forehead, glistening eyes, the scent of cologne and Vicks VapoRub assailing our noses whenever we went into his room, his cough, his hands caressing mine. "Don't go, Daddy." How could I leave? I would stay there until he fell asleep. If necessary, I would call in to the office from his room so as not to leave him alone. So that he would feel supported, loved, and accompanied.

In order to avert a scene, however, I would leave the sickroom and head straight for the living room the minute I heard Antonia's car in the driveway.

There I would pretend to read or watch television, so that she would not suspect I had spent all afternoon with the little one.

Were she to find out, a jealous rage would ensue. She could not stand the thought that the child might love me more than her. "All you're trying to do by spoiling him like that is turn him against his mother," she constantly reproached me.

It seemed as if her goal was to maintain an ongoing state of conflict. And naturally she was never to blame for the shouting matches. The blame always lay elsewhere: with the servants, her aunt, Berta and, needless to say, her husband.

The arguments were so unreasonable as to border on the ridiculous. In an attempt to justify herself, she often would bring up issues that were completely unrelated to whatever had set her off.

"I don't know what my father saw in you to have made so much effort to get me to marry you." And if I ignored the comment, "When we met they were always raving about how intelligent you were, but they were deceiving me. You're just a clod: nice-looking maybe, but not much in the way of brains."

I would merely nod in silence. But she never tired of her efforts to degrade me. She would assure me that even she could do my job at the company. "In the end, your job comes down to selling books just as if they were potatoes. It's anyone's guess what kinds of tricks you'll come up with to improve your book sales."

It was all about humiliating me. She especially enjoyed pointing out my weak points to others. "My husband into sports? Hardly. I've never seen him do any sports." And if it seemed helpful, she would actually point to me with her finger. "The only thing I've seen him do is swim. Yes, mostly the dog paddle. He doesn't have a whole lot of style. He can do the back stroke, but only long enough to fool you. He says his sport is exercising his brain muscle." And she would burst out laughing so that they would all join in. "It's so flattering the way he saves up his physical strength for his wife."

Those sorts of conversations—entertainment of the cruel and idiotic variety—delighted her circle of friends. And feeling clever and smug, she would top it off by flirting shamelessly with any man she saw.

It was clear that her flirtations could not be taken seriously. It was another one of her tactics to elicit a reaction, to force me to pay attention to her.

In her fantasies, I would rise up to defend "my honor," confronting the alleged offender with my fists held high. I was supposed to throw down the gauntlet and demand satisfaction just like in the old days when honor was in style. But styles do not last forever and honor is a word that is rarely heard these days.

Therefore, whenever her pretend advances towards her friends' husbands were actually reciprocated, she would reproach me for my passivity as soon as we arrived home. "You have cool-aid instead of blood running in your veins, that's for sure. I cannot believe you didn't protect me from that kind of harassment. Or don't you call a kiss on the lips harassment?"

Once I responded that in her case the best thing I could do was pretend not to notice. "Essentially, you're the one provoking such advances, so you have to deal with the consequences." And to sidestep an argument, I added, "I've always trusted in your fidelity. One kiss more or less is irrelevant in the bigger picture."

Obviously nonplussed by that, she would try threats. "You'll have a surprise coming to you one of these days." She pronounced it like a sentence. "You might not believe it, but I've been rejecting propositions for years. I never mentioned it to you because I didn't want you to worry. So I may have been faithful up to now, but things can change."

I had trouble suppressing a laugh. For all her beauty and extravagant gossip, most of the men she knew would never have gotten involved with her as I had. Most men with any sense at all tended to defend themselves against women like Antonia. They knew her too well to expose themselves to what I had to put up with. It was enough to hear how she talked about me to understand that any attempt at intimacy with her could end up being terribly dangerous, less in terms of destroying home and family, than having to put up with her whims, her outbursts, her demands, and her self-centeredness.

And of course she too was aware that no one else would put up with her as I had. So infidelity was not really in the picture. What she needed was a poor "clod" incapable of deceiving her and equipped with enough patience to tolerate her nonsense without coming down on her like a ton of bricks. Who else would go along with her inane pantomimes in front of the mirror, her diva imitations, the vast repertoire of facial expressions and poses that she would later trot out at her friends' parties?

I imagine most men would have gotten fed up with her long before I did.

So on one of those occasions when she threatened to fall into the arms of another man, I had not a moment's hesitation. "Go ahead. Don't hold back on my account. Cheat on me. Turn me into a cuckold. Let some other poor sod deal with your ranting and raving, your obsession with being crushed to death, your obscene narcissism, with all that kissing yourself in the mirror to show how much you're in love with yourself."

After I said that, the last thing I remember was thinking that the world had collapsed.

Bristling with malice, she came towards me with the open umbrella just as I was putting the key in the front door of our house.

We were just coming home and it had been raining. Everything around us was blurred by wisps of clouds that were slowly amassing into fog.

I suddenly felt a powerful blow to the head and as I turned, I saw her poised to bring the umbrella down on me once again with all her strength while I, dazed and in pain, tried in vain to defend myself against her furious onslaught.

Instinctively I backed up against the wall and raised my arms to shield my head from blow after blow.

Then she stopped. She was panting. Her hair was disheveled and the umbrella was a tangle of bent wires and tattered fabric, as she vacantly regarded the blood diluted with rain streaming down my face onto my jacket and tie.

Recovering myself, I opened the door without a word and ran to the bathroom to staunch the wounds. And there in the mirror I saw Anton's tiny form in the doorway, his eyes fixed on my wounds, and his face wearing the anguished expression that always tore me up inside. "Mommy hit you again," he said.

I tried to smile to allay his fears. But his desolation was total. "Oh, we were just playing around," I lied.

But he did not hear me, only repeated, "Mommy made you bleed."

In the child's mind, "making someone bleed" was against the rules of any game. It was beyond the pale of any sort of pretending or game. "Why does Mommy always hit you?"

My God, I'm not sure how I managed to maintain my composure. I called Berta to take him. It took me to the limits of my endurance to see him there suffering, unable to assimilate such an aberration, covered in red, covered in bruises, in cuts, in incomprehension.

Seeing my injuries, Berta brushed aside my stubborn insistence. We have to treat those wounds, Sir. They might get infected." And forgetting the child, she began to daub at my face and apply bandages. "You need to see a doctor."

Suddenly we heard three muffled, rapid blows as if someone had tripped, or bumped into a wall, along with the sound of tearing fabric and anguished moans.

Alarmed, I rushed to open our bedroom door.

And I saw her.

She was ambling half-naked about the room, advancing gingerly as if she were blind and bumping into the furniture and the walls: her dress was torn, there were welts on her shoulders and her body—except for her face—was covered in scratches.

For a moment everything went blank. I had no idea what was happening. She looked as if she had been thrashed, abused, battered.

"What the hell are you doing?" I yelled at her.

She started to bite at the air as if she were biting my skin. "I'm not doing anything," she responded. "You did it." And with a sadistic expression, she showed me all of the wounds, each painful mark that she herself had caused. "If I report this, you can say goodbye to your son." She spat out the words. "And when I show the judge what you've just done to me your shitty little scratches will seem like nothing. A battered woman has the right to defend herself."

Right now Eladio is thinking that the word "burst" has so many different uses. Wind. Instants. Dreams. Hopes. Rain. Regrets. A whole host of things that come and go.

And this is what Eladio is now trying to classify in his tumultuous mind. Why not try to find a friendly burst. One that lasts, that leads to repose and that might somehow erase the dreadful burst that has reverberated in him ever since Antonia died, as if even in death she will not leave off torturing him?

Is it possible that some memories can never be extinguished? he wonders.

Maybe a case of amnesia would save the situation. But amnesia only occurs in old movies.

The plane is a muffled drone that discourages thinking. But Eladio cannot stop his thoughts from running together, from forming abstract shapes that cannot be properly classified and jockeying for position in his mind until he is completely spent.

The important thing right now is to find a way to justify what would have seemed completely unjustifiable just a few minutes ago. I have to find a way to compensate for my problem, rationalize my reasons, turn the partial into impartial, he repeats over and over again in his mind.

But no matter how hard he tries, the rationales escape him. They transcend his sense of balance, his entire being, everything that might merit a favorable verdict.

In his effort to stay on course, he tells himself again that life is full of bursts and the one that is now tormenting him is really just one more.

"Bursts are always fleeting. You don't have to give them a second thought," he tells himself. But he is not convinced. He cannot be. Memory has swelled all those things that were hunched in the shadows, has eliminated their right to be forgotten.

From the adjacent seat, Daniela is regarding him in confusion. Although she does not know why, she understands that her friend is experiencing a hard moment. She probably sees it in the stillness of his body, the way he is staring at the seat in front of him as if watching a film that only he can see.

What alarms her is how much time Eladio has spent submersed in silence. Or rather the way he is acting, as if he wants his silence to speak for him.

Maybe he wants the conversation that has progressed so openly up to now to recede into the background. Maybe it is because what they have not said to each other is more important than the things they have gradually revealed during the course of the flight.

Suddenly the pilot's voice—with the usual hearty inflections—is heard over the loudspeaker explaining the details of the flight.

These routines are familiar, but everyone is cheered by them. So the passengers fall silent and listen with interest to what the pilot has to say.

And the flight continues. The expanse surrounding them is still filled with light because the hours have been immobilized by the rhythm of a world that metes out time in exact measurements and compels space to bow to its dictates.

When the pilot is finished speaking, the passengers become more expansive. They look at each other, stand up, search around for papers, make small talk and return to their seats with the conviction that their destinies consist of sitting down and waiting patiently until the plane lands.

But the gentle milling about seems to have roused Eladio from his silence.

"Whenever the pilot speaks it is as if he is saying, 'Ladies and Gentlemen, the flight is approaching its conclusion.'"

"I was thinking the same thing," says Daniela.

Eladio turns towards her with a curious look. He would like to be able to guess what she is really thinking deep down.

"Sometimes when I look at you, despite your self-assurance and firm course in life, I can't help but think you need someone to protect you," he remarks, no longer looking at her.

"I've always been an independent woman. I've never needed anyone to protect me," she exclaims, perhaps slightly affronted.

"Don't you think that 'feeling independent' is tantamount to feeling lonely?"

"I'm not afraid of solitude. It helps me think. Solitude is what enables me to imagine, create, come up with new ideas. In fact, I need it in order to keep from stagnating."

Eladio nods his understanding of what Daniela has said.

"I have the opposite reaction. Solitude scares me. It blows the memories up out of proportion, makes them cruel." And after a brief pause: "People need company. Someone to give them a reason to go on living."

"And yet given what you've told me, it's going to be hard for you to find that 'someone.' What I mean is, hard to find a woman like the one you had."

Again the silence. And all that he has kept silent threatening to burst forth.

There is Antonia, bleeding from the mouth, eyes desperate, her fear of being crushed to death vanquished forever.

"Didn't you say you were 47?" Daniela asks abruptly, as if his age might hold the key to his secret.

"Which is old enough to begin to ask myself what I have really accomplished with my life."

"That's not an answer."

"You're right. It's not."

"Well, I'm not quite forty and I've already asked myself the same question."

"And what have you answered yourself?"

"That I haven't even begun to live."

She's said it looking him straight in the eyes, firmly, as if driven by an internal force.

"In contrast, I feel as if I've lived way too much," he returns, frowning. My life has been extremely intense—and exhausting."

"It's also exhausting to feel empty."

"What kind of emptiness do you mean?"

Daniela smiles and endeavors to be frank.

"I've never experienced real love. What I mean is a love that is complete, reciprocated and profound, as you have."

"Maybe if you had you wouldn't have felt fulfilled either. And that exhausting emptiness would have been even greater. It's possible to feel lonely even if your love is reciprocated. Nothing and no one can ever achieve total satisfaction." And

seeing his response has left Daniela looking pensive, "Don't worry. As you just said, you're still young. You still have time to fill the void."

"We all have time, as long as we still have the energy."

"My energy waned considerably when I lost my family," he replies distractedly.

But he does not name them. It is essential to be cautious. He thinks that by remaining silent he might be giving Daniela the wrong impression, but he doesn't have the strength to tell her the truth. If he explained to her the horror of living with Antonia, she might think less of him. So he only mentions the little one.

"The worst thing was losing my son," he says.

"It must have been terrible."

But Eladio does not respond. And silence reigns once more. It is a dense silence, gagged by those terrible bursts of memory.

Daniela intuits that something is tormenting Eladio so she makes an effort to change the subject.

"You know what I say? I'm sure the greatest mistake of my life was wanting to be so independent. Why shouldn't I acknowledge it? I was obsessed with freedom," she exclaims, laughing. "But I often think I ended up a slave to my own desire to be free."

"We're all slaves to one thing or another. No one is truly free. We become trapped when we least expect it." And by way of emphasis, he shakes Daniela's hand lightly. "I also longed to be independent, but I failed. I never was."

"Yet by all appearances, you're the kind of man we call a 'success story' in the States."

"Haven't we already established that appearances can be deceiving?" he asks.

"But there is nothing in your appearance to indicate that life has treated you poorly."

Eladio does not respond. He prefers to let the lie repose in the corrupt terrain of imprecision. To open up right now would be like noticing that the plane's engines have stopped and the vessel is about to plunge to the ocean floor.

So he remains silent, his failure a knifepoint piercing the silence. Leaving it so that Daniela, ignorant of his true life, will not have the right to judge him.

"Do you like music?" he inquires abruptly.

And Daniela realizes that Eladio's question is an excuse to cover up something he does not wish to divulge.

"I'm no connoisseur, but soft music helps me work. I can't stand anything loud and blaring, so I never go to discotheques."

And Antonia again. An anathema to peace and quiet. Out circulating all night long looking for noise, psychedelic lights, commotion, anything that would help her restless, narcissistic mind get attention.

And he sees himself too, wasting away the hours at whichever club was in vogue while his wife was busy enthralling all her friends with her infantile behavior.

He sees her on the dance floor twisting and turning to the grating sounds she loved so much.

"I hate it too," he exclaims.

"I can't understand how those places can have so much appeal for young people today."

"Don't wear yourself out looking for an explanation," he jokes. "There are very few reasonable things in this life. How do you explain the lines that formed when Franco died, first to pay respects to his corpse and then to heap scorn on it? Can you explain the kind of nationalism that orders you to kill? Or the costumes worn by some homosexuals as if the normalcy they preach can only be justified by such displays of ostentation? Don't their own extravagances turn them into a grotesque parody of the normalcy to which they aspire? And going back to the discotheques: can you believe the wink and nod of a bouncer responsible for overseeing the entry of dozens and dozens of unruly people can be bought with so many coins, no matter how generous the amount? And how to defend against drug addicts, skinheads, fascists, and all the other various and sundry lunatics who frequent such places?"

They both look away at the same time. Something out of place and troubling is erecting a barrier between them. But Daniela does not seem willing to let the communication slip.

"Why don't you explain to me once and for all why the devil you're getting so worked up?" she asks in an even voice. "What are you trying to hide from me? Why do you let fly an arrow and then do everything possible to make sure it misses its mark?"

Eladio pretends to laugh but cannot help but notice that Daniela's words carry more than simple questions.

"I guess it's that obvious I'm trying to change the subject?"

"Indeed. It's as if hitting that mark might cause something akin to an explosion inside you."

But Eladio does not offer his arm to be twisted and tries to brush off Daniela's assertion.

"Tossing bombs mid-flight is not a laudable measure."

"If it scares you so much to actually hit the target, why don't you just tear it up and forget about it?"

"Because to forget would be to give up."

"Give up what?"

"The chance of finding a way to actually get it right. What I mean is, I'm afraid of losing something I never thought I'd ever know. And now that I know it, I'm horrified at the thought of losing it. The truth is I've been mulling it all over for a while now, trying to find a solution."

"I don't quite understand what you're saying," she persists. "Please, you're not trying to confuse me, are you?"

"Sometimes creating confusion is the only viable way to establish pacts of concord between the confuser and the confused."

"Since you're not making yourself clear, the confusion will only deepen, rather than diminish."

"Have you ever stopped to think that it might be better to swim in digression than to sink in dangerous emotional waters?"

"You still haven't clarified anything for me."

"Maybe that's precisely my goal. To avoid clarifying any-thing for you."

"Why?"

But Daniela does not obtain a reply. It is clear that Eladio wants to dodge the question. Turn it back. Let it float off into the void.

He suddenly sees clearly that if he yields to the temptation to tell her the things he does not even want to admit to himself, he will surely lose her. "I cannot," he repeats to himself. He must strangle by whatever means available the terrible truth he has been carrying alone since Antonia's death.

"What I've been thinking is that if I am completely frank with you, I might lose you. I have to gauge my confidences. It

may seem strange to you, but nothing would hurt me more than to know I'd lost you"

Daniela seems to rebel at this notion.

"You and your silences. But I warn you that you can't lose what you've never had."

There is an edge to her voice, as if she is irritated by Eladio's secretive behavior.

"You're right. We can't lose what's never been ours. We can only lose what is ours to begin with."

And as he speaks, Eladio observes his companion's reaction out of the corner of his eye.

Right now Daniela appears reflective, brooding, and there is a touch of sadness in her gaze that Eladio compares with the feeling his son's lost expression used to evoke in him.

"It's true," he says quietly. "Maybe I've never had you, but I can assure you that you have had me."

"If so, I wasn't aware of it," she exclaims, her voice still slightly guarded.

But Eladio persists. "To have does not only mean to own something. It can also mean to capture it. To take what it communicates to us and make it ours, to touch it with affinity, even if that affinity is intangible. And that's what I mean when I say that you've had me."

Somewhat appeased, Daniela attempts a reassuring smile.

"Maybe you have a point."

"It's not a matter of whether we see each other again," he continues. "Distance is not an issue when it comes to feeling connected. And one thing is for sure: there will never be indifference between you and me."

"So you think indifference is more realistic between two people in close touch than between those who can never meet again?"

"I'm sure of it."

Instinctively Daniela's gaze turns to the stain on her skirt. The color has faded over the hours. Indeed it is now a distant memory rather than a recent stain. As distant as the thirty-eight years she has lived without knowing Eladio.

But she does not say it. She covers up the thought as if confessing that she will never take that skirt to the cleaners would be tantamount to expressing a very intimate feeling that confuses her and that she is afraid to accept.

"Do you believe in platonic love?" she asks abruptly.

"Perhaps."

But both of them now seem to be talking about extraneous subjects, as if the word love could never be a reality they would have in common.

"They say platonic love never ends," he finishes.

"Do you know that from experience?" she asks.

"I intuit it."

Daniela lifts her gaze from the skirt and turns towards him.

"So do I."

They regard each other for a few instants, totally absorbed. There were no more questions or answers. Just an overwhelming need to look at each other, to communicate without words, to breathe the same air, and to try to forget that the plane is moving inexorably forward.

Both of them start suddenly. They look away and Daniela remarks,

"We'll be arriving in the United States soon."

When I saw Antonia so destroyed and so out of her mind, I was afraid. I had never seen such a pathetic and appalling sight. If Berta had not been there to witness the self-inflicted wounds, she would probably have come to believe that I had caused the whole debacle.

I remember that it had been a harsh winter of brittle trees, torrential rains, and winds that easily tore of branches, threatening to disrupt traffic and injure some unsuspecting pedestrian. But not even the fury of that winter could possibly compare to the violence of Antonia, virtually torn to pieces by her own hand just so she could claim that I had been the one to inflict her wounds.

I immediately called Aunt Luisa and told her what had happened.

"I'm convinced that Antonia believes that the injuries she has inflicted on herself were caused by me," I told her.

As always, Luisa arrived without any outward sign of distress. "Don't worry, Eladio. I know my niece well enough to know that it wasn't you."

The thing was that whenever I went anywhere near Antonia, she would shrink back. "Don't hit me again, Eladio. I haven't done anything to make you keep hurting me." And she would add that the umbrella had only been a means of defending herself against my harassment and violence.

As usual, her father was traveling abroad and Aunt Luisa's support was no small comfort.

Antonia gradually calmed down, especially when she threw herself across the bed to cry.

What I remember most about the whole episode was Berta's expression and my son's trembling.

There is Anton again, his face pale as he regards his mother. His pain is stripped of all innocence. Once again, he is struggling to "understand" without an adult's ability to reason. He is storing up rancor without knowing why and wishing at any cost that what I had referred to as "play" was not really a punishment.

I asked Berta to go look for some Valium. "The lady is suffering from nerves."

I gave it to her myself, as if there had never been a nasty altercation between us.

Under my ministrations, Antonia seemed to recover her grasp on reality. She stopped threatening to "speak seriously with her father about firing me." And I promised her that despite our difference, we were joined by a powerful bond. "All marriages have their rough spots," I assured her.

And she ended up hugging me and promising me that she too would do whatever she could to avoid more friction. "I love you so much, Eladio. No matter what you do to me, I'll still love you."

Instinctively I turned to the window. It was still raining although more gently now. It was a strange rain: slanted, or as if it came from the ground rather than falling from above.

I imagined that perhaps the episode had changed her and, therefore, I was baffled a few days later when I heard her talking to one of her friends about the "bodily injuries I had caused her in a jealous rage." She was pulling aside her clothing to reveal still visible bruises and cuts. The friend was astonished: "How could such an apparently peaceful man like Eladio possibly have done all that to you?"

And she, with a resigned expression, had responded that appearances aside, I was an extremely violent man. "He becomes consumed with jealousy. He can't help himself. That's why he hits me."

Since things had calmed down, I often tried to analyze whether Antonia actually believed the lies she spread. Once again, I was assailed by guilt. Maybe something about me disturbed her, wounded her. But it was impossible to know what that "something" might be.

More than once I tried to have a reasonable conversation with her. If we could only talk calmly, I might learn that the episodes I considered unfounded actually related to mistakes on my part which, being a man, I was unable to discern. But every time I tried to clear the air with her, Antonia would retreat.

I soon learned that it was impossible to have a normal conversation with my wife. She would invariably go off on a tangent. My questions were met with trite assertions that had nothing to do with the point I was trying to make.

Maybe she was trying to avoid any acknowledgment of the things she did not admit even to herself. She had to escape reality. Had to keep herself from becoming mired in her own fantasy world.

The fact is that no matter how hard I tried to describe how imbalanced she was, no one save Luisa and Berta would have believed me. And I could not even count on them, because they had never turned their backs on her.

When it came to her friends, at first, while they may have considered her "different" they still fawned over her for her beauty and because she was adept at endearing herself to everybody.

And then there was the farce of her marital bliss. She lied. She made up scenarios, which were always premised on my alleged jealousy. She created irrational tensions and once, when I tried to make her see reason in front of her friends, she did not hesitate to tear my assertions to shreds with humorous half-truths so that her listeners would take what I was saying as a joke.

On one occasion she told me that she had consulted a psychic. "They are infallible, Eladio. Everything this woman predicts happens. If you only knew what she has seen in my future."

She spoke nervously, her emaciated frame half-reclining on the sofa, her legs crossed, as she regarded the clock on the wall that always gave the wrong time. "I'm going to receive a very lucrative proposition to become a professional model."

It was her dream. Nothing would please her more than to imagine herself parading her body down a runway, her public fawning all over her and not even noticing her apparel. And then to appear in the romance magazines, while the top designers vied for her collaboration.

"She has assured me of it. It will not be long before I receive an offer." And as I regarded with a mixture of pity and exasperation, she continued, "You know what, Eladio? Fashion is very important. And not everyone has what it takes to make it as a model."

I told her I was delighted and wished her every success, "presuming the psychic is correct," I added.

And she: "How can you doubt it? She never makes a mistake." And in a rather tense tone of voice, "You're problem is you have no idea what kind of woman you married." And quickly rising, she stood before me, pulled her skirt up to her hips and struck a provocative pose as if I had never been introduced to the wonders of her thin figure.

I have to admit that I found those scenes extremely disconcerting, so unlike the innocent child who had been described to me before we married. It was as if I had married two different women: the naïve girl aroused by sexual discovery and the sexpot who sought to arouse me with the twisted mind of a nymphomaniac.

At the time I still had enough presence of mind to avoid being swayed by her constant aberrations.

Lately nothing about her appealed to me. It was as if we no longer had anything in common except for our son.

Our increasingly rare conversations—if they did not deteriorate into a squabble—were vague and aimless. Meaningless words that simply evaporated into thin air. Of course her fear of being crushed to death was nearly always brought into play, especially when she complained about my absences. "You're always so busy."

As time passed even her friends realized she lived in a fantasy world. They gradually began to keep their distance from her. Perhaps they had finally wearied of her constant criticisms and the ignominious fallout from her gratuitous remarks about everything and everyone around her.

In the end, the only unconditional friendships that remained were her schoolmates from Switzerland. But those girlfriends had become nothing more than slips of paper in the form of letters or photographs, with trite, saccharine messages that had nothing to do with reality.

Indeed, they were more relics than relevant. Fragmented reminders of something that no longer had a reason to be. So when Antonia spoke of them she did so as if they were already dead. "You know, I can't really recall what they were like or the color of their eyes."

The fact was, the past had no meaning for Antonia. She was only interested in the "new," or the "unexpected." Anything that might garner unexpected flattery from others.

And change. She hated routine. Loved to feel herself at the center of unfamiliar vibrations, stand out, attract attention.

The only habits she followed faithfully were the gym, her power walks, her skin treatments using an array of exotic creams recommended by her beautician, and of course, starving herself.

And she was obsessed with tanning. As soon as spring came, the first thing she did was run to the tanning salon.

It was futile to tell her that an excess of the sun's rays could be dangerous. She stubbornly resisted all advice. Anything that did not fit in with her preconceived notions or her "made in Antonia" agenda, was summarily rejected.

I remember now the summers we spent together.

Every year in July we would install ourselves, together with Aunt Luisa, at Mahler's house in Marbella. I would then return to the city and rejoin the family on the coast every weekend. The month of August, however, was sacred.

I remember that Antonia, true to form, would always rise late, since the parties tended to last well into the morning hours and all her friends would still be asleep at noon. I, however, rose early to have some time with my son.

The neighborhood was huge and its extensive lawn and gardens were shared by the wealthy residents, most of whom used the same interior designers and landscapers. Indeed, the lavish homes all looked alike, with their shades of light green, pink and yellow.

Antonia loved her father's house. She was convinced that the color scheme set off her tan perfectly. "Haven't you noticed, Eladio? My tan is not like everybody else's. It's sexier than any conventional tan."

Antonia always spent three full months in Marbella. She said that the climate of the White Mountains kept her from getting sick and warded off the psychological malaise that tended to afflict her in Barcelona.

What really attracted her was the fast-paced lifestyle. There was always a party in the offing, a dinner dance, a gathering of international high society types, or filthy rich Magrebis, or world famous movie stars.

I would only spend August there. An August devoted to playing with Anton by the pool and quiet mornings enjoying the lawn and gardens spanning the neighborhood.

On those summer days, Antonia often stopped being so demanding and forgot to visit the accustomed humiliations upon me. Her one strict demand was that I not bring "that cell phone contraption" down to the swimming pool with me. "When you're on vacation it only sets people's nerves on edge."

Otherwise, Marbella was an absolute paradise according to her. Every day she had what she called a "plan." "I've been invited to ———." Or "I had to attend three cocktail parties yesterday." Or "A famous artists has decided he wants to paint me in a bikini."

And I would simply nod, without paying much attention to her frivolous comings and goings.

The bad part was when the plan was conspicuous by its absence for two or three days. Then she would revert to her old habits. "So, Mr. Executive. What the devil have you been doing while I've been so busy?"

I sometimes asked her questions, just to shut her up. In her usually over-excited mind, my interest in her activities was flattering, especially when I pretended to be fascinated by her psychics or gurus or clairvoyants. "Somebody very well-versed in this has told me I'm going to have a long life, although I will have some trouble finding happiness."

And when I did not seem impressed: "They also told me to watch out for a dangerous woman who is hovering around our family."

I laughed. "Now you're going to tell me who this woman might be. I suppose they weren't referring to Berta or Aunt Luisa." But Antonia persisted. "They were very serious about it: 'Your husband is a very attractive man and he inspires hidden passions. You'll have to tread carefully. Any day you might find yourself with the proverbial horns growing out of your forehead.' "

That particular summer the neighborhood was in a state of excitement because we had all come together to have an upscale open-air eatery set up in the gardens. That way the neighbors could eat lunch by the pool instead of having to return to our respective houses.

The grand opening was magnificent. The bar and tables were full of neighbors anxious to sample the cook's delicacies and discuss the benefits the new restaurant would bring to the community.

To render the occasion more festive, music had been wired in so that it could be heard throughout the garden. We had even planned a champagne toast to wish ourselves a long, prosperous and marvelous life.

I remember that afternoon the sea flashed silver glints that could be glimpsed from behind the bougainvilleas separating the garden from the pristine empty beach, the bathers having already taken refuge from the hot midday sun in the commercial establishments along the boardwalk.

I also remember that the music was soft enough so that the muted sound of traffic could be heard on the far side of the buildings and, in the stillest moments, one could hear the slender branches of the weeping willows gently keening as if they guessed what was to come.

And the child. There he is again, smiling at me in contentment because we have been playing for hours and frolicking in the pool as I clumsily attempted to teach him to swim.

And once again I perceive his damp skin sticking to my chest as his arms circled my neck. "Don't leave me, Daddy."

Antonia was late coming down to the pool that morning. She looked exhausted. "I hardly slept a wink last night. I didn't get to bed until 5 a.m."

And as was her habit, she dropped into the lounge chair to sunbathe. Once again, seeing her there oblivious to the neighborhood, to me, to everything around her, I had the feeling that nothing would ever bring us together again. I asked her whether she was going to join in the small party at the café. "With that worthless crowd? I think not. Anyway, I've decided not to eat today. I prefer to sleep. I'm very tired."

My total lack of interest in anything she said, or did, or knew divided us. What could we possibly have to share when we were growing farther apart with every passing day?

I see Berta hugging the child. "What a romp you had with your father," she teased him.

And Anton prancing around his nanny like one of those puppies that express their exuberance by jumping in circles, tails waving madly.

She told me then that she was going up to the house to prepare Anton's lunch. "I won't be long."

I told her not to rush. I would watch over the little one.

There was an instant in which it sounded as if someone had turned up the volume of the music coming from the café and the people milling about seemed to be talking more loudly.

It was a fleeting moment, but it was enough for Antonia, with a sour face, to twist her body around towards the din and snap, "Don't people have the right to rest peacefully on their own property?"

Then she abruptly recalled that she had not applied the lotions she carried in her beach bag. "Dear God what a thing to forget!" And she began to rub her body agitatedly.

I am seeing Berta's back recede towards the house, the garden virtually deserted, the restaurant a cage of voices and merriment that even an unexpected blizzard would not have dampened.

At that moment the assistant who worked from the house came down to inform me that my father-in-law was calling from Barcelona and needed to speak with me urgently.

I see myself turning towards Antonia and asking her to keep an eye on the child. "I'll be right back, just as soon as I've spoken with your father."

And she, waving her hand from the lounge chair as she massaged her stomach with her scented lotions. "Don't worry. I'll keep an eye on him."

And I see Anton smiling. "Come back soon, Daddy." God how many times I have heard that voice in my dreams.

I cannot recall what Mahler and I said nor how long our conversation lasted.

What I cannot forget is returning to the garden. A crowd was gathered by the side of the pool. Strange bodies gesturing as if they were statues that had been given dispensation to move.

The circle of people parted at my approach. They did not speak to me. They just stared.

And then I saw him. He was on the ground, motionless, his arms shrunken, hair wet, and the sadness in his eyes gone forever.

Apparently he had fallen into the pool while his mother slept. She'd gone to bed so late the night before . . .

"Yes, we're nearly to New York. It's the final leg of the trip," replies Eladio, trying to ignore the pang he feels at the thought.

It occurs to him that "final" might be the most important word he has pronounced throughout the entire trip. As soon as the plane touches solid ground the strange peace and happiness he has felt during this conversation with Daniela will vanish like a puff of smoke. She will say goodbye to him and make her way towards the gate for her flight to Los Angeles while he will head for the exit to find the vehicle Woultmand & Starky will have sent to take him into New York city, that giant nest of skyscrapers piercing the atmosphere much like the Tower of Babel must have done in bygone times.

And he wonders if people then—convinced of their own importance being as they were contemporaries of such an unprecedented structure—had moved about the city with the same degree of dehumanization as people traversing the cities of the world today.

And he sees himself too, gazing indifferently at the anthill of strangers: tall, short, black, white, fat and thin, all with their own painful histories and perhaps—as is the case with him—carrying an invisible burden of guilt, even though their expressions and manners seem serene and their reputations as honorable and peaceful people remain intact.

The plane, which will be landing soon, is probably also full of unconfessable silences: hidden tales of cruelty suspended beneath the calm and innocuous surface of the person who experienced them.

"Have you ever wondered just how many of the hearts sardined on this plane just like ours are beating in fear, or anguish, or remorse over some unconfessable shame?" Eladio asks suddenly.

Daniela is taken aback by the question but feels compelled to respond.

"It's possible. But I've also thought about their potential heroism. Not everything in this life is ignoble."

But Eladio is having a hard time accepting that some passengers might be free of painful, shameful silences.

"Human heroics are very rare," he says halfheartedly.

And once again his mind takes him to the city that awaits him: streets teeming with anonymous people, the vague almost dead stares of its vagrants, its street vendors, its automobiles circulating endlessly on worn-out roads in a chronic state of disrepair.

"But they happen," she insists. "Anything we do to try to stop someone else's suffering can become a heroic act."

"Even if it means deepening our own suffering?"

"That's what heroism is: self-sacrifice."

Eladio frowns and with a preoccupied expression asks, "Have you ever been afraid of happiness?"

"I'm not sure what you mean."

"Feeling a deep sense of joy but knowing that it would be a cruel mistake to show it."

"Maybe I felt something like that a long time ago when I got off that train," she admits.

She is looking at Eladio, half-squinting as if she would like to penetrate his brooding thoughts.

"There's no doubt about it. Pronouncing the word 'goodbye' is like dying a little bit," she affirms.

"Maybe that's why nowadays everybody says 'see you later' instead of goodbye, even though that 'later' always has a sense of finality."

"And yet there's still the hope that the 'later' will come true," exclaims Daniela, possibly hoping to avoid the eventuality of a final goodbye.

But Eladio is reluctant to accept what she proposes: "We should probably find a replacement word for when we part, just in case. Can you think of one?"

But Daniela shrugs and shakes her head. Suddenly her expression changes and she blurts out softly, "Yes. Until God wills it."

"And if God doesn't will it?"

"No one can predict God's plan. Besides, why wouldn't he?"

Eladio lowers his gaze, crosses his legs and does not answer immediately. "Second meetings can sometimes be destructive." And before she can reply, "It's best to let destiny take its course. Go back to our jobs, deal with the daily challenges and, at least in my case, reminisce about this trip constantly."

"That's all well and good," she asserts, "but I still don't see how that will stop us from simply parting for good."

"Well what do you do about the magic?" he asks with an attempt at lightness. "I mean the magic that has united us during this crossing. In order for the magic to last, it is often important to 'remember' without falling into the trap of trying to obtain the object of your remembrance," Eladio insists.

"So to you, what you call magic is more important than whatever it was that caused it?"

But Daniela's question has too many meanings to be answered in a single reply.

"In any case, I refuse to let this flight get lost forever in the fallacy of forgetfulness. And while you might not believe it, it may be that the only way to remember it and prolong it indefinitely is never to see each other again."

Daniela's gaze is full of doubt. Eladio's vague responses are intriguing and surely hurtful as well.

"I understand," she replies, disappointed. "You're a cautious man. You don't want to make a mistake. It's a good reason. Right now you're probably at a crossroads of sorts and it's frightening to choose a path. I'm sure if I were in your shoes, I'd hesitate too."

Although Daniela cannot help sounding upset, Eladio understands that she too is navigating in a sea of doubts.

He also does not discard the notion that at the slightest indication on his part, her doubts would vanish into thin air. But he cannot do it. He must not. What he is hiding from this woman is precisely what would cause him to lose her should he own up to it. There are some compartments that must never be opened. He must therefore remain silent, must lock the vault of his truth with secret keys, even if in doing so, he must disappoint and even hurt her.

But Daniela is not ready to give up. "Sometimes it's a matter of time. Of allowing the passage of time to confirm or discard what you call magic."

But this argument does not seem to convince Eladio either. "No, it is not a question of time."

"So what is it? You're not ill are you?"

And Eladio thinks that he is in a way. But there is no cure for his disease because, although his body is sound, his soul has reached the end stages.

"No," he replies half-jokingly. "I am in good health. And, as I've already mentioned, my problem has nothing to do with time."

"I didn't know you had a problem."

"It's a problem of space," replies Eladio without looking at her. "A problem that nobody knows about and because of that, is likely to keep on expanding the distance that might separate us."

Daniela does not understand. She is becoming slightly impatient.

"Why don't you just come clean and explain to me once and for all what is going on?"

181

"Because if I do, it will be all over. What I mean is, I will have lost you without any hope of getting you back. And that's why I cannot talk about it."

Daniela crosses her arms: Eladio's response confuses her. She cannot possibly imagine the reason for so much mystery.

"You're about to be married," he reminds her gently. "Don't look back. From what you've told me, your producer is a good match for you." But his initial alacrity recedes and he continues in a muted voice, "I could lie to you, do you know that, Daniela? Lies can cover over the wounds for a time. But you don't deserve that."

Daniela looks at him, her pupils a halo of misery.

"And what are you going to do?"

Eladio smiles as he gently strokes the hand resting on her skirt.

"Remember you. Hear your voice. Reflect on all the things you've told me. Close my eyes and contemplate over and over again the stain on your skirt. Imagine you wearing the scarf I bought you around your neck. And know that my silence is the best wedding present you'll ever receive." And, as if he has forgotten something, "Oh yes. And I'll do one other thing: I'll talk to you every day. I'll reconstruct our conversation, accentuating the most relevant parts, and I will rely on them to keep on living."

At that moment everything (except the drone of the engines) has descended into silence once again. A silence severed from any past and powerless to change the future.

It is an unyielding silence that refuses to become voice and "explain," and "compare" and "decide."

"It is my fervent hope that you have a lot of children," he says suddenly. "You will be a wonderful mother."

"I'll talk to you too," she murmurs, but she does not look at him. She says it as if she were thinking aloud, as if he were not there by her side. "Talking is important. It's what distinguishes us from the other animals."

But from the sadness permeating her voice, it is clear that Daniela is miserable inside.

Eladio takes her hand, kisses the back of it, and returns it gently to her skirt.

"I'll never forget what you just said," he responds, without looking at her.

It is absolute torment to recall those moments: to hear the beating wings of the flock of birds that came out of nowhere to flutter over the body of my son, as the people around me struggled in vain to explain to me what had happened.

Everyone seemed to feel guilty. They tried to blame the scorching sun combined with the headiness of too much alcohol and the soft music that muted the splashes and cries from the water.

Each explanation was an incoherent blur: a what the hell are they talking about. The phrases made no sense: ". . . child drowned . . ." ". . . distraught mother . . ." " . . . couldn't be revived . . ."

And the music. The unrelenting music. Could not someone disconnect the speakers?

The explanations blended together, interrupted each other. Strange tales that traveled beyond the pool, the empty lounge chair, the child laid out on the grass his eyes open and the contour of his mouth rigid for all time.

And the weeping willows. And the sparkling water belying irrefutable facts. And my refusal to accept the truth as I tried with all the strength in my lungs to bring my son back to life. "It cannot be. It cannot be."

I did not give a thought to Antonia. They had taken her to a hospital in a fit of hysterics.

And then I saw Berta, her face distorted, stretching her arms towards the boy as if waiting for someone to place him there. "My God, my God." It was all she could say as I hugged to my chest the remnants of the son who would never again call out for me, or laugh, or run, or play.

He was so cold, his small form chilled by the poisonous waters of a pool that had become nothing more than a puddle of stinking rotten misery.

Someone—I don't know who it was—patted me gently on the back as if such absurd topical maneuvers could console me. And everything seemed frozen in stale routines: things that crumbled to pieces while nothing could be done to keep them from being lost forever.

And Berta repeating, "My God, my God." As if God were a magician willing to bring him back to life with a flick of his cape. God wanted him dead, wanted to take him because Anton was suffering too much and because God wanted to turn that place into the most hated corner of the earth. It was impossible to comprehend that death. It was impossible to comprehend anything at all.

And my rebellion. An intransigent rebellion, desperate, reeking of indispensable things that were lost forever, dead and buried.

And later.

Little by little I began to assimilate what had transpired. No one there by the pool had wanted to tell me the truth. They felt they were to blame for not noticing that Antonia had dropped back to sleep, lulled by the music, the murmur of voices, her lotions and a scorching sun with no ozone layer.

It was all so hard to believe, so simple, so uncommon. How could those residents, focused as they were on superficialities and idle thrills, possibly have imagined the tragedy that was unfolding in the now-deserted swimming pool?

I do not recall clearly when I saw Antonia again. I think the child's body had been taken from the garden. An autopsy had to be performed: a long incision made, his still pliant body poked at, his organs removed, all so that his "non-life" could be given an official meaning. So that the judge could assert that he had drowned like any other summer resident, as if his motionless form, his swollen belly and his full lungs were not enough evidence to certify his death.

I saw her come into the house, supported by two nurses because she could barely walk. A young doctor trailed behind them issuing terse orders that she was not to be disturbed. "She is in a critical state. The poor thing is devastated."

But when Antonia saw me, she seemed to recover her vigor. She came towards me, raised her right arm and with all of the strength she could muster, began to pummel me until the nurses and the doctor managed to restrain her. "Murderer, negligent parent, criminal shit." She spat insult after insult at me, while no one intervened for fear of making the situation worse.

Seeing me standing there so impassively, some of those present finally moved to stop her from attacking me. "She can't help herself. The pain has driven her out of her mind," they remarked.

They said it with conviction. No one could have imagined that this violent reaction was just a small taste of her constant rages. No. They felt for her. "It's understandable," they affirmed. "The poor thing had no idea that no one was watching over the child."

The doctor decided to administer a hefty sedative. "She should be put to bed and left to sleep."

Of course I made no effort to defend myself. I also did not explain that I had told Antonia to watch him before leaving the garden. No one would have accepted that she was exclusively responsible for the tragedy. "Fate, adverse circumstances, the unexpected: these things happen and no one is to blame."

Any hypothesis might be construed as reasonable, except the true one: the one premised on the negligence of a mother who was sleepy, on her dulled and disturbed mind, on her indifference towards everything that did not have to do with her: her lotions, her "sexy tans," her "escapes," her fake nails and her fears of being crushed to death.

And also the prohibition on taking the cell phone down to the garden, "because those screeching, interfering contraptions just don't go with summer relaxation."

It appears as if I did make an attempt to defend myself, to explain what had really happened. But they did not let me speak. "Don't get upset, Mr. Escalante. We all know that you are not to blame. Your wife doesn't know what she is saying. She has lost her son, after all."

And mine. The person I loved most in this world. The only thing that managed to turn my existence into something reasonable and sane.

"The poor thing had no idea the child was alone."

But I did. I knew. I remember perfectly well that arm waving me off, letting me know that she would watch Anton: "Don't worry. I'll keep an eye on him."

The rest is consigned forever to a morass of details combined with an overpowering hatred that surpassed any other I might have experienced before in my life. What I felt went beyond hate, was more akin to a mortal abhorrence, a repugnance nourished by contempt, rage, and an insane desire to never see her again for the rest of my life.

Aunt Luisa and my father-in-law arrived in Marbella that afternoon. The house was full of people. Everyone was talking at once.

And at last the truth of what had happened was brought to light. Berta had taken it upon herself to convey the bare facts. "Your daughter fell asleep when she was supposed to be watching the child," she told Mahler openly. "But you must not tell her. The pain would kill her. She's convinced it's her husband's fault."

I remember Mahler's strong embrace. "I called you at the wrong time," he apologized in tears. He too had loved his grandson. He had not seen him all that frequently, but he had loved him. Then there was Luisa looking terribly distraught. Despite her cold and austere bearing and her tendency to withdraw from anything and anyone that annoyed her, she was visibly distressed, as if she too felt to blame for the death of my son.

"I know how you must feel, Eladio. I don't know what to say. Such a horrible thing to have happened, may God have mercy on us." I'm not sure why, but I had the impression she was apologizing for having allowed me to marry Antonia. For having hushed up her unpredictable and incoherent nature.

The days that followed are nothing but a blur. Days for which time had no meaning, as if they were suspended in a strange paralytic state, without beginning and without end. Days of darkness devoted to insipid and gloomy tasks that seemed to carry no weight at all.

Fortunately, Antonia slept on. The doctor assured us that given the immensity of the shock, it was best that she be kept sedated to give the emotional wounds time to heal and enable her to recover her equilibrium.

Berta also fell ill. The fever plunged her into fearsome chasms of pain and regret. "We have to feed him," she said over and over again. "Even though his mother doesn't want him to eat, we have to do everything possible to make sure Anton gets enough nutrition."

And I? What can I say? Everything was just a painful haze of unrelenting shapeless torments. Already prone to insomnia, my nights became groaning living beings drenched in fury and hatred and desperation.

I also cannot recall exactly when I returned to the city, nor my comings and goings between home and the office. I see only the profusion of photographs of Anton that had suddenly invaded my bedroom and my office.

And my colleagues' concerned faces. And my long intimate conversations with Mahler. Conversations that mixed grief with codified measures to address work-related problems. Systems to boost the company's revenues. Ideas that, despite my grief, somehow seemed to come out of nowhere and grow into new projects and bureaucratic undertakings that my father-in-law never failed to applaud.

At one point, Mahler made an attempt to help mend our marriage. "You must forgive her, Eladio. My daughter is not a bad person. She is mad with grief."

And in order not to make things worse, I pretended to accept what he was saying.

I remember Douglas Raft's constant presence, his way of quietly conveying his understanding of how empty my life was. "I know what that is," he said. "Your pain forces you to swim against the current and it's exhausting." Maybe he was speaking of himself too. Of the things he had to endure as a homosexual man. "In any case, please let me know if there's anything I can do."

But what could Douglas Raft do except spend the evenings with me, talking about Anton, reminiscing about what he was like and about all the things I would never recover? What can anyone do in the face of that terrible certainty? Those kinds of certainties have no silver lining. They are inflexible. They do not give the benefit of the doubt. No. Certainties do not lie. They simply drive in the nail and force one to bleed tears and mull over monstrous notions.

And yet life went on. The meeting with Antonia after her sleep cure was not an encounter of absolute contempt in search of an exposed flank, but rather a tenuous somewhat awkward communication fraught with memory lapses and unlikely to cause a scene.

She did not attack me again nor did I throw in her face her negligence when Anton was in her care.

We barely spoke and when we did converse about some detail of the daily routine, we were careful to keep it to superficial topics that would keep the memory of our son at bay.

Mahler visited us frequently during that time and I now believe those visits helped maintain a semblance of calm between us.

Luisa too tried to get us to smile now and again. And Douglas Raft.

Indeed, Douglas was the only one who really knew how to handle the situation. He did not try to coax us out of our lethargy. He would simply come to the house, sit with us and use his presence as a buffer against any possible conflict by keeping up a constant chatter. "I've brought you some marzipan from Toledo." Or "I've heard about a new restaurant we should try out."

It was also he, together with Aunt Luisa and Berta, who cleared out the closets and disposed of Anton's things. Neither Antonia nor I could bring ourselves to go into that room and contemplate all that the child had left behind.

Douglas let us know later that the clothing and toys had been donated to a charity.

Antonia remained impassive at this news. She simply thanked him and asked if he would like a drink.

I am not sure why, but her patent indifference raised my hackles. So much docility and self-possession was inconsistent with my wife's supercilious and volatile nature.

Her "normal" behavior lasted no more than a couple of weeks. Until the afternoon she showed up at the house a different person.

Wearing a black ankle-length dress buttoned up to the neck, she settled herself in the living room, saying she wished to speak with me.

"From now on everything is going to change," she informed me. "I've decided I'm never going to suffer again."

I noticed then that she was not wearing fake nails or make up and that her usually curly hair had been pulled back into a severe bun that certainly did nothing to enhance her appearance.

I only half understood what she was trying to say. She finally explained, "I've thought about it a lot, Eladio, and I'm going to change my life. I'm done with all the frivolity and psychics, gyms and race walking, discothèques and most of all, being beautiful."

Detecting my confusion, she continued: "I'm going to adopt a reclusive lifestyle. I will visit hospitals and work on behalf of the poor. And I'm going to speak with my father about an important project: I want to found a home for sick children. I will name it after Anton of course."

I did not know what to say. Coming from anyone else, it would have struck me as an admirable proposal, but coming from her, it sounded like a pipedream. Just another one of those ridiculous whims she suddenly took into her head.

She had also been struck over the head by religion, just like that. She had, of course, tailored it to suit her needs, creating a unique amalgamation of several different faiths. All sorts of disparate beliefs replete with reservations, egotism and criticism levied against anyone who might question her.

It was more like a sect featuring mystical and largely irrational exaggerations, self-idolatry and chaotic inventions. Rooted in an entire spectrum of austere practices, her newfound faith was harshly critical of all the things she had once considered indispensable and admirable.

More than religion, she was accumulating archaic and uncompromising doctrines removed from their actual contexts. "I've prayed to the sea," she told me once. "The sea is the god of water and water was in the world before land. The Bible says so."

In her feverish mind, her personal hypotheses were jumbled together with scraps of mythology and Christian principles: "The sea is probably the gateway to heaven," she insisted. "That's why Anton died surrounded by water, so that God could gather him to his breast."

She spoke as if she were paranoid, but as soon as she had gleefully fired off some of the most demented and incoherent statement, she would issue her disclaimer. "I know you're thinking I'm crazy, but you're mistaken, Eladio. What I said is merely a metaphor for my true beliefs."

And to persuade me of her sincerity, she filled our bedroom with Christian symbols, obscure saints, bleeding Christs and anachronistic relics of all sorts that resembled amulets more than religious objects.

Everything became a sin through the lens of her accusing eyes. Objects or habits that had enjoyed her enthusiastic approval prior to Anton's death had become "evils" that were not to be tolerated under any circumstances. "How can people take Communion after exposing their bodies to so many lascivious looks?" Or "Don't pay attention to anything so and so says: she only looks at people's faults and doesn't hesitate to pick them apart. There was even a new justification for her anorexia. "I'll eat everything, with one exception: one day a week we'll just have bread and water."

But the main thing was her obsessive anathema to the things she had previously defended, especially if the object of her censure had some bearing on her friends.

The sudden change soon raised hackles among her circle. Especially when in a fit of fanaticism, she would predict celestial punishments usually associated with her fear of being crushed to death.

"You're all going to be flattened under the weight of an immense ruin," she would predict with the air of a Wagnerian prophet.

Seeing her so unhinged, many of her girlfriends deserted her. But Antonia never yielded. To the contrary, the more they withdrew, the more she "excommunicated" and "censured" the deserters.

While her anorexia improved somewhat, it did not disappear entirely. Instead of fasting to preserve her "model's figure" she did so to expose the sins of others. "Since men all like voluptuous women, I'm going to try to stay as thin as possible to keep them from having disgusting thoughts."

I can see her now proposing to her father the establishment of a charitable foundation to immortalize the name of our son. "It will be called Anton Mahler Escalante," and she added that reversing the last names was allowed in Spain.

Her father replied that he would think about it but that he would need time to make sure the project was sound.

That was when Mahler unburdened himself to me. He said he feared for his daughter's mental health. "The child's death has deranged her," he told me. "She should be seen by a psychiatrist." And seeing that I was not shocked, "She's always been a little erratic," he admitted, "but I never imagined she would take it to such extremes. Have you seen how she dresses now? What bee has she gotten stuck in her bonnet that makes her go around looking like a suffragette?"

And as he spoke, I contemplated once more the Louis XV table situated between the two light-filled windows. And the photograph of Antonia when she was eight years old. The same photograph I had seen the first time I set foot in that office. It had become yellowed over the years because Mahler never had gotten around to replacing it with a more recent one. Maybe because as a child, Antonia did not resemble the woman whom her father would choose to recommend to me years later. "I am not unaware of what you have had to endure, Eladio. You may well judge me to be a fairly uninvolved parent. But though you may not believe it, I am fully informed of all of my daughter's erratic behaviors."

For the first time I understood that Mahler, despite his status as a powerful and important man, was just a poor wretch who had evaded the truth about his daughter through piecemeal methods that were becoming increasingly less effective.

With regard to Antonia's imbalances, I tried to reassure him. "Don't worry. I'll talk with the doctor myself to fill him in on all the background. It's better that she not know it's a psychiatrist. I'll figure out a way to make her think she is seeing a regular internist."

Mahler embraced me. "Thank you, Son. I don't know what I'd do without your support. My sister-in-law is not the best one to handle such delicate matters. And she is weary of it all. I can't rely on her anymore."

I could tell by his voice that he was having trouble keeping his spirits up. No matter how much he tried to keep his head above water, he was a man brought low by his age and by the problems his daughter had caused.

I thought of the immense fortune that would fall into Antonia's hands when he died. But I was overwhelmed, rather than overjoyed at the thought. "No one is poorer than a helpless rich person," I thought. What was the value of having all that money when it only served to keep alive a person whose mind was in shreds?

I remember the dusk came quickly that day, because autumn was taking hold of the city with the urgency of a sudden death. The light that had illuminated the office when I arrived was quickly retreating to reflect on the streetlamps of a street swathed in shadows.

Night had fallen by the time I went out onto the street. And night it remained a week later when Antonia fell ill. At first she could hardly breathe or speak and she had chest pains. Then she began to cough up blood and the fatigue was evident in the cold sweat that drenched her body.

She was immediately taken to a clinic and diagnosed with a pulmonary embolism. "Don't worry, you've gotten here in time," they reassured me.

It seemed that the embolism was caused by a clotting problem due to a Vitamin C deficit. "This deficit," I was told, "can lead to venal thrombosis."

I asked if it was a serious condition and they assured me that it was. "But if she follows a strict treatment regimen, it can be cured."

I remember that they injected her with heparin and that during the two weeks she remained hospitalized, she was like a dry branch on a neglected vine. She barely spoke and never complained. She did not dare even move.

She gradually began to recover her senses. She no longer had tantrums and some semblance of reason—that scrap of reason I had fallen in love with before—was restored. The sectarian craze vanished along with her fears of being crushed to death, her criticisms of her friends, and all the other things that had formed part of her derangement after Anton's death.

When I went to visit her, she even smiled just as she had when we were engaged. "You know what, Eladio? They say I nearly died."

I admit it: at that moment, all I felt for her was pity.

"So you haven't told me about that missed train yet," Eladio exclaims suddenly. "What was he like? What did he do?"

Daniela smiles. She must find it amusing that Eladio should be interested in her hidden past.

"He worked in a gym. He was the director of a physical education academy and the trainer for a women's basketball team."

Eladio frowns and ponders Daniela's reply. He cannot imagine her falling for someone so diametrically opposed to the things he admires in her.

"And what did you have in common? I cannot imagine you playing basketball or him undertaking artistic projects."

Daniela tries unsuccessfully to suppress a chortle. Eladio's reasoning is too logical and categorical to deny.

"We've already established that when it comes to falling in love, reason is conspicuous by its absence. Falling in love can be as contradictory as knowing that the rain has fallen in love with the sun. Or the sun with the glaciers. But those sorts of love affairs occur, exist, they become powerful and tumultuous." And laughing again, "But then they burn out. The glaciers melt and when the sun tires of the rain it has no difficulty proclaiming that fact by carefully crafting a rainbow. Hadn't it ever occurred to you that rainbows are always symbols of a tumultuous ending?"

The rainbow metaphor impresses Eladio and he tells himself that Daniela, besides being intelligent and attractive, is also full of surprises.

Without knowing why, he suddenly recalls the highly controversial painting: the Garden of Earthly Delights. Nothing in the painting gives the impression of being delightful. And enamored as she might have been with her physical education professor, nothing about Daniela fits with the image of a gymnasium.

"But," she insists, "he was the prince charming of my dreams. It's funny isn't it? The truth is, separating from him and telling myself I had to forget him was just like throwing myself onto the tracks in front of that train."

"You loved him that much?"

"I'm not sure 'love' is the best choice of words. I was in love.

In other words, dazzled, bewitched, how do I know? But I felt the same way about my career."

"So your preference was to leave him."

"It wasn't my preference, but that's what I did."

"Were you sorry after?"

"I was at first. But as I said before, my career was pushing me to leave him. I needed to prove to myself that I could get ahead on my own."

"And so you lost the chance to be happy."

"I'm not so sure my happiness would have lasted anyway. When you expect so much from a love as intense as the one I was feeling, exhaustion soon sets in and starts to chip away at it. It is diminished. And a diminished love affair isn't worth it."

"Was it hard for you to get over him?"

"Very."

"Did you ever try to see him again?"

"No. I found out that he married one of his students about a year after we separated. So I said to myself, 'that's it.' I tried not to think. I buried him."

"Completely?"

"No. I still had the incipient happiness I'd felt with him. And a hint of regret at having said no to him. But I soon realized that it hadn't really been love."

Eladio is now comparing Daniela to a straight path leading to an impregnable fortress.

"In order to be complete," she continues, "love must be accompanied by faith and hope. And my trainer lacked both of those things."

"I understand," murmurs Eladio.

"In contrast, while I've never felt those innermost, earth-shattering emotions about the man I am going to marry—as people who say they're in love claim to feel—he has pledged his support to me and will generously accept mine. We know each other very well. We respect each other. And we both know that true love is not so much about feeling as about giving."

"And that is enough for you?"

"I haven't stopped to think about it. In any case, it seems pleasant and reasonable to me."

Listening to her, Eladio feels trapped in a circle of envy that is pushing him to leave caution aside, to confess what is

torturing him, and to say straight out what he intuits Daniela
is also feeling.

"So what you two have is a loving friendship. Am I right?"

"Yes, that's right."

"And you think that's enough?"

Daniela does not reply. She remains motionless, as if
Eladio's question has had no effect on her whatsoever. She
is probably thinking that if she answers she'll have to lie to
him—and that her lie will be unacceptable.

But Eladio persists.

"That was one of the things that I first noticed about you,"
he says impulsively. "Your discretion, the unassuming way
you have, and especially your reaction when my tomato juice
spilled on your skirt."

"Are you saying that because I didn't answer your question?"

"Perhaps. But also because I wanted to tell you how much
our conversation has meant to me. For example: the way you
don't wear make up, your slightly tousled hair, your natural
beauty. Those are the details that delight one." And as he
speaks he does not stop searching her dark eyes with his light
ones. "I think I told you already. I don't remember ever hav-
ing had such a complete feeling as the way I've felt in your
presence."

He suddenly falls silent. Sometimes you have to stop if you
want your words to make a lasting impression. And what
Eladio needs most of all is to last in Daniela's mind, to remain
there for the rest of her life.

Although she does not seem perturbed by Eladio's unflinch-
ing gaze, Daniela also does not give in to it. She pretends she
is not interested, raises her hands to her face and covers her
eyes. It is as if the pleasure she feels when he looks at her is
triggering sensations in her that she refuses to feel again.

"Sometimes those feelings are just preludes," she replies to
the question that is hanging in the air between them.

"Preludes to what? Preludes without a continuation don't
make sense."

"Nor do continuations that harbor secrets."

There is an edge to her voice as if she can no longer endure
Eladio's metaphors to cover up whatever it is he is hiding.

Eladio understands perfectly well Daniela's exasperation
at his constant digressions. He also knows that the slightest

allusion to his feelings for Daniela will be enough to change both of their lives forever.

But life is not a matter of doing whatever you please as Antonia did. Daniela herself had said it just moments before when she had explained that heroism requires sacrifice.

"Do you think it was somehow predestined that we should meet?" he asks, disconcerted.

"Who knows?"

"In any event, maybe it was also predestined that once we had met, we would have no other choice than to go our separate ways again," he muses.

"I don't understand why," replies Daniela. "The city of Los Angeles has an airport, airplanes, and an unfailingly clear sky."

"Maybe despite the clear sky, I would be the one to fail you."

"No," she responds in a low voice. "You could never fail me."

And hearing her, it is as if the entire plane has become a dream filled with vagrant illusions, marvelous impossibilities, and hopes that might not be disposable after all.

And right at that moment, he is able to feel happy and he thanks Daniela with all his heart for the new sensation surging within him, a deluge of promises that will now always be real, even if they are never kept.

It is as if the plane they are in did not exist and the flight were taking them to an unknown world where everything has a solution, even the most acute pain, even the most deeply rooted shame.

"May I say something very personal to you?" he asks.

"Yes."

"I swear on my son's memory that after having made this flight, I will never be the same again. Daniela, you have no way of understanding this, but you have changed my life."

The doctors were very clear: "with the right medication, your wife can get well. But it's going to be a long road."

It seemed that pulmonary embolisms are more common than one would have thought. The important thing was to monitor the patient carefully to ensure the proper dosage of medication.

"She'll need an INR test every month to make sure the prescription is correct."

The medicine was named after a Roman warrior: Sintrom. It's as if I can see her, with her detailed prescription and a bag of medications with the usual warnings: "consult your doctor." The consultations were to be monthly, to draw blood and monitor her progress. "She must rest. No excitement."

The truth is that no one could explain where the problem had come from. The doctors said it was due to a vitamin C deficiency, while the popular wisdom attributed it to the shock of losing the child.

"She is so thin. How could she have a blood clot?"

But the doctors were not surprised. "Such physical anomalies have nothing to do with weight fluctuations." What happened to Antonia could happen to anybody.

The most important thing was not to upset the patient. "If administered properly, Sintrom can cure the problem permanently."

Antonia was heartened by the doctors' confidence. It is as if I am seeing her again, her eyes desperately searching the doctors' faces for the reassurance she needed.

Everything in life boils down to this: to feeling that one is safe, marshaling one's defenses, avoiding risks, striving for calm, and fleeing danger.

When I first saw her in the hospital room with the sheet pulled up to her chin, afraid, watching the doctors as if looking out over the edge of the abyss, I felt the strange compassion one sometimes feels at seeing a beggar asking for a handout. Especially when, terrified, she reached for my hand. "Please, Eladio. Don't let me die."

I tried to soothe her. I did not want her to die either. I was even moved at seeing her so helpless, so unlike herself, so horrified by her own illness. "Relax, Antonia. I'm not going to let you die. Trust me. I'll do everything I can to help you get well as soon as possible."

I was not lying. I can swear that right then Antonia was nothing to me but a helpless and frightened human being desperately in need of comfort.

Her voice was at once plaintive and insistent. "Don't leave me alone, Eladio, no matter what. Don't go. Stay with me. I need you."

She needed me. She always needed me: sometimes to torture me and sometimes to act the docile lamb and make me her slave. One way or the other, my presence completed her, changed her back into the old Antonia—with her ups and downs, her rages and loves, her moments of reason and of incoherence—longing for my presence, my devotion, and the trust I inspired in her.

Now I see the doctors going into her room at the hospital. They are walking in slow motion, their gestures lethargic, murmuring unintelligible questions and answers full of technicalities that left a bad aftertaste in the mouths of the uninitiated.

I remember them mentioning the word "rigor" over and over again and volleying sometimes contradictory but always painstakingly analyzed ideas back and forth to make sure that hopeless-looking wisp of a woman might remain among the living.

I also see Mahler, looking at me with a mixture of hope and anguish, echoing his daughter's entreaties: "Don't leave her. Stay with her. I beg you, Eladio."

And Luisa too, her habitual severity tempered by the scare. Her eyes dry and darting anxiously about the room as if to ward off the tears. "Help her, Eladio. Antonia trusts no one but you. Maybe if you take good care of her, this illness will change her."

I believed it to. The Antonia of those days was nothing like the hateful woman who had so abused me.

And she: "Eladio, I'm begging you. Don't fail me." She said it in a cowed voice, as if lost in the silences that sometimes seemed to plunge her into murky dreams. "They said that if the embolism happens again it will kill me."

I do not know who had told her that. Antonia could be fairly adept at guessing what was being whispered around her, but that time I am sure she had heard it from the doctors themselves as she feigned sleep.

My response was indignant. "Who has put that ridiculous notion into your head? The doctors are convinced that you will make a complete recovery with the proper treatment. I'm going to make sure that all the instructions are followed to the letter. You're going to live, Antonia. I promise you that. I'm not going to let another embolism happen."

How well I remember those days. Everything was smooth, free of ambiguity, lies and artificial explanations.

Excuses were unnecessary. Sincerity was gradually permeating an overarching truth. And the truth was the desire for Antonia to get well, to return to life, and for us to recover our lost path.

But the specter of death did not recede. Antonia's fear of being crushed to death seemed to have been replaced by her obsession with a blood clot.

I can hear Mahler promising his daughter that he would make sure I would not have to leave her side if she did not want me to. "We'll set him up at the clinic so he can work from there."

That was just what she needed. That I not leave the hospital. That I sleep with her, eat with her and work in a little space just off her room. "Don't let him leave, Daddy. If Eladio leaves me alone, God knows what will happen to me. People are bad and I don't trust anybody."

And her father saying first things first. She was not to worry. "Your husband will not leave the hospital."

I remember that severe winter weather had set in and torrential rains had fogged up the windows of the room.

And the days passed with the smell of food, flowers, and the indistinct odors created by the accumulation of medications permeating the halls, especially when a patient was brought back from surgery.

I also see myself talking to my secretary and the various executives at my disposition from the small room Mahler had ordered set up so that I could adequately keep up with my daily tasks.

I was not to leave the hospital even for an instant. The supreme daughter of the boss was to feel sheltered, and the doctors were to be able to count on me at all times to soothe the patient.

Whenever I evoke the constant whine of the windowpanes I don't know why I associate them with Antonia's pale, desiccated face. Her ashen complexion was frightening and every time I entered the room nothing except her weak smile seemed to have changed.

I had never seen her so immobilized, so fearful that her blood would bubble up and detach her from this life forever.

The days and nights rolled into one, each twenty-four hour block the same as the one before.

So as I reminisce about our stay there, I find it hard to reconstruct the details. Only instants stand out in my mind. Inconsequential moments such as the glow of the moon in a dark sky before drawing the curtains, or some light comment Antonia tossed out to thank me for my presence, or the relief I felt when her doctor assured me that my wife was improving and would be able to go home soon.

Then there was the opinion of the psychiatrist who pretended to be an internist so as not to offend her. "You can rest assured, Mr. Escalante, that your wife is mentally sound. It's possible that her personality is somewhat infantile and therefore scattered. She still needs to mature. But I can guarantee that I don't detect any sign whatsoever of paranoia or uncontrolled inhibitions."

I was relieved by his opinion. He was a highly regarded specialist who, at my father-in-law's urging, had visited Antonia on the pretext of examining her in relation to her illness.

To bring him up to date and avoid any confusion, I had met with him to discuss her erratic behavior, her rages, and her obsession with losing weight. "Malnutrition can often contribute to such episodes," he told me. And he added that those sorts of reactions were common in women who married very young. "They feel confused and they're not sure how they're supposed to behave. They think that since they're married, they should be considered the cat's pajamas," he joked. "But it's a huge leap from there to mental illness."

He later told me that after having talked to her at length, he had noticed that she was very much in love with me and that she sometimes seemed to feel as if she was unable to get my attention. "I often have the impression that my husband doesn't love me," she had apparently told him.

Mahler seemed relieved when I filled him in on my conversation with the specialist. "She shouldn't have gotten married so young," he admitted. "But she was dead set on having the wedding as soon as possible and I didn't know how to argue with her."

Amidst all of those crosscurrents however, the anorexia receded. Although she never finished her meals, she no longer rejected them outright. The hospital routine did not leave room for changes or whims and she had no choice but to partake of the same food as the other patients.

Accustomed to going hungry at first she only picked at the food on her plate. It must have been her fear of losing her strength that compelled her to eat, albeit in small doses, but at least taking in enough calories to prevent lethargy due to lack of nutrients.

Nonetheless, she not only remained extremely thin, she continued to insist she was putting on weight. "If I stay in this hospital much longer I'm going to end up as big as a cow."

To calm her down, I would assure her that even if she put on weight, she would still be the most beautiful woman in the world.

And I would kiss her, caress her. Let her know that everything between us was going to change from then on. "When you're better we're going to go away together, just the two of us, just like our honeymoon." And needless to say, that happy prospect was enough to help her relax.

She was so serene that she did not even complain when my job kept me in the little room adjoining hers hour after hour. She knew I was close by, so she did not mind it when I spoke with my staff or spent a long time glued to the telephone or receiving visitors as necessary to get my work done.

She was also able to receive visitors during her two-week stay in the hospital. The same friends as always who, alarmed and sorry for having deserted her because of her excesses, immediately came back upon hearing that she was so ill.

Now, as I look back on those days, I can still hear the laughter and high-pitched babbling, which was sometimes irritating because it kept me from concentrating on my work. Yet I never complained.

Occasionally I would catch some of the well known phrases: "The executive doesn't leave my side now." Or "When I'm better he's promised me a second honeymoon."

After two weeks, we were able to return home. She spent the first week in bed and would not let anyone but me administer her medication. "I trust Eladio. You don't know anything about medications," she told Berta and Aunt Luisa.

And Berta, acquiescent, gave into Antonia. "Of course, my girl. No one can take better care of you than your husband."

She no longer mentioned her former religious zeal mixed in with her superstitious predictions. She also seemed to have forgotten her sectarian principles of austerity.

She soon recovered her interest in fashion, in anything new that came out, in the need to be *au courant* and modern. "The truth is that Anton's death completely unhinged me," she confessed in a woeful voice.

But the months passed by and the immediacy of Anton's death had begun to recede.

At one point I even said to her, "You're very young. You'll have more children." But Antonia hurriedly rejected that notion. "No way. I will never make the mistake of becoming a mother again. I've suffered too much to repeat the experience."

She said the same thing when I entreated her to stop taking the damned birth control pills. "It's no use, Eladio. You can get on your knees and beg me but I'm never going to run that risk again."

Once we were home, it appeared I was going to have a bit of a respite. Two weeks of hospital imprisonment hermetically sealed in a state of constant tension had left me completely exhausted.

In the hospital, Antonia's non-stop vigilance had been oppressive. Especially the way she picked apart my every expression, posture, gesture, or escape into the hall for a change of scenery.

And though I knew my enforced bondage had contributed to her recovery, it was still an effort that, like it or not, had only alienated me from her still more.

Mahler was aware of my situation. "Patience, Son. You'll be back at the office soon."

And I did indeed return shortly after that.

Antonia initially accepted by return to the office without any outward signs of distress. "But please don't be long. You know I need you here."

According to her, she counted the hours that I was away. "You're late," she would rebuke me if I did not appear at the door the second she expected me.

But her recriminations were not as virulent as they had been before her illness. They were limited to off-hand remarks, small slights thrown out as neutral observations that were not really meant to accuse.

As time passed, however, her equanimity gradually began to crumble again. "Who knows what you've been up to?" Or "Do you think you may have gotten lost at the wrong 'domicile'?" The word domicile had a pejorative connotation in her mind: she associated it with a whorehouse.

And, to keep the peace I was once again obliged to invent silly excuses and outlandish explanations because if I told her the truth, mundane as it was, she would never have believed me. The important thing was to make sure she did not suspect I was lying. My explanations had to convince her because if they did not, she might become agitated and that would not be good for her.

The constant need to invent plausible excuses to coincide with the various time frames began to take their toll on me, and I felt myself slipping back into my former miserable state.

Somehow, though, her first month back home was characterized by the calm that the doctor was constantly recommending. "A lot of peace. No commotion."

The one thing Antonia was unyielding about was that no one but myself should take care of her things. I had to help her dress, accompany her when she bathed, decide on her meals and most importantly, prepare the proper dosages of Sintrom according to the doctor's prescription. "I don't trust Berta. She's not all that bright and I'm afraid she'll get the dosage mixed up." And as if I did not know it already, she never tired of repeating over and over "It's up to you to make sure I don't die, Eladio. You know what they told me: If I have another episode, I'll die."

How often have I heard that phrase in my head during my long nights without Antonia. Nights that seem confected of grinding absences, of crossroads offering no real choice, of confusions begging clarity and darknesses kept brightly lighted to prevent me from crashing headlong into ghostly skeletons of remorse.

Horrible nights in which the mistakes made swell up beyond the scope of any possible remedy. Instead they propagate and expand, imposing their realism and poisoning any potentially positive insight to make sure it can never be accepted.

Nights in which guilt is not even entitled to an antidote. Nights of prodigal sons having no parents willing to forgive them or envious brothers to corroborate that forgiveness.

There is no appeal for clemency during those nights of mine, those anterooms of hell. Even if such an appeal were possible, forgiveness would not be forthcoming. Because forgiveness requires "knowledge" and the nights I live through keep me from allowing anyone else to "know." They just accuse and blind, creating solitudes that can never be shared.

Of course I had to accompany her to the technician each month. The dosage of Sintrom was contingent upon the results of the INR.

But the doctor was optimistic: "Everything is going very well at this point. Within a year the danger will have passed and you'll be able to resume your normal activities," he assured my wife.

Everything was progressing smoothly. The blood tests were always within the range the doctor anticipated. "Just make sure you don't overtire yourself," he would insist.

In any event, Antonia's lifestyle did not pose any risk. She was able to cautiously resume her social life with no difficulty.

Gradually the Antonia whom everyone had always fawned over was recovering her status as the clever conversationalists, the scintillating center of attention at all the parties where gossip and lurid stories were the drug of choice. It's as if I'm seeing her, telling stories that no one had heard before. Stories she had probably made up using her sharp intuition.

And once again the insinuations that gave the wrong impression. And the indiscreet, slightly lewd comments. And the sullying of reputations directed at anyone who had a reputation to be sullied.

The exaggerated asceticism that had followed our son's death became a thing of the past. No more anathema towards her friends. No more Wagnerian prophesies, or sectarian terrors, or any of the other paranoid behaviors.

She no longer spoke of foundations for children. Perhaps her father had gotten that notion out of her head. It was more effective to make sizable contributions to existing charities devoted to caring for needy children and that would take care of the matter.

The only thing that still filtered through now and then was her fear of being crushed to death. "Sometimes I dream about it, you know that, Eladio?" It's as if I can hear her voice. She spoke in a voice heavy with sleep, like the guttural sound of doves. "You have to keep an eye on the balconies."

And all I had to do to allay her fears was stroke her half-sleeping form. "Don't worry. They're just dreams. Silly little gusts. Sometimes I dream I'm drowning in the sea."

And she would fall back to sleep, her premonitions anesthetized for the time being.

Eight weeks transpired in that manner, focusing on the trivial, looking for formulas to recover lost pasts that did not veer too close to the memory of Anton, and planning the hopeful things to come that felt bleak and sterile only to me.

During that period, my father-in-law was traveling again. As for Luisa, once she saw that her niece was back on track, she returned to her own devices and we no longer saw very much of her.

I do not know much about her life. If you listened to Antonia, the only sign of life displayed by her aunt Luisa was breathing. "She's like a stick of furniture, Eladio. I'm telling you, she doesn't have much to say about anything."

But there came a point when I missed her. Having her in the house was a way of knowing that Antonia had someone to help her whether she appreciated it or not. That allowed me some respite that simply dried up when she was not there. In a way, Luisa was my back up squad: her presence enabled me to support my wife without always having to do it myself.

The worst thing was to leave her alone with her frailty, her digressions, her imagination aimlessly navigating the rivers of the household and creating detours that she mistook as the true course.

She often pointed out things that I could not possibly do but that were imperative to her. "Have you forgotten what you promised me while I was in the hospital? You said that as soon as possible we would go away together, just the two of us."

To a certain extent, she was right. "Things have changed, Antonia. Business has picked up and I cannot take a vacation right now," I said.

But she was not to be appeased. "Excuses. The problem is that you don't enjoy traveling with me any more."

So I talked to her about her father, about my obligations as a partner of the publishing house and as CEO of Woultmand & Starky to step into his shoes on certain tasks. "The economy is changing and we have to be alert to the consequences of globalized finances on the publishing market."

She did not listen to me. My responses struck her as insults. "Do you think I'm an idiot?" And absolutely nothing bothered her more than to be trapped by her own ignorance. "Those are all just lies to get out of keeping your promise."

It was impossible to reason with her. There is nothing more difficult than battling against the vanity of the ignorant. And Antonia was useless when it came to financial matters.

There was no question that the arguments were heating up again.

Unpleasant memories came flooding back. The tensions, charged with emotional violence. Memory can be the worst counsel—and Antonia remembered. I too, without realizing it, was acting out of my recollection of past scenes: the upheavals and the manipulation that had led to violence, intimidation and abuse.

And Anton: the reproaches, the blame, the insults. The sadness in the child's eyes as he stared uncomprehendingly at his mother. And the times she had cruelly thrown him out of her room as she was fixing herself up. The kiss on the mirror. Everything.

Yes. Everything. One by one the accusations burst out like mushrooms in autumn. Neither of us could help it.

When the heart fills with ashes, try as we might to sweep them out and leave it spotless, traces will inevitably remain. There is always something rotting in a corner, an evocation that reeks, a filthy intensity that disgusts us as much as when it first happened.

Memory is a bad thing. It always wants the past to continue on in the present. It is memory that propels us towards resentment, vengeance and insult.

So despite our constant "togetherness" the homey interludes were beginning to disintegrate. The lazy days reading or watching TV hand in hand, the Saturday afternoon shopping and the Sunday matinees together were replaced by bridge games at friends' houses, or psychedelic nights at the same discotheques as before, and lascivious arguments upon arriving home, nearly always provoked by the alcohol ingested. Ridiculous wars about nothing: just a bad habit and completely devoid of affection.

When life begins to sink, there is nothing for it but to cling to the ridiculous and the artificial, and to fake sexual desire when there's nothing left but going through the motions. And give up on a thousand things that had once seemed salvageable.

The thing was, Antonia was gradually reverting to her old self: to the Antonia of confrontations, verbal abuse, and attacks on my person.

It did not matter that I was standing right in front of her. "In the end, the executive married me for my money."

It did not even matter that her humiliating comments about me reflected badly on her. She had to lower me, beat me down, and take advantage of my silence to reinforce her insults. "You can even discern his low origins in his breath." Or "Despite his spectacular presence as an important executive, he has no class whatsoever." Or "Did you know that his father was an usher in a movie theater?" Or "If you'd only met his mother. The poor thing had a hump from cleaning so many stairs."

I'm not going to deny that when I heard her go off like that I sometimes had the urge to smack her. But I never dared do it. It would only have given her an excuse to play the victim.

The most I ever did was leave the house, returning only when I thought she would be asleep.

She would wake up the next morning as if nothing had happened, having slept off the effects of the alcohol. She would claim not to remember having attacked or insulted me.

But during one of her onslaughts, I finally ran out of patience. It did not have to do with my family, or her jealousy over my absences, or the obscene questions she would pose: "Who were you taking your chances with tonight?" Or "Were you able to swing that little cord of yours okay?"

It happened when, after one of those nocturnal adventures of hers, drunk on hate and alcohol, she started to yell that the problem with me was that I was a "faggot" and that was why I was such good friends with Douglas Raft. "The truth is I don't understand how I could have fallen for a borderline queer."

And as if that were not enough, she explained to anyone who would listen that I had Douglas Raft to thank for my job at Autumn Books. "Douglas made him into an executive."

Her intimations spread rapidly. They took root. Those kinds of slurs are like a treadmill: it does not stop turning even if a donkey is activating it. No one spoke of my professional merits. My efforts to remain faithful to my wife did not count. To the contrary, my fidelity only buttressed Antonia's assertions: "We're all familiar with how effective those gay mafias are."

And the gossip spread. It was easy to detect in the insinuating remarks directed my way. The lie had been planted, the conjectures multiplied and women began to regard me with a certain disappointed reticence. Meanwhile, the men pretended not to give any credence to what they secretly believed. They acted as if they were above such talk, that they simply let it "wash over them" in their words. "After all, we are living in a democracy, aren't we?"

Two or three months went by in this way. Her imputations became increasingly frequent and brazen, and my reputation as a man and a husband was thoroughly sullied.

Naturally, she would not countenance any potential absence on my part when it came time to visit the doctor to have her blood drawn for the INR test. "It is your obligation as a husband to be right there beside me."

It was a sacred rite. Her own father had asked it of me. "Take care of her. If you don't take her to the hospital, Antonia is quite capable of forgetting all about her ailment."

He was right. Antonia had forgotten she was sick.

Fortunately the visits were brief. So were the days. The incipient spring was still being sabotaged by winter. And although the trees tossed in a temperate breeze, their pale green leaves were still just barely perceptible.

I remember those details because the hospital had a garden. A spectacular garden totally incompatible with the sorrow and misery that simmered in the facility's inner chambers. And on that particular day I'm not sure why it occurred to me that life was a study in contradictions. That, more often than not, things are not in their place. And that to persevere in pain was something that did not fit with the profusion of life the hospital's immense garden had to offer.

Once more the doctor indicated to me the exact dosage that I should administer to Antonia. "Don't forget, Mr. Escalante. Any change can be fatal to your wife," he told me when she was out of earshot. "Up to now, her progress has been favorable. The results are perfect."

I remember that when they first warned me of the danger of an incorrect dose, it left a bitter taste in my mouth, as if those warnings contained an ominous portent that was completely on my shoulders.

I did not realize that most of the things that happen in life are governed by signs, even when we are not paying attention.

Unperceived by us, these signs gradually embed themselves in our beings like bad habits inherent to a second nature. An invincible hidden nature that leaves us hopelessly mired in intangible stupors and clouds our vision with an appearance of normalcy underneath which lies unexpected cruelty.

When we arrived home that day, therefore, I had no inkling whatsoever of what was to come. And even now, when I think about what happened, I have the impression that I did not actually live that scene, that it was all nothing but an accursed dream.

Antonia turned on me in a sudden fury screaming wildly, "You killed him. You left him alone by the pool."

And just that once, I could not contain myself. I lost control. I allowed my revulsion to get the best of me. I told her I could no longer endure her incoherence, her slurs, her whims, and that I was going to separate from her even if it cost me my job.

She did not hear me. Once more, hate pervaded everything and the past came rushing back as if Anton had only just died.

It was inevitable. Every corner of the house was impregnated with a past that both she and I had attempted to bury with lies.

She suddenly drew close poised to strike me. She had a letter opener in her hand and she was about to attack me with it. But once again, I grabbed her by the elbows and threw her against the sofa.

And there she remained until Berta, alarmed by her screams, came into the living room. "She needs her medication," I told her icily. "The lady is having a bout of nerves."

I prepared it myself.

There is no chronology to describe what came next. It is unthinkable to try to evoke the exact details of that day. I believe I left the house. She was asleep when I returned. I cannot remember it all exactly, or maybe my subconscious mind needs to forget. The impression I have now is that of a man who did not feel, did not think, was not in control of his own actions.

The next day I prepared the Sintrom dosage as usual and I gave it to Berta to administer to her.

Three days later we were notifying the emergency room doctor, Aunt Luisa and her father.

No one could possibly have suspected that I administered an incorrect dosage to her. Even I could not believe it. I heard without comprehending. They spoke but I could not absorb what they were saying. I remember the doctors crossing themselves. They could not understand why the pulmonary embolism had returned. The test results had been so good.

The plane is preparing for landing. The designated path has run its course.

The flight attendants are checking whether seat belts are fastened and seatbacks have been returned to their upright positions.

Once more, the anxiety of the passengers as they attend to any unnecessary pressing detail to remind themselves that they will soon be leaving behind the vast emptiness to walk again on terra firma.

As the plane begins its decent, the atmosphere clears to reveal a calm, transitory sea that no longer threatens ruin.

"It looks as if the sun is out in New York," exclaims Daniela.

"We're on a different continent."

"It's curious," she replies. "It is as if the unpredictable weather has no idea that time has stopped. After all, the time on the clock here is more or less the same as when we left Spain."

"Maybe these seven hours didn't really happen," he responds, trying to inject some lightness into his tone.

"It's possible. Just like imagining that our conversation has ended in a paradox."

"Or in a dream," he rejoins. "To exist without time is like falling asleep and losing out on what that time might have had to offer us."

And after a brief silence:

"It's probably just getting dark in Spain now," she remarks, just to say something.

And Eladio thinks that for him Spain and everything he has left there—home, friends, dreams, the dead, torment and revelations—will always be an interminable night to which he will never return for anything in this world.

"You have to be optimistic," she says. "Instead of thinking we've been cheated out of several hours, we could also imagine that the trip has lengthened the day."

But neither of them manages to assimilate that this "lengthened" day will ever be anything more than a flimsy patch, altogether lacking in substance.

And although they do not understand why, a tepid or apathetic sensation is welling up in both of them. It is an uncomfortable feeling, as if a metaphysical tumor were growing between them.

Daniela reacts abruptly.

"Maybe this is a little out of place, but I want to thank you for what you just said about my changing your life. I never imagined I could have an influence on someone of your stature."

"Do you really think I'm so important?"

"We all are to God. But the importance I'm referring to has to do particularly with the grace with which you've accepted the tragedies in your life: the loss of your son, your wife, you're mother's struggle to put you through school. To face all of those things as you have done is what makes a man important."

But Eladio signals for her to stop.

"I prefer not to remember. Memory can be very cruel. One has to forget if one is to go on living."

But although Eladio tries to sound convincing, he knows that forgetting is a delusion.

There is Antonia again, imprisoned in the ignoble trap that he has set, taking advantage of a trust he did not deserve.

And he contemplates her eyes, wide open and pleading for help that he cannot provide, although as soon as he realized what he had done, he activated all possible mechanisms to prevent the inevitable. And he sees himself thinking; "It isn't possible. It isn't possible. Why? It wasn't me. It was someone else. Someone who imposes and influences." And he hears her gasp for breath as the doctors struggle in vain to save the life of that scrap of a woman who was refusing to die.

And he recalls Luisa's despondence. A Luisa who is nothing like the woman Antonia had reviled. Her eternal veneer of calm rent by sobs that no one understood or tried to stem with useless condolences.

And the empathetic silence of Douglas Raft. The close friend who perhaps "intuited" God knows what stifled torments, but who only hugged him and offered his understanding. "I know how you must feel, Eladio. Count on me for whatever you need. I'm not going to say anything more. I don't want to overwhelm you."

That was when Eladio entreated him to intercede with Mahler to send him somewhere far from Spain. "I can't go on here. I can't endure it," he said. And Douglas promised to help him.

The worst part was his father-in-law's return. Seeing him there impotent, an incredibly wealthy man impoverished as he gazed at his daughter's body—her face pale and ashen, her legendary beauty gradually receding—as if he were a beggar dealing with his terrible failure, appalled by the pointlessness of his own life, of his own efforts to reach the goal of those glory-seekers who invariably end up as "nobodies."

And he observes Mahler embracing him, making no effort to hide his sobs as he sought much needed consolation from his son-in-law. "My God, Eladio. We've lost her, Son. We've lost her."

He also cannot forget the chill he felt then. A chill that sought "not to be" but that "was." So cold it stopped any tears from falling. But Mahler did not notice and continued speaking: "I'll never be able to thank you for everything you did for my daughter. She loved you so much."

And Berta.

It would be impossible to forget Berta. There she is now, wearing an expression of mute anguish. As if she were half-ashamed of her apparent composure. As if the death of "her baby" did not affect her.

Despite Berta's outward calm however, her face did not suggest indifference. To the contrary, everything about her was a suppressed wail that gravitated about the house like the howls of a mute dog. It was a frightening look: neither reproachful nor comforting. It was as if she "knew" yet refused to know. As if feigning calm might confuse the pain.

And he sees her as she was this morning when she said goodbye to him, extending her hand forcefully, as if that gesture could absolve him of that for which no absolution was possible. "Try to forget, Sir. Try to forget everything."

"There is no doubt about it," Eladio thinks now. "Berta intuited it. Berta was the only danger."

The others were mere spectators in a nebulous reality that—as is so often the case—was destined to be sucked into the vacuum of the unknown, of what no one could ever have suspected much less proved.

And as if Daniela were reading his mind, she suddenly asks, "Do you think someday you will be able to forget?" Eladio does not respond. "I understand that forgetting would be hard for you," she persists. "When you've loved someone as much as you loved Antonia, it takes a long time."

"I may never get there," he replies. "In any case, no one is perfect. Perhaps what I saw in her wasn't real."

"If that were the case, you might get past your grief sooner," she concludes.

"Don't believe it. Sometimes it's not just the loss of our loved ones that hurts us."

"What do you mean?"

"I'd rather not say."

"Why not?"

Eladio turns to her rather brusquely, takes her by the arm and shakes it lightly.

"Because if I tell you I will have lost you forever and that is what I'm trying to avoid at all costs."

He quickly removes his hand from her arm and, pretending to contemplate the sun that continues to illuminate the earth below, he looks out the window, turning his back to her.

Confused, Daniela regards his curved back, the crease of his neck, his somewhat tousled hair and the harmony of his body in a seat that is much too far away from her own.

"You've already lost me forever," Daniela asserts, somewhat testily. "Haven't you already assured me that we will never see each other again?"

Eladio straightens himself in his seat and then turns towards her again.

"You know what, Daniela? Never seeing you again is one thing, and losing you is quite another. Please remember what

I'm going to tell you. It's important. The word 'tomorrow' no longer has any meaning for me. Or to be more precise, now that I've met you, what normal people call 'tomorrow,' will be a never-ending 'today' to me. A memory that can never die. That's why I am working so hard to preserve it. I'm going to need that memory. It may be the most important thing that has ever happened to me."

"If it's so important, why do you underestimate it?"

"It's not that. I'm protecting it. I'm 'guarding' it like you might guard a treasure. Surely that greed will force me to lose a happiness that I've never known and perhaps could come to know. But between the 'perhaps' and the certainty, I prefer to stay with the perhaps. Certainties tend to be deceiving."

Daniela's eyes are moist. She does not understand. She does not know. She might guess and yet she only asks:

"What about me? Why don't you think about what I stand to lose?"

She has allowed it to escape in a tremulous voice, as if the dampness of her eyes were about to turn into a sob. And Eladio is once again caught up in the temptation born of doubt. Now he thinks that if he opens up his heart to Daniela, she would understand. "Maybe what I did wasn't so bad," he repeats to himself over and over. "It was probably my subconscious mind and I had no control over it."

And without realizing it, he is unraveling all the reasons for his silence: a man has a right to be happy, to have a family, to have dreams, to create hope, he thinks all at once.

Perhaps if he had the courage to unload on Daniela the dark truth of his secret, she would understand and forgive him. Might even become an accomplice in what he has done. But was what he did really that bad? Sometimes when one has reached the extremes that he has, it's possible that the future might allow one to slam the door on the past and glimpse new horizons, new frontiers, new perspectives.

The plane slows and gradually begins to descend. It is a slow descent that quickly changes the contours of each false possibility and inexorably establishes the truth of the matter.

And Eladio knows he will never tell Daniela what his own desperate need demands that he should confess.

All at once the wheels make contact with the runway and the passengers share a sense of collective relief.

212

And then the voice of the flight attendant is requesting that they remain in their seats until the plane has come to a complete stop.

And Eladio is promising himself once more that what he has not told Daniela will remain forever sealed in a disconcerting state of nothingness.

Once more the coats, bags, the book on the harmony of visual aesthetics, the sick child leaning into his mother, the heavy-set gentleman adjusting his tie, and the businessmen gathering their equipment. And the silence between them as they file through the tunnel towards the airport.

And suddenly the cold. And the tumult of customs. And then the claim area where the luggage will distract memories and heighten vigilance.

And the carts. You have to wait by the railing with the cart in tow and hope that your suitcases have arrived intact and without complications.

At this point, Daniela and Eladio are barely looking at each other. They both know the conversation is over. They know the routine of landlocked things is always more powerful than the free-flow of words lost in the evanescence of space.

The suitcases take their time in coming.

"Always," remarks Eladio, to say something. "So much progress in some areas and so much regression in others. When will they grasp that the process of surmounting long distances through flight is completely out of step with the process of recovering your suitcases?"

But Daniela does not reply.

Every so often a shout is heard coming from the people waiting outside the baggage claim area: surreal, meaningless sounds. Insignificant tributes that the human genus pays to the silence of those awaiting only God knows what types of solutions.

And finally the luggage.

The carts are filled with suitcases, bags and packages. Daniela and Eladio head wordlessly towards the exit. "Anything to declare?" Both say no. But Eladio is aware that they have both lied.

Not declaring usually consists of more than concealing prohibited objects. It can also mean concealing pitiless acts, painful sensations, futile hopes, emotions and renunciations.

And countless fragile and fleeting substances that, though ephemeral, may still cause misfortunes capable of altering the very essence of life.

There is the exit. Instinctively, they both stop. To the left is the sign that wants to separate them: CONNECTING FLIGHTS and an arrow indicating where the passengers should go to find the plane that will take them to Los Angeles.

"We've reached the end of the line," remarks Daniela. "An end with no horizon in sight, right?" she asks, as if she is still sure Eladio will hold her back and beg her not to go, even as she extends her hand for him to shake.

"Maybe some day," he murmurs.

"Maybe," she repeats.

"Good luck," he tells her.

But Daniela does not answer. The arrow and the sign seem to be urging her on. The flight to Los Angeles awaits her.

"I also wish you luck," she says finally as, without looking at him, she begins to walk in the direction indicated by the arrow.

Eladio allows her to go and stands before the automatic door.

But he does not move forward. Unable to stop himself, he turns to look at her as if he can feel that she is doing the same.

And there they are, standing motionless several meters apart, gazing at each other. He unable to stop the knot from forming in his throat. She, tall and slender, her eyes brimming with tears, the stain on her skirt barely visible.

Unable to stop himself, Eladio runs to her, takes her in his arms and covers her damp cheek with his kisses.

They do not speak. What for? Sometimes silence is the most eloquent form of expression.

They do not even say goodbye. There is no more definitive goodbye than the passion of a silent embrace.

www.ingramcontent.com/pod-product-compliance
Lightning Source LLC
Chambersburg PA
CBHW030518020726
47494CB00004B/1147